TESTING
RELATIONSHIPS

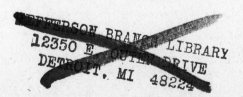

TESTING RELATIONSHIPS

Brittney Holmes

www.urbanchristianonline.net

Urban Books
1199 Straight Path
West Babylon, NY 11704

ISBN-13: 978-1-60162-963-0
ISBN-10: 1-60162-963-X

First Printing: June 2008

Printed in the United States of America

10 9 8 7 6 5 4 3 2 1

Submit Wholesale Orders to:
Kensington Publishing Corp.
C/O Penguin Group (USA) Inc.
Attention: Order Processing
405 Murray Hill Parkway
East Rutherford, NJ 07073-2316
Phone: 1-800-526-0275
Fax: 1-800-227-9604

Dedication

I would like to dedicate this novel to all of those who have supported me throughout the years, but especially to my parents Jonathan Bellamy and Kendra Norman-Bellamy. I appreciate all you've done for me and I love you.

Acknowledgments

Always first, I would like to thank my Lord and Savior, Jesus Christ. I cannot thank You enough for the gift You've given me in the form of writing. I vow to always use it to praise and uplift Your name.

To my parents, Jonathan Bellamy and Kendra Norman-Bellamy, thank you for supporting and believing in me. I thank you for all you've taught me. I promise that, as I begin this next phase in my life, I will remember all of the morals and values you have instilled in me.

To my grandparents, Bishop and Mrs. H. H. Norman, Mr. Jesse and Mrs. Dorothy Holmes, and the late Elder Clinton and Mrs. Willie Mae Bellamy, and the rest of my extended family (uncles, aunts, and cousins): whether you're here with me physically or spiritually, I carry you in my heart always.

Terrance, my cousin and publicist, you've done so much for me. I especially appreciate how much patience you had while teaching me to drive. God bless you!

To my best friends, my close friends, and my acquaintances—I love you guys for your continuous support and encouragement. Thanks to my true friends for letting me cry on your shoulders, trusting me with your secrets, laughing with me, and telling me the truth. I pray that our connections will never fade. To all of my educators at Redan High School, thank you all for your support in and out of school. To the magnificent RHS class of 2008: WE MADE IT!!! May all of our dreams and goals become reality as we embark on this journey called adulthood. Keeping focus and faith are the only true keys to success.

To the members of National Honor Society and Beta Club, the P.I.L.O.T. Program, and to the fabulous divas of Silver Essence Auxiliary—thank you for keeping me busy when I wasn't in school.

To my 2007–2008 SM-LAC Delta Debutante sisters and chairpersons: it was a blessing to share that bonding experience with you all. Mrs. Rachel Zeigler, Ms. Renee Thomas, Ms. Erika Jenkins, Ms. Erreka Reed, Ms. Marie Dunn and all of the other fabulous Delta Sigma Theta alumni who assisted in my journey from childhood to womanhood—I appreciate you all and I will never forget how instrumental you were in my life. To my Deb sisters: all of the laughs, the tears, the aggravation, the time, and the money were not in vain. We put a lot into this program, but we received so much more from it. We are sisters for life and I love you all!

Thanks to Toschia Moffett and the Divine Literary Tour, the Anointed Authors on Tour (AAOT), Hank Stewart, Sherri Lewis, Tanya Finney, Shonta Bass and GAAL Book Club, Tee C. Royal and RAWSISTAZ, and all other authors and literary supporters for your love and encouragement.

All of my love to my spiritual family at my home church, Revival Church Ministries, and my home-away-from-home church, Church of God by Faith Ministries: you all have been by my side from the very beginning and I plan on taking you all the way to the end.

To my publishers, Urban Books (Urban Christian), I thank you for making all my dreams come true. A special thanks to my editor, Ms. Joylynn, for your constructive criticism, challenging my creativity, and helping me improve as a writer.

And finally, to my readers: This book will make you laugh and cry; you might even get angry. But I hope entertainment is not all you get out of it. I pray that you will learn what it means to put your faith and trust in God so that no matter what you go through in life, you'll always know that He is with you.

Chapter 1

June 4

"Happy birthday to you. Happy birthday to you. Happy birthday, dear Ebony. Happy birthday to you!" Shimone Johnson helped her three-year-old daughter blow out her birthday candles as their family and friends clapped.

"Yay!" Ebony Amana Anderson clapped and laughed with her family.

"Shimone, hold her in place so I can get this picture," Robert Anderson said.

Shimone tried to hold her very active daughter down in her seat. "Ebony, sit still," she instructed.

Robert snapped the picture as his son, Marques Anderson, walked through the door. Shimone looked at her boyfriend and father of her child as if he was an intruder. Marques was supposed to have arrived at her apartment hours ago to help decorate for the party. Ebony had been asking for her "daddy" all day long and Shimone hated not knowing where he was.

"Hey, baby," Marques greeted, kissing Shimone like nothing was wrong. He walked toward his daughter and lifted her up into his arms. "Hey Daddy's big girl. Happy birthday," he said, kissing Ebony on her forehead and chubby cheeks.

"Daddy," Ebony squealed. "Daddy here!"

"Yeah Daddy's here," Shimone said, taking Ebony from him and sitting her back into her chair. "Who wants cake?" she asked as she gave Marques a look of displeasure.

After they graduated from high school, Marques had been very attentive to Shimone in the last stages of her pregnancy. They'd made a pact that if Shimone birthed a baby girl, Marques would cater to her every need and desire for two weeks, and vise versa if she gave birth to a boy. After having their daughter, Marques waited on Shimone hand and foot for months longer than their two-week deal. Back rubs, foot massages, her favorite meals—whatever her wish, he was there to fulfill it.

When they, along with their friend, Ronald McAfee, entered Clark Atlanta University in Atlanta, Marques frequently visited Shimone's off-campus apartment. But after Ebony's first year of life, Marques's everyday visits began to dwindle to every other weekend. Since he was enrolled on a full basketball scholarship, Shimone knew he had to be present at all games, home and away. She understood that he had classes, but she did too. After taking Ebony to daycare, she went to early morning classes and then rushed to pick her daughter up in the evenings so she could settle Ebony in for the night. Things were worse after nightfall when Shimone would have to forgo sleep to do homework during Ebony's late night cries. Marques's distance had raised several questions, but Shimone had very little luck in finding any answers.

After eating half of the cake, everyone settled in the living room.

"Shimone," Nevaeh Madison spoke as she walked over to her best friend of thirteen years, "don't you think it's time to let Ebony open her presents?"

"No," Shimone said through clenched teeth. "I think it is time to give Marq a beat-down. I know you saw him come in here late like it's no big deal. This is his daughter, too, you know."

"I know," Nevaeh tried to calm Shimone. "But at least he is here."

"His own parents didn't know where he was," Shimone said, refusing to acknowledge the positive side her friend was trying to present. "That's a shame and you know it."

"Well, if you want to yell at him, go ahead," Nevaeh shrugged, "but wait until the party is over," she added, knowing Shimone didn't mind making a scene.

"Fine." Shimone walked back over to her daughter who was trying to open a gift from her grandfather.

"Here." Robert kneeled on the floor next to his granddaughter. "Let Papa help you with that." He ripped the paper off the box as Ebony squealed.

"Look, Mama," Ebony said, pointing to the doll that was in the box.

"Yeah, that was on the TV last week," Shimone said. "What do you say to your Papa? Say 'thank you.'"

"Thank you, Papa," Ebony said.

"You're welcome, precious." Robert stood next to his wife. "Grandma got you something too."

"I sure did," his wife, Shundra, said, taking an unwrapped gift off of the table. "Here you go, baby."

"Thank you," Ebony said, hugging the brown teddy bear.

"You are welcome." Shundra looked up at Shimone. "We're going to get her a few outfits tomorrow."

"Thank you." Shimone smiled with much appreciation. "Lord knows she needs them."

"Here's a gift from me and Uncle Ron," Nevaeh said to her goddaughter as her boyfriend, Ronald, got up to help Ebony open the gift.

When they finally got all of the wrapping paper off the box, Ebony took the top off, threw it to the other side of the room, and pulled the pink and yellow sundresses out.

"Put it on now, Mama?" Ebony asked Shimone as she held the pink dress up in the air.

"Not now, sweetie." Shimone placed the dress back into its container. "Maybe later, okay?"

"Okay," Ebony replied. "Where Mama Ma?" Ebony said, asking for Shimone's mother, Misty.

When Ebony first learned to talk, she'd been confused when Shimone and Marques had taught her to call both their mothers "grandma," so Shimone clarified, "Grandma Misty is Mommy's mama." Partially comprehending her mother's explanation, Ebony began calling Misty "Mama Ma." Shimone didn't feel a need to correct her daughter until she was old enough to fully understand. Misty liked the nickname, so it sufficed.

"Mama Ma didn't forget about you," Misty replied in response to Ebony's call and approached her granddaughter with a large gift bag in hand.

Ebony stood and tried to look inside the bag, but nearly toppled over. Shimone grabbed her by the hand. They watched Misty pull out several items of clothing. While Ebony couldn't stop smiling, Shimone was near tears. It had been hard to provide for Ebony. Her family helped from time to time, but Shimone never took advantage of them, despite Marques's desire to do so. Shimone wanted to be responsible for the life they'd created. But she thanked God daily for her supportive family.

"Thank you so much, Mama," Shimone said, allowing Ebony to walk toward Misty.

"Thank you, Mama Ma," Ebony said, getting off the floor to kiss her grandmother.

"You're welcome," Misty said.

"Save a kiss for me, baby girl," Marques said as he walked out of the apartment door and wheeled in his gift.

"Oh, look Mama," Ebony shrieked with wide, excited eyes as she pulled at Shimone's skirt. "Look what Daddy got!" She jumped.

Marques rolled the life-size, toy Corvette in the middle of the living room. He picked his daughter up and placed her in the driver's seat of the car. Ebony turned the wheel and clapped her hands when she pressed against the horn and a loud beep filled the room. Marques turned on the car's real-life radio, placed sunglass on his daughter's face, and smiled.

"Marques, don't you think this is a little too much?" Shundra asked her son. "She can't even reach the pedals."

"Naw, Mama," he said. "She'll grow into it. I got it on sale down at Toys R Us. Fifty percent off."

"How much was that fifty percent?" Robert asked skeptically.

"Umm . . . 'bout two hundred dollars," Marques shrugged.

"*Two hundred dollars*, Marques!" Shimone nearly screamed. "You know we don't have that kind of money to be throwing around on a car for a three-year-old!"

"I've been saving up so I could get something nice for her," Marques said with a flaring attitude. "I don't see the big deal."

"Marques, man," Ronald said, stepping up and placing his hand on Marques's right shoulder, "go look in that cabinet, and tell me how much food y'all got. Or look in Ebony's room, and see how many clothes she has to wear."

"Man, what is your point?" Marques asked, moving out of Ronald's grasp. He was getting annoyed because everyone was ridiculing him just for getting his daughter a birthday gift.

"His point," Misty said calmly, "is that you should have spent that money on something this child needs."

"So y'all want me to take it back?" he said, turning the car's radio off and taking Ebony out of the car. She began to kick and scream immediately.

"Marques, stop it," Shimone scolded, taking Ebony from her boyfriend and placing her on the floor. "You are upsetting her. No one is saying you have to take it back. Just try to spend money on something that we need, and then use anything extra on something like this."

"Fine, I'll just save the money next time."

The room was silent as Shimone placed her daughter's gifts on the table and threw all of the wrapping paper and trash away. Ronald, Nevaeh, and Ebony's grandparents sat on the sofa and watched as Ebony showed them a new dance she'd learned in daycare. Marques was sitting in the corner of the living room, pouting like a baby. He was sick of Shimone and her overbearing ways. He had purposely come to the party late, knowing that it would upset her.

They had been dating since their senior year in high school, but now as they were about to enter their senior year in college, Marques noticed that Shimone wasn't as happy as she used to be. It was probably because he had been spending less time with her and their daughter and more time with Alexia Harrison, a recent graduate who had been throwing herself at him since he entered Clark Atlanta as a starting point guard. Their "no-strings at-tached" agreement was what had kept him in a relation-ship with her.

Marques loved Shimone; she was the first girl he'd ever stayed in a relationship with for longer than a month with-out cheating or even thinking about being with another girl. But after entering college, his pre-Shimone habits began to seep back into his soul. He wanted to go out and get with every girl he could, as if he was proving to himself that being tied to one woman for so long hadn't damaged his ability to attract other women. But with Shimone always on his mind, that mission was almost impossible.

A year after Ebony was born, Marques noticed that Shimone was becoming more and more possessive of her relationship with him. She would show up at his basket-ball practices *with* Ebony and wait for him to finish so they could go out. She would call his dorm room con-stantly just to see how he was doing, which was her way of checking to see if he was there or not. She always wanted to know of his whereabouts. Everything, even the most minute things, she did would get on his nerves.

Marques looked at Ronald, his best friend, cuddled on the couch with Shimone's best friend. He wished he and Shimone had what Ronald and Nevaeh shared. He and Shimone used to share a deep connection, but somehow it had dissipated. Marques had envisioned himself spending the rest of his life with Shimone, but, at the rate they were going, he didn't know how much longer he'd want to be in the same room with her.

"Okay," Robert said nearly thirty minutes later. "It's time for us to go."

"No, Papa go," Ebony said, holding onto his leg.

"Papa has to go," Shundra said as she picked Ebony

up. "And so does Grandma. We have to go to work in the morning."

"I have to go, too," Misty said. "I have to get paperwork started for the new dancers who signed up for the summer," she said, referring to her dance class.

Misty had been the sole owner of Misty J's Dance Studio for nearly thirteen years, having purchased the building that housed the studio after her late grandmother had left her thousands of dollars to do whatever she pleased. In the last few years, business had blossomed tremendously and Misty had left her corporate job so that she would be able to devote all of her time to her eager students.

"Okay, Mama," Shimone said, hugging Misty, Robert, and then Shundra.

After seeing them to the door, Marques asked Ronald if he wanted to play a round of basketball.

"Naw, man," Ronald declined, "I wanna get Nev home before it gets too late."

"What are you talking about? It's only eight o'clock," Marques said.

"I know, but Nevaeh wanted to go out to dinner tonight," Ronald said, "and who am I to deny her?" He smiled, looking into Nevaeh's eyes.

Nevaeh returned the smile and turned away from his gaze. "Shimone," she said, walking over to her friend who was busy taking plates into the kitchen, "thank you for inviting us to the party." She hugged Shimone. "Don't let him stay too late," Nevaeh whispered in her ear.

"Oh, trust," Shimone whispered with indignation, "he won't be here long."

Nevaeh pulled back. "Please don't make him mad. I can't stand to see when y'all are mad at each other."

"I'm not making any promises," Shimone said.

Nevaeh bent down and picked Ebony up off the floor. "Bye, Auntie's baby," she said, kissing Ebony's cheeks.

"Bye bye," Ebony said. "Bye, Uncle Ron." She ran into his arms for a hug.

"Bye, sweetie." Ronald kissed her cheek and then looked up at Shimone. "She is going to be thick just like you."

"I know. That's why I'm trying to stop feeding her so much so she won't get fat," Shimone laughed, "but she just won't quit."

Ronald stood up and grabbed Nevaeh's hand. "Well, I'll see you later, man," he spoke to Marques. "Bye, Shimone."

"Bye." Shimone waved, closing the door after they walked to Ronald's car. "Ebony, go sit on the sofa," she said to her daughter who was sitting on the floor. "Sit here and play with your bear while I finish cleaning," she instructed, handing Ebony the stuffed bear she'd just received from Shundra before walking past Marques and into the kitchen.

"Are you going to ignore me all night?" Marques asked, following Shimone into the kitchen.

"Marques, I really don't feel like arguing tonight," Shimone said as she ran water in the kitchen sink. "So if that is what you stayed around for, you could have gone home."

"I don't want to argue with you either, but what am I supposed to think if you give me these looks like you wanna kill somebody every time you look at me?"

"I don't know." Shimone began washing the dishes that sat in the sink. "I just hoped that if you wouldn't come on time for me, at least you would do it for your daughter. She was asking for you all this morning, and when everyone else had showed up and you still weren't here, she was in tears. You didn't call to say you were

going to be late. Then you walk in here like it's no big
deal, with gifts that cost too much, knowing we hardly
have any money for food around here. And Ebony needs
some summer clothes; she is growing so fast. She can't
wear the same clothes that she wore last year.

"I don't know what has gotten into you. It's like I don't
even know you anymore. You totally ignore me unless
it's to ask me something about Ebony. You don't call, and
when I do hear from you, it's like someone made you call
me, 'cause you never have anything to say. I hardly see
you around campus, and when I do, you act like we're
not even together. So you tell me what you thought when
I kept giving you those looks, 'cause I hope it had something to do with your daughter, and how we need things
around this house other than a bunch of toys, and *not*
about how I can get on your nerves."

"Shimone, no one said that you get on my nerves,"
Marques said, although her assumption had been true.

"Nobody *had* to say it," Shimone snapped, wiping tears.
"Your actions say everything, especially in the few times
you do visit. It's like you just pop up out of thin air and you
spend all of your time with Ebony. Not that it's a bad thing.
I'm not saying that you aren't a good father or anything,
but I am still your girlfriend." She stopped rambling and
turned to face him. "At least I hope I am."

"Baby, you are," Marques said, hugging her close. This
was one of the few times when he realized how much he
loved Shimone and didn't want to lose her.

"Well then, it would be nice if you started acting like
it," she told him, slightly pulling back. "It would be nice
to see you more than just every other weekend, and it
would be even better if we started going out more often."

"We can go out this weekend," Marques said. "Me,
you, and Ebony. We'll go somewhere."

"Thank you," Shimone said, kissing him lightly on the lips.

"Mama," Ebony moaned as she walked into the kitchen, rubbing her eyes.

Shimone and Marques looked at their daughter and smiled. Ever since Ebony learned to walk at fourteen months, she could hardly stay in one place for too long. Shimone was surprised she'd stayed in the living room for as long as she had.

Shimone moved toward her daughter and picked her up. "What's wrong?"

"I sleepy," Ebony said.

"That means it's time for bed," Marques said, taking Ebony out of Shimone's arms. "Let Daddy tuck you in before he leaves." He walked across the living room into Ebony's bedroom, which was decorated with Mickey and Minnie Mouse furnishings. He placed her in her "big-girl" bed, tucked her in under the covers, and then kissed her forehead.

"Mama sing, please?" Ebony asked her mother.

"Okay," Shimone said. She sat at the foot of the bed as she looked into her daughter's brown eyes. She softly sung "Rock-a-bye Baby" as Ebony's eyelids became heavier and heavier.

Marques was still amazed at Shimone's gift of song. She even made the lullaby sound like a hit record. That was another thing he loved about Shimone. She had the voice of an angel straight from heaven, and no one could deny that. But after recording an album three years ago, Shimone requested that the record company release her from her contract because they wanted her to start a tour. She didn't have time to promote the album. Mostly because she was too busy with Ebony and school to take on any more work. Luckily, the company consented. But

Marques knew that if Shimone asked the company to re-instate her contract, they would do it in a heartbeat.

Shimone pressed her lips against Ebony's forehead when she finished the song. She got up and turned the lights out, leaving the door open as she left the room with Marques behind her. They sat on the sofa and Shimone placed her feet on Marques's lap.

"I am so tired," she moaned as he began to massage her feet. "Ebony is starting to be a handful. At first she was just a baby and she couldn't walk or talk, but now she can do both and she wants everything. Every time we go into a store, it's 'Mama I want' or 'Mama, can I get.' It's just so nerve-wrecking."

"If you let me move in, I could be of more help," Marques offered in a soft, coaxing tone.

Shimone cocked her head to the side and stared into his eyes. Before getting an apartment with Ronald last year, Marques had been hinting about moving in with her, but she had a feeling it had nothing to do with being helpful. He had been trying to bring sexual intimacy back into their relationship, but Shimone was completely against it. When she had found out that she was pregnant with Ebony, she had decided to stop being sexually active. Not only did she not want to risk the chances of getting pregnant again, or even becoming susceptible to an STD, but she felt the need to stop participating in sexual activity so she could have a better relationship with God. She didn't want to be tempted. She knew she would be if he moved in. She thought that after he gave his life to Christ, he would change his way of thinking, but not much had changed over the past three years.

"Marq, now you know there is no way I can let you move in here. As a matter of fact, *you* were the one who suggested that I live here by myself, so there wouldn't be any temptation. I plan to stick to that agreement."

"Okay," Marques easily yielded, getting off the couch and pulling her up with him. "Have it your way." He leaned down and kissed her softly.

She walked him to the door and kissed him again. He smiled as he looked into her eyes. *God help me be strong,* she thought. Marques walked down the steps to his car as Shimone watched him climb into the vehicle and pull off with his radio blasting. She closed and locked the door before going into Ebony's room to make sure she was asleep. After pulling the covers up around Ebony's neck and kissing her cheek, Shimone walked to her bedroom and climbed into her bed without bothering to take off her clothes.

After knocking on the door twice, Marques was tempted to leave and go home to his empty apartment, but just as he turned to walk away, the door opened. He walked into the condo and closed the door behind him. He swore he'd never go back to this place, but being denied by Shimone so many times began to wear on him. He needed something, or *someone,* to fill in the gaps in their relationship. And Alexia was the right woman for the job. She took his hand and led him to her bedroom.

Two hours later, Marques lay awake in Alexia's queen-sized bed, unable to sleep, not only because of the snoring beauty to his right, but because of the guilt he felt from being back in this situation again. The last time he left her, he promised himself and God that he would never lie in this bed again, but here he was. He wiped the tear that threatened to roll from his eye. Quietly, he climbed out of the bed and put on his clothes. Leaving the house, he said a silent prayer. *Lord, forgive me. I swear this was the last time.*

Chapter 2

After hearing a door slam and the garage door rising, Nicole McAfee watched, from her bedroom window as her father sped out of the driveway and onto the surface street. It was the second time this week Malcolm McAfee had left the house after fighting with his wife, Angelica. In the last year, all Nicole's parents did was argue. She knew their relationship wasn't going to last much longer if things continued like this.

At first, they argued over little things. They argued over who was supposed to pick their youngest son, Jeremy, up from school. They fussed about which high school courses would best prepare Nicole for the field of pediatrics. They screamed over who was the last one to use the grill just to see who was supposed to clean it. Now it seemed like they argued over bigger issues; things like how much money was being spent, why Angelica was being so overbearing, and why Malcolm came home after ten o'clock at night when he was scheduled to get off of work at seven.

Nicole had gone to her mother to ask what was going

on with her parents. Angelica had told her daughter that they were having serious differences and that she didn't know how much longer she would be able to take it. Nicole knew that her mother was seriously thinking about leaving her husband, to whom she had been married for almost twenty years.

Nicole sat on her bed and sighed. Ever since her older brother, Ronald, had gone off to college, things in the McAfee household had not been the same, and Nicole had felt like she'd lost her best friend, despite the fact that he was less than an hour away. Ronald had always been there for her when she needed someone to talk to, but now that he was no longer around her all the time, she had no one to carry her burdens to.

Nicole knew she could talk to her best friend, but ever since Imani Madison had started dating Eddie Fulton, Nicole hadn't seen much of her. Imani and Eddie had been going out for almost two months, and Imani was already saying she was in love. When Nicole and Imani were about to enter their senior year of high school, Eddie had just graduated from their school and was about to enter Emory University on a full academic scholarship. With his hazelnut skin complexion, dark eyes, full lips, and always neatly braided hair, Nicole had to admit that he was very easy on the eyes. He was gentle and caring, and he loved the Lord. But Nicole believed Imani was allowing her emotions to get the best of her. Anyone could see how much Eddie liked Imani, but Nicole doubted he was already in love with her.

Nicole's eleven-year-old brother, Jeremy, burst into her room, breaking into her thoughts. "Where Daddy goin'?" he demanded.

"I don't know," Nicole said with a shrug. "He just left."

"He always leavin'!" Jeremy said angrily. "Why don't he just stay away?"

Nicole looked at her brother solemnly. Jeremy stood with his hands shoved into his pockets and his eyes were glazed with anger. She remembered when he used to be a nosy, annoying, but fun-loving little brother, but after turning ten last year, he had become a rebellious brat who didn't listen to anyone other than his mother, of whom he was very protective. Nicole didn't know what had changed him, but she wished he'd return to the person he'd been before.

"Why don't you go check on Mama?" she suggested as she picked up her ringing phone. She waited for Jeremy to shut the door behind him as he left before she greeted her caller.

"Wassup?" the person said.

Nicole rolled her eyes and tried to be as polite as she could. "How did you get my number, Shawn?"

He laughed into the phone. "I got my resources."

"What resources?" Nicole asked, annoyed.

"That's for me to know and for you to never find out," Shawn laughed.

"Boy, stop playin' and tell me who gave you my number without my permission before I hang up on you."

"Oh, you wanted me to have it," he said softly. "You just ain't want me to know you wanted me to have it."

Nicole hated the way Shawn played mind games with her. She could never get a direct answer from him; he always had to make everything complicated. Shawn Underwood had been trying to get Nicole to go out with him for months, but he was not her type. Although they had been friends—more like acquaintances—since they were freshmen, she was well aware of the disrespectful manner with which he treated girls, and she didn't want to fall for any of the games he played. He had a way of making her feel special, though, and it scared her. He treated her differently than other girls and that frightened her even more. What was so special about her that made him want to treat her better than the rest? She'd pondered upon the question many times, but hadn't a clue as to what the answer could be.

"Kiki, you still there?" Shawn asked. "I ain't make you mad, did I? If you don't wanna talk to me, that's cool. I'll just let you go," he said.

He was the only person who called her Kiki. Nikki was already the abbreviated version of Nicole, but he had to shorten it even more with Kiki. For some strange reason, she liked it.

"No," Nicole said, wanting to see what was really going on with all the attention he had been showing her lately. "I don't mind that you called. It's just that you asked me for my number, I said 'no,' and somehow you managed to get it. I just want to know who gave it to you."

"If it's really that important," he said with a sigh, "Imani gave it too me."

"She did?" Nicole said, not surprised that Imani would give him her number.

It was no secret that Imani thought Shawn would be good for Nicole. She'd said that they'd make a cute couple and that Nicole should give him a chance. But Nicole felt that her best friend's comments had been made during the height of her infatuation with Eddie. She was sure that Imani had been thinking about her own relationship when she'd suggested that Nicole "give love a chance."

"Yeah," Shawn replied, bringing Nicole out of her thoughts, "she said you probably wouldn't mind 'cause you were really feelin' me, you just won't admit it." Nicole could tell he was smiling. "Why wouldn't you want to admit you like me?"

Nicole couldn't believe Imani had told Shawn something she'd shared with Imani in confidence. She did like Shawn, but she didn't want to like him because he didn't seem like boyfriend material. She didn't need to get caught up in something she may not be able to get out of if she wanted to.

"I never said I wouldn't admit that I like you," Nicole said.

"So you are saying that you *do* like me?"

"No. I . . . umm." Nicole didn't know what to say. "I'm just saying that I never said I wouldn't admit it *if* I did like you."

"So . . . *if* you did like me, would you tell me?" Shawn asked.

"I don't know." Nicole found herself falling into the softness of his voice, though she tried to resist it. "It depends on your response."

"What if my response was that I'm feelin' you, would you tell me if you was feelin' me, too?"

"Maybe," she teased with a smile.

"See now, you don't like it when I play games, but you can act like you don't wanna be real after I just told you I was feelin' you," Shawn said. "That's messed up, Kiki."

"Okay," Nicole gave in and decided that being honest with herself and Shawn could have its benefits. She desired to be in a relationship and if Shawn was willing to give her that, then who was she to turn him down? "I do like you a little. I just don't know if I should like you at all."

"Why would you say that?" Shawn asked defensively.

"Don't get upset," Nicole told him. "It's just that I have known you for almost three years, and every time I've seen you with a girl, it's like she's not even there. I know 'what's-her-name' got mad the other day when you were all up in my face, while she was standing right beside you."

"You talkin' 'bout *Shelia*?" Shawn said the girl's name as if it left a disgusting taste on his tongue. "She ain't even my girl no more. She just be followin' me like a stray dog. If she got mad 'bout anything, it was probably 'cause you are much finer than her."

Nicole knew he meant that as a compliment, but she didn't accept it as one. "See, that's what I'm talking about. How can you sit there and talk about that girl like she's nothing. I can't see myself with someone who can't see every person as a person. You cannot be around me talking about people like you do, 'cause you'll end up making me see *you* as less than what you would want me to see you as."

"Dang," Shawn chuckled, "all I said was that you looked better than Shelia. I ain't mean to make you lecture me. But I feel what you sayin.' I shouldn't have called her a dog, but she do be following behind me like she's lost or something. What am I 'posed to do?"

"Tell her, *nicely*, to give you some space," Nicole advised. "Then, tell her that you would like to be friends, so she won't feel like you don't want to be around her."

"Then I'd be lyin,' 'cause I *don't* want to be around her," Shawn said, and then paused for a moment. "But if you do a lil' somethin' for me, I'll do what you asked."

Nicole didn't like where this conversation was headed. There was no telling what Shawn wanted her from her. If it was something stupid, he could forget it. "What?"

"If you hang wit' me this weekend, I'ma try to treat girls better."

Without thinking, Nicole laughed out loud. She hadn't meant to laugh, but it just seemed like he was joking.

"Why you laughing?" he asked. "I'm serious."

Nicole thought about his proposition. She did like him, but she didn't know if going out with him would be a good idea. Then again, if he was genuine in his approach, their friendship could turn into something more. She thought that going out with him might not be so bad. She thought he was cute, tall, had nice caramel skin, a gorgeous smile, and he was fun to be around most times. But he was not her type. He was a wannabe thug who thought he was God's gift to women, and Nicole preferred the more romantic type. *Girl please,* her conscience said. *Stop looking for excuses and just admit that you want to go out with him.*

"Okay," she said before she could change her mind.

"For real?" Shawn sounded surprised. "Don't play me. You serious?"

"Yeah, I'll go out with you, *if* you start treating girls with some respect."

"Then consider it done," he said.

Nicole's phone line beeped. "Shawn, I have to go. Someone is on my other line."

"Okay," he said. "I'll call you later to see what you wanna do."

"Alright, bye," she said as she clicked over.

"Dang, how long it take for you to answer your phone?" Ronald said, knowing his sister was on her other line. "Just 'cause you got your own line now, don't mean you can be tying it up all day."

"Well, hello big brother. Oh, I am just fine, thank you. How are you doing?" Nicole said sarcastically.

"Whatever," Ronald replied. "Tell Imani that she needs to find something to do other than talk on the phone all day."

"For your information," Nicole responded, "I was not on the phone with Imani. I was talking to . . . a friend."

"A friend?" Ronald questioned, suspiciously. "What kind of friend?"

"A friend. That's all you need to know," she said with a laugh.

"It bet' not be no boyfriends," Ronald retorted. "Don't make me beat him down."

"Ronald, I am seventeen years old," Nicole stated as if her brother needed to be reminded of her age. "If Mama says I can date or have guy friends call me, then I consider her word to be final, not yours. And just to push your buttons, it *was* a boy, who happened to ask me out this weekend *and* I accepted."

"You keep on and you are going to end up in trouble," Ronald said seriously. "Just 'cause you *think* you grown, don't mean that you are."

"Whatever you say," Nicole sighed.

"Anyway, where is everybody? I've been trying to call the house all day, but I've been getting a busy signal. I just tried your number 'cause I figured you were holding up the main phone line."

"No, Mama probably took it off of the hook just in case Daddy called," Nicole stated as if it was a normal, everyday occurrence.

"Why would she do that?" Ronald asked, confused.

" 'Cause lately they've been arguing a lot and Daddy just stormed out of the house. He hasn't been here for the past thirty minutes."

"How long has this been going on? Why didn't you tell me?"

"It's been like this since about a year after you went to college, but it has gotten worse since you moved out."

"Again, *why* didn't you tell me?" Ronald asked.

"I didn't want to bother you. You've been so busy

lately with work and football practice. Then you spend whatever spare time you have with Nevaeh, Marques, and all of your other friends. I just thought you wouldn't have time to hear about this stuff."

"Girl, this is family," Ronald said, not understanding why his sister would feel like she couldn't come to him. "Just because I'm not at the house doesn't mean that I am not here if you need to talk."

"Thanks," Nicole sighed, feeling the need to release the burden she'd been carrying for the last few weeks. "I really needed to hear that, because I wasn't sure when I should tell you this."

"What?"

"Mama is thinking about getting a divorce."

Chapter 3

Shimone had just walked out of the kitchen after sitting Ebony down at the table with a plate of food in front of her. As soon as she entered her bedroom, she heard a crash and then Ebony screaming. She rushed into the kitchen to see her daughter's plate on the floor. Mashed potatoes, macaroni and cheese, and chicken were splattered across the kitchen floor.

"What's wrong?" Shimone said, looking at her daughter with concern.

"I no want it," Ebony said. "I want ice ceam."

Shimone's concern quickly turned into anger. Just before she'd left the kitchen, Ebony had requested a bowl of chocolate ice cream, but Shimone had denied her request, saying that she had yet to have dinner. She could not believe her daughter had just knocked her food onto the floor just because she didn't want it. She walked swiftly to the table and lifted Ebony out of her high chair.

"Don't you ever do that again," she said as she hit Ebony's thigh over and over again. "Do you understand me? You do not waste food 'cause you don't want it."

"Yes, ma'am," Ebony cried.

Shimone walked Ebony into the living room and sat her on the sofa with her drinking cup. Just when she was about to go back into the kitchen to clean up the mess, she heard the front door being unlocked. At first, it frightened her, but then she remembered she'd given Marques a key a few weeks ago.

"What's up," he greeted, walking over a few of Ebony's toys.

"You really need to call before you come over here," Shimone said before greeting him with a kiss. "One day it's going to be late at night and you are going to be trying to unlock the door, and when you walk in you are going to find a frying pan upside your head."

Marques laughed. "Yeah right. You'd be so scared that you wouldn't be able to even hit me."

"Try me if you want to," Shimone said as she walked into the kitchen to clean up the mess.

"What happened here?" Marques asked as he looked at the wasted food.

"Why don't you ask your daughter," Shimone said.

He looked at his daughter who still had tears in her eyes as she sipped apple juice from her cup. "What did you do?"

"Mama hit me," Ebony tattled, pointing to her left thigh, which Shimone had disciplined, allowing her father to see the light red bruise.

"Want me to do it again?" Shimone threatened as she got up from the floor and walked toward her daughter with a stern look on her face. "Don't blame it on me. Tell him what you did."

"I knock it over," Ebony said, pointing to the food that was still scattered across the floor.

"You knocked your food onto the floor?" Marques asked for clarification as Ebony nodded. "Why?"

"I want ice ceam," Ebony said, rubbing her eye.

"You don't throw tantrums just because you don't get your way. Do you understand?" Marques said in a firm voice.

"Yes, Daddy," Ebony said.

"Now we're about to go back into the kitchen and Mommy's going to fix you another plate of food, and what are you going to do with it?"

"Eat," Ebony said with a pouted lip.

"Good girl," Marques said. "Now go back to the table and stop pouting before you get in trouble again."

As Ebony somberly made her way back to the table, Shimone suppressed the laugh that tickled the pit of her stomach. She'd never imagined Marques being such a disciplinarion. He was usually a softy when it came to chastising Ebony—most times getting on Shimone for being too hard on their daughter. But he'd made some serious progress in that area in the last year.

Marques placed Ebony in her high seat as Shimone cleaned the wasted food, washed her hands and Ebony's plate, and then went to the stove to prepare a fresh plate for her daughter.

"Marques, do you want something to eat?" Shimone asked.

"Yeah, I'll take a plate," he said.

Shimone fixed Marques a plate, placed it in front of him, and then sat Ebony's in front of her. She walked back to the stove and prepared herself a plate also. When she came back to the table, she noticed that Marques had started eating before blessing his food.

"Marques," she said as he bit into his fried chicken.

"Huh?"

"Did you forget something?" Shimone asked, holding her hands in prayer position.

"Oh, my bad." He said as he put his chicken back on his plate and clasped his hands together.

"Daddy, I can pray," Ebony volunteered, seemingly recovered from her earlier disappointment.

"Okay, go ahead." Marques bowed his head along with Shimone.

"God's great. God's good. Thank You for my food. Amen." Ebony raised her head and smiled.

"That was great, Ebony," Shimone praised.

They ate in silence as Marques secretly continued to check his watch for the time. He only had fifteen more minutes before he had to be at Alexia's condo. She had called him right before he had come to see his daughter and said she needed to see him. Marques hadn't objected at all. Although he had been seeing Alexia behind Shimone's back for more than four months, he had no growing feelings for her. Their relationship was strictly sexual as far as he was concerned. It seemed, though, that Alexia was getting more and more attached to him. Their once-a-month "meetings" had turned into once or twice a week.

At first, Marques didn't concern himself with feeling guilty about the whole situation, but now, as he looked across the table at his girlfriend who could be a pain, but seemed to grow more beautiful each day, and his daughter who was the light of his life, he noticed a mounting sense of shame. He wanted to tell Shimone what was going on, but was afraid of losing her. And if he lost Shimone, he was sure to lose Ebony also.

Marques had given his life to the Lord on Easter Sunday three years ago, but he didn't see himself changing like he thought he would. In the beginning, he tried to do things the right way by going to church and learning more about the Lord. He would pray daily and ask for wisdom and understanding. He would go to church every Sunday, hoping to come out of the service full of desire to do the Lord's will. But after entering college, he found himself back in the same place he'd been before. He wanted to live college life to the fullest by partying and having endless fun. He experimented with drinking and girls after resisting both many times. Shimone would ask him to go to a church service or to come over to the apartment so they could study scriptures together like they used to, and he would turn her down so he could go to a party or hang out with his friends.

When he met Alexia, his first thought was that although she wasn't his type, she was beautiful. She was almost as tall as he was with smooth, dark skin. Every strand of her long, jet-black hair was in place and her outfit looked like it had been designed just for her lean body. He was even more attracted to her after she boldly approached him. They began to hang out, and soon their friendship turned into something that Marques didn't want to control.

But now all of his sneaking around was getting to be a burden that he didn't want to carry any longer. When he looked across the table at Shimone, she smiled. He looked at his daughter, and she laughed. He knew he needed to end his relationship with Alexia, and he needed to do it tonight.

Marques pushed back from the table. "I have to go now," he said to Shimone and Ebony's disappointment.

"Daddy leaving?" Ebony asked sadly.

"Why?" Shimone asked. "This is the first family dinner we've shared in a while. I know I don't like you being here too late in the evening, but it's only seven-thirty. It's not that late. You can stay."

The distressed look in her eyes made him want to sit back down at the table so she wouldn't worry. He knew if he didn't break things off with Alexia now, he wouldn't have the courage to do it later. "I know it's been a while and I wish I could stay, but ... I gotta work tomorrow and I need my rest," he lied, knowing full well he could sleep tomorrow morning away and be rested enough to work in the afternoon.

"Okay, I understand," Shimone lied as well. She didn't understand much of anything Marques did or said lately.

Marques walked over to his daughter and kissed her on the forehead. "Bye, pumpkin."

"Bye bye, Daddy," Ebony said, pushing a spoonful of macaroni into her mouth.

Marques walked to the end of the table and leaned over to kiss Shimone. When he tried to stand up straight, she gently pulled his face back down to hers and looked into his eyes.

"I love you," she whispered.

Marques swallowed the truth that tempted to erupt from his soul. "I love you, too," he said as he kissed her again. He walked to the door and turned around to see both of them watching him. "Tomorrow we will spend the whole day together," he promised. "We'll go to the movies or something. Okay?"

"Movie!" Ebony squealed as Shimone nodded without verbally responding.

Marques saw something in Shimone's eyes that frightened him. He didn't know if she could sense that something was wrong or if she was just tired of him not being around. Whatever it was, he wanted to fix it so that he or anyone else would never hurt her. He stepped outside into the humid air and locked the door. Walking to his car, he practiced what he was going to say to Alexia as soon as he arrived at her apartment:

"I'm sorry, Alexia, but I love my family and I don't want to keep lying to them. They need me and I want to be there for them, so I have to stop seeing you."

* * *

"What do you mean you have to stop seeing me?" Alexia shouted as Marques stood in the living room of her condo. "I call you over here so we can spend some time together and you walk through the door and start saying stupid crap like this! Where is this coming from? Since when do you need to stop seeing me so you can be there for your daughter?"

"I'm not just trying to be there for Ebony," Marques said as Alexia continued to pace in front of him. "I need to start being faithful to Shimone. I'm tired of lying to her."

"How can you be faithful to someone you are not even in a relationship with?"

"Shimone and I *are* in a relationship. We've been going out for nearly four years. You knew that, so don't even try to front like you didn't, 'cause I told you all about my relationship with her when I told you I had a daughter."

"Marques, do you really think I would have let you into my life or my bed if I had known you and Shimone were together, in a committed relationship?" Alexia asked as she stopped pacing and stood toe-to-toe with him. "Do you really believe that I would even consider having any type of relationship with you if I knew you were with Shimone?"

"Apparently so, since you did," he said, folding his arms across his chest. "You knew I was with her when we started this whole thing, so I don't have the time or the patience to stand here and argue with you."

Alexia dropped onto the sofa. "Well, I don't see why you have to stop seeing me. Why can't you break things off with her?" she asked in an exasperated tone. "She's the one you are always complaining about, and you are the one who is always talking about how she gets on your nerves and how you wish she would leave you alone sometimes. So I don't see why you have to leave me. I love you."

Marques didn't know how to respond to Alexia's declaration. He knew she had gotten attached, but it hadn't occurred to him that she could actually have serious feelings for him. Although he was really close to feeling sorry for her, he stood his ground. "I have to leave you because I love my family. I don't feel any love for you like I do for Shimone. I don't have a child with you. I want to be a real family with my family."

Alexia sank further into the sofa cushions and buried her face in her hands. Marques heard her sniffle. He stood in the middle of the living room as deep sobs erupted from the pit of her stomach. He knew he couldn't leave her like this. He had to stay at least until she calmed down. He sat on the sofa and tried his best to comfort her, but all he felt was uncomfortable. She looked up at him and rubbed his bald head, then she placed her hands on his face and began moving them down toward his neck. Marques abruptly ended her exploration and stood to his feet. He looked at Alexia's face and sighed as tears continued to stream down her cheeks. He didn't need to fall into temptation. Not now. He didn't want to leave her in this condition, but he needed to go before he found himself in a position he didn't need to be in.

"Alexia, I really have to go," Marques said as he backed away. "I'm sorry." He walked to the door and turned the knob.

"Marques," Alexia called with tears still flooding her eyes, "I'm pregnant."

His hand dropped from the doorknob as his eyes slowly met hers. "Excuse me?" he asked as his jaw clenched.

Alexia stood up and pressed her hand against her

stomach. "I am two-and-a-half months pregnant and you are the father."

Marques walked into his apartment at a quarter 'til eleven. He had been driving around for almost two hours. After Alexia had told him she was pregnant, he walked out of the door. Before he left the porch, he could hear her cries and had forced himself not to walk back inside the house to comfort her. He couldn't believe she was pregnant; it just had to be a lie. She couldn't be; he always used protection. She was lying; he knew she was. She was trying to trick him into staying with her, but it wasn't going to work. He was going to confess to Shimone and try to start being a real family with her and Ebony.

Deep down in his soul, though, Marques knew Alexia was being honest. Just the look in her eyes said that she wasn't trying to be deceitful. He could tell it was hurting her just as it was killing him. He also knew she was going to keep the baby. Alexia had told him many times before that she didn't believe in killing an innocent child just because the parents weren't ready to care for it, so he knew for a fact that she was going to go through the nine months of childbearing and the hours of labor.

What he was mostly concerned with was how he was going to tell Shimone. She was going to kill him. And he would deserve every punch, every kick, and every insult she would give him. She could do anything she wanted to do, he just didn't want her to leave him and take their daughter with her. He wouldn't be able to bear it if he never saw his family again.

He wished he could just take the past four months back. He wished that when he first met Alexia he would have told her that he had a girlfriend that he loved and didn't want to hurt instead of saying he had a girlfriend that got on his nerves 24/7. He wished he had stuck with his commitment to God instead of turning his back on the people who cared about him the most.

Marques walked into the den and the blinking voice-mail light on the telephone that sat on a stand in the corner of the room caught his eye. He pressed play.

"Marques, it's me," Shimone said frantically into the phone. "I've been trying to call you for hours. I don't know where you are. I left several messages on your cell. But I need you to come down to Emory. Mama was in an accident. She had a heart attack. Please come. Ebony is asking for you. Nev, Ron, and your parents are down here already. I love you. Pray while you drive, okay? Bye."

Marques pulled his cell phone out of his pants pocket and shook his head. He always kept his phone on silent when he was with Alexia, so that if Shimone or someone else called him, he wouldn't have to lie about his where-abouts. But, tonight, after leaving her house, he'd forgotten to check his phone for missed calls. Taking notice of it now, he had five voicemail messages on his phone.

He quickly forgot about his problems as he ran out of the house and hopped into his car, praying that all was well with the woman who had become a second mother to him.

Chapter 4

Shimone sat in the hospital's waiting room as she watched Ebony play with Marques's nephews, Bryan and Brandon, on the floor near their grandparents. Nevaeh sat beside her as Shimone continued to wipe tears from her eyes and pray silently.

"It's going to be okay," Nevaeh consoled as she rubbed Shimone's back. "Your mother is strong; she will pull through this. It was just a mild heart attack. She's just in shock."

"But from what?" Shimone asked. "All I know is that she was driving somewhere and the doctor said that something might have taken her attention away from the road, but I don't know what could have scared her so much that she would swerve off of the road and into a ditch."

"Maybe it was an animal or something," Nevaeh said, wiping Shimone's face. "Maybe she saw a dog and tried to miss hitting it."

"No," Shimone said, still not convinced. "I don't think so. Mama knows how to handle stray animals in the street; she even knows how to handle people who honk at her or pedestrians or other drivers who don't have the right-of-way. She's really calm about those types of things. I think that something or someone really scared her."

Ebony walked over to Shimone and Nevaeh. "Mama Ma okay?" she asked her mother.

"I don't know," Shimone said, pulling Ebony onto her lap. "We have to wait and see what the doctor says."

Ebony gazed at her mother and placed her small hands on Shimone's face. "Mama okay?" she asked as she noticed her mother's tears.

"Yes, I'm fine," Shimone smiled.

Ebony's gaze lingered on her mother for a minute longer, and then she smiled. Shimone kissed her daughter's forehead and placed her back on the floor.

"Uncle Marq," four-year-old Brandon shouted out as he ran toward Marques who had just walked through the hospital doors.

"Wassup, Uncle Marq?" seven-year-old Bryan said, running behind his brother.

"Daddy, Daddy," Ebony called, her little legs trying to catch up with her cousins.

Shimone looked up and saw Ebony running toward her father. She was glad that he had come, but she wondered what had taken him so long. Marques had been late every time Shimone needed him to be somewhere, and he never had a valid excuse. When Ronald and Nevaeh had arrived at the hospital about a half-hour after Shimone received the call from the paramedics, Ronald had informed her that Marques hadn't been home since leaving for her apartment earlier in the evening. Shimone wasn't naïve; she knew something wasn't right with her relationship with Marques. She just wished that she knew what it was so that they could work on it before the matter grew worse.

"Wassup, man?" Ronald greeted his friend. "What took you so long?"

"I just got home an hour ago and got Shimone's message on my voicemail," Marques said, bouncing Ebony in his arms.

"You look tired," Ronald said. "Are you okay?"

"Naw, man."

Ronald looked at Marques and knew they needed to talk later on. He took Ebony from Marques and motioned to Shimone who was sitting in the back corner of the waiting room. Marques walked toward Shimone, who seemed to be extremely emotional. He didn't want to hurt her any further, so he decided to confess his wrongs later.

Nevaeh stood and hugged him. "She really needs you right now."

"Okay," Marques said as he released her. He remembered a time when Nevaeh despised him, but now they were as close as family.

Nevaeh walked toward Ronald and the kids in order to give the couple their privacy. Marques reached for Shimone and she immediately wrapped her arms around him. She cried on his chest as he held her and assured her everything was going to be fine. Even though she was upset with him, Shimone was glad he was there to comfort her.

"Ms. Shimone Johnson?" a male doctor asked as he walked into the waiting room.

"That's me," Shimone answered as she tried to dry her tears.

"I am Dr. Ingles," he said. "I am happy to inform you that your mother is going to be fine. She just had a mild heart attack and she was in shock for a moment, but we've got her in stable condition and she will most likely be able to go home in two or three days."

"Did you find out what caused the heart attack?" Nevaeh asked the question that everyone had been wondering since they had been called to the hospital.

"Well, the EMTs found her in a ditch, and when they brought her in on the gurney, she seemed delirious and she kept mumbling a name. I think it was 'Taylor,' " he said, checking the details on Misty's chart. "No, I'm sorry. It was Tyler; she kept repeating 'Tyler' over and over again. Does the name ring a bell?"

Nevaeh's eyes shot in Shimone's direction. Her reaction made everyone else look to Shimone for an answer, but she was nearly speechless. "My . . . my f–father's name is Tyler," she whispered as tears began to stream down her face.

"Mama, what's wrong?" Ebony asked as Shimone sank into a chair.

"Ebony, go over there with Uncle Ron," Marques instructed as he held Shimone.

"Mama okay?" Ebony continued to ask worriedly as she climbed in the chair next to Ronald.

"Mommy is going to be fine," Nevaeh assured as she sat on the other side of Ebony. "She is going to be okay."

Nevaeh tried to make herself believe her own words as she watched Marques hold Shimone, who had become hysterical. Brandon, Bryan, and their grandparents sat near Shimone and Marques; they watched as she rocked back and forth and muttered a prayer that no one could decipher. Dr. Ingles had called a nurse to help calm Shimone down as everyone looked on and wondered why Shimone's father's name would upset her so much.

*   *   *

Misty lay asleep in the hospital bed as Shimone stood and watched the monitor measure her mother's heart activity. She said a silent prayer of thanks that her mother was alive. Yet, she still wondered what her father had to do with this whole situation.

Shimone had never met her father. All she knew about him was that he was a handsome white man and he and her mother had attended the same private high school. They dated for several months, then broke up after Misty told him she was pregnant. As far as Shimone was concerned, her life would be perfect as long as Tyler Calhoun stayed out of it. But now, knowing that he had something to do with her mother being in this hospital room instead of in the comfort of her own home, Shimone wanted to find him and make him feel every ounce of pain he'd caused her mother.

Misty's eyes opened and she smiled when she saw her daughter. Shimone hoped she had done a good job of washing her face before coming into the room, so her mother wouldn't detect any evidence of lingering tears.

"Hey, Mama," Shimone said, taking Misty's hand. "How you feeling?"

"Good." Her voice was weak, but Shimone was glad she was able to talk.

"Everybody is here praying for you. Even Ebony was asking God to make you better."

Misty managed a weak smile as a tear rolled down her cheek.

Shimone reached down and wiped it away. "Mama, what happened?"

Misty closed her eyes to prevent more tears from releasing themselves, but it was no use as they trailed down her cheeks and onto her pillow. Shimone took a tissue out of her purse and wiped her mother's face and then wiped her own.

"Mama," Shimone said, softly, "did you see my daddy?"

Misty nodded slowly as more tears streamed down her face. She closed her eyes again and this time she revisited the night's events.

"What else do I need?" Misty asked herself as she went down the next aisle in the grocery store. She didn't usually grocery shop on weekdays, but when she went into her kitchen, she noticed there was nothing in her cabinets or refrigerator that she wanted to eat. So she decided to pick up a few items.

She picked up a couple loaves of bread and moved toward the poultry section. She selected two whole chickens and a few vegetables before heading toward the checkout counter.

"A pretty young thing like yourself should never have to shop alone," the tall, dark, and handsome cashier flirted as she placed her items on the conveyer belt.

Misty shook her head and blushed at his comment. He smiled as he totaled her items, and then she swiped her checking card through the card reader.

As she punched in her pin number, a gentleman in the next line caught her eye. He was a tall, handsome, white man with light brown hair—like Shimone's—and light brown eyes—just like Shimone's. The man caught her staring and returned her gaze. When Misty looked into his eyes, it seemed as if her daughter was staring back at her. He seemed like he thought he recognized her, but was unsure of himself. However, Misty knew exactly who he was and quickly turned her attention back to the cashier who was handing her a receipt. She took it and walked briskly out of the store.

After placing her groceries in her trunk, she got into her car and turned on the engine. Through her rear view mirror she could see the man looking in her direction as he climbed into his vehicle. Misty pulled out of the parking lot and sped onto the surface street. At the red light, she continuously checked her mirrors to see if he might be following her. She spotted his car three cars behind hers in the far left lane. When the light turned green, she kept straight as she tried her best to hurry home. She looked through her mirrors again and saw that he was in the lane right next to her, only one car behind. She sped up, and when she looked over in the next lane he was driving right beside her. She tried to stay focused, but when she glanced in his direction again, he looked into her eyes. She panicked and lost control of her car. The next thing she knew she was strapped to a gurney and was being brought into the hospital for testing.

Shimone cried as her mother told her what had happened. She couldn't believe after years of not seeing Tyler, he'd just popped up out of nowhere and scared the living daylights out of her mother. And he had to see the accident, so where was he now? He could have at least tried to see if Misty was okay, but, once again, he was running from something he had caused.

"Mama, I'm going to let you get some rest okay?" Shimone said. "Try not to think about that man," *If you can call him that,* "or the accident." She kissed her mother's forehead and pulled the covers up around her neck. Shimone walked out of the room and into the waiting room where her friends and family hoped for good news.

"How is she?" Marques asked.

"She is doing fine," Shimone said, wiping leftover tears.

"Thank You, Jesus," Ronald proclaimed with exhilaration. "You hear that, Ebony? Mama Ma is going to be fine. Can you say, 'Thank You, Jesus'?"

"Thank Jesus," Ebony said, holding her hands in the air and clapping them together.

"That's right, baby," Shimone said, taking Ebony into her arms.

As they began to relax in the waiting room for a few more minutes, a white male walked through the doors and up to the receptionist's station. Shimone looked at the strange man who seemed to be very familiar.

"Are you okay, sweetie?" Shundra asked Shimone.

"I don't know," Shimone responded as she continued to stare at the tall, brown-haired man.

"May I help you?" the receptionist asked in a professional tone.

"I think you can," the man replied in a strong voice. "I'm here to see a woman who was involved in a car accident about three hours ago. She drove into a ditch and they say she had a heart attack. I have been trying to get information on her. I saw the accident, but I had another emergency to attend to, so I was not able to get here sooner. But I'd really like to see if she is okay."

"I'm sorry. I cannot let you in the room at this moment, sir, considering it is past visitation hours. But the accident victim's family is in the waiting room right over there." The receptionist pointed in Shimone's direction. "You may be able to see her if they allow you and if one of them accompanies you into the room."

"Thank you," the man said as he walked toward the waiting area.

As he neared them, Shimone's heart began to beat faster. Marques looked at her and wondered if she was about to pass out.

"Baby, are you okay?" he asked her. Marques followed her gaze and saw the man standing next to him, staring down at Shimone. "May I help you?" he asked the man.

The gentleman couldn't seem to take his eyes off of Shimone who was still staring at him as if she knew who he was, but didn't know what to do in his presence. Nevaeh and Ronald looked at each other and back at the man, and then at Shimone, who stood up and placed Ebony in Marques's arms.

"What are you doing here?" Shimone asked him.

The man seemed to be at a loss for words as he stared into what he knew were his daughter's eyes.

"What are you doing here?" Shimone asked, louder this time as tears began to stream down her face.

"I . . . I came to see Mis–Misty John . . . son," he stammered. "I was won-wondering if you would permit me . . . to . . . to . . . see her?"

"Why?" Shimone spat. "You haven't wanted to see her or me since you found out she was pregnant. So why?"

Her family finally realized who the man was.

"I . . . I just tho– . . . " He cleared his throat. "I just thought that I could see if she . . . was well," he said as he continued to look at Shimone with a mixture of love and regret.

"Well, you thought wrong. *No* you cannot see if she is well," Shimone said as tears clouded her vision. "You didn't care about her well-being when you told her she should abort me. And you didn't care when all those kids treated her mean just because they thought she had gotten pregnant to trap you into a relationship, and you surely didn't care when you waited three hours before you even came to the hospital to see if she was still alive after you scared her half to death on the road. You didn't care then and it's a waste of time to even care now, so you can leave."

Tyler stood in front of her with tears in his eyes. "I know you are angry with me. I don't blame you. I should have been there, but I wasn't and I am sorry." He searched her face. "You look so much like her," he whispered.

"I said leave!" Shimone screamed as she hit him repeatedly on his chest. "Just go, now. Leave!"

"Mama!" Ebony cried as she reached for Shimone. "Daddy, why Mama crying?"

"Is there a problem here?" a security guard asked as he walked over to the waiting area.

Tyler curiously gazed at Ebony as Marques stood and pulled the child away from Shimone. He watched as Nevaeh pulled Shimone into a hug. Ronald stood next to Marques as both men told Tyler, with their stares, that he needed to leave.

"No problem, officer," Tyler said as he walked toward the doors and left the hospital.

Nevaeh held Shimone in her arms as she cried. "That was my daddy," Shimone said over and over.

"I know, sweetie," Nevaeh said. "Everything is going to be okay."

Shimone cried as she wished Tyler would come back to embrace her and tell her that he loved her and that he would never leave her or her mother again. She wanted him to come back and stay, so they could make things right together. She wanted him to come back and be the father that she missed having for the past twenty-two years. But he didn't.

Chapter 5

"Yes, and I have a design that is going to be in the fall fashion show," Sierra said into the phone.

"Sweetheart, I'm so proud of you," Christopher applauded. "I can't wait for the day when I go into a store and your name is printed on the back of a pair of jeans."

Sierra laughed. "Me either. Well, Daddy, I have to go because Corey will be here in a few."

"Okay, baby girl, tell everyone I said hello," Christopher said, "and I love you."

"I love you, too, Daddy." Sierra smiled. "Bye."

Sierra Monroe placed her phone on its hook before walking out of her bedroom and into the den of the apartment she shared with her best friend, LaToya Thomas. Sierra looked around her living space and sighed, "Girl, where are they?" she asked LaToya.

"I don't know," LaToya responded. "Jamal called about twenty minutes ago and he was at Corey's house. He said that they would be here in fifteen minutes."

"Well, they need to hurry up before I decide not to go," Sierra said as she plopped down on the sofa. "I could've called Nevaeh by now. You know we haven't spoken to her in a while," she pointed out as LaToya nodded in agreement.

Nevaeh, Shimone, Sierra, and LaToya had attended high school together and during the four years of their secondary education, Sierra spent the majority of her time trying to outdo Nevaeh. Anything Nevaeh had, Sierra wanted, including Ronald. Their strained relationship had prevented either of their best friends from associating with each other as well, but in the last few years all four women had laid the past to rest and had grown to be close friends.

"Oh," Sierra moaned, "They need to come on. My feet are starting to hurt."

LaToya laughed. "Well, nobody told you to wear five-inch heels to the park."

"Whatever," Sierra said. "You know I don't go nowhere looking like a bum off the streets."

LaToya laughed, but remembered a time when Sierra came to school dressed in baggy jeans and a sweatshirt, starting two weeks after she had found out she was HIV positive. Before that, Sierra had been the queen of six-inch heels and mini skirts. She always looked like a runway model or like someone who had just stepped off the cover of a fashion magazine. But for many months after receiving her test results, she wore nothing but jeans, T-shirts, and tennis shoes.

Even while dating LaToya's brother, Corey, she dressed down. But after receiving counseling and attending classes for people who had HIV or full-blown AIDS, Sierra returned to her normal self, which made everyone happy, including her father who had never seen his daughter so distraught.

Christopher had hardly been around for Sierra. Between picking up court cases and women, it seemed like she didn't exist. But after finding out about her condition, he immediately began to spend time with Sierra hoping to make up for years of lost time. Ever since she had told him about her disease, they had been as close as they could get. Even, now, when they were a time zone apart.

"I think that's your little man crying for you," Sierra said as she got up from the sofa

LaToya went into the room she and her twenty-one-month-old son shared and turned on the light. Jabari was kicking and screaming as usual. She pulled back the bed sheets, picked him up out of her bed, which he had just gotten used to sleeping in, and tried to calm him down. She rocked him and walked back and forth in the room as she hummed a soothing tune.

When she first got pregnant, LaToya had thought about aborting the baby. She was in the second semester of her freshman year and knew she didn't have the time or the patience to take care of a child. But after talking about it to Sierra, who had been through an abortion and a miscarriage within the course of a year, LaToya decided to have the baby. At first it didn't sit well with her boyfriend, Jamal, who was a junior at the time.

Jamal Lowden was Corey's friend and LaToya remembered thinking how cute he was when she first saw him. He had a flawless smile with an even set of pearly white teeth and the most impeccable shade of dark chocolate skin with the perfect shade of dark brown eyes. In her eyes, Jamal was just perfect. He had been a rising junior at Missouri College, majoring in Business Management when she met him. When he asked her out, she immediately accepted. After dating him for a few months, they made the mistake of spending one night together, and the result was Jabari Bernard Lowden.

When Jamal suggested that LaToya have an abortion, she told him about what Sierra had gone through, and then she explained to him that she didn't want to have to deal with the same emotional turmoil. He decided that it was okay for her to have the baby, but they should give it up for adoption. LaToya knew she wasn't going to carry her baby for nine months and then give him up to some stranger, so immediately after turning down that option, she went to her brother and pleaded with him to step in and handle the situation. Corey finally talked, maybe even threatened, some sense into Jamal's head and he decided that he would be there for LaToya and Jabari.

Hearing the solid thuds against the front door, Latoya walked back into the living room with her son in her arms. When Sierra opened the door, LaToya had to suppress the fluttering she felt in her stomach at the sight of her boyfriend. Jamal looked extremely handsome in his khaki shorts and white polo shirt. Her brother looked nice in his jeans and his custom made "Got Jesus?" muscle shirt also.

"Hey," Jamal said as he leaned down to lightly kiss LaToya on the lips.

"Hi." She smiled.

"How is Daddy's lil' man?" Jamal took Jabari out of LaToya's arms.

"Cranky," LaToya said. "He just stopped crying. I don't think he got enough sleep last night."

"Daddy," Jabari squealed.

"Well, he seems fine now." Jamal smiled. "C'mon, we need to go before it gets really hot."

"Whose car are we taking?" Sierra asked as she placed her purse on her shoulder.

Corey placed his arm around her waist and led her to the door. "Baby, do you even have to ask? We always roll in the Navigator."

They laughed as they headed out of the apartment and toward the car. They pulled up at the park fifteen minutes later. Corey helped Sierra out of the car and they waited while Jamal and LaToya changed Jabari's diaper before heading to the playground. They found a grassy spot and Sierra opened the checkered blanket out onto the ground. LaToya sat down next to Jamal, placed the picnic basket on the blanket and sat Jabari next to her. Sierra sat in front of Corey and rested her head on his chest.

"How are you feeling today?" Corey asked, fingering a strand of Sierra's hair.

"Good," Sierra answered. "I took my medicine and I don't feel tired, so I'd say I'm doing well today."

"You look like it," he said, pulling at her skirt.

She laughed and stood up. "Come push me."

"What?" Corey asked, confused.

"Come push me on the swing." Sierra laughed at his expression.

"Sierra, you are twenty-one years old," Corey said. "So what do I look like, at twenty-three, pushing you on the swing?"

"You'd look like you were trying to make your girlfriend really happy," she said with a pouted lip and a pleading expression covering her face.

Corey got up and took her hand. "Okay, Daddy's baby," he said in a sarcastic tone.

Sierra sat in the swing as Corey pushed her gently. She looked toward the sky and wished she could see God's face so she could thank Him for giving her life. She realized that she could have not awakened this morning, but God allowed her to live another day and she was grateful.

"What are you thinking about?" Corey asked.

"God's goodness," she responded honestly. "I could not be here right now, but I am and I know it is because of God."

Corey smiled. He remembered when Sierra had called him, three years ago, after coming from an Easter service. She sounded so excited when she told him that she had given her life to Christ. He had been surprised to find out that both of their fathers and his sister had done the same.

"You know," Corey began, "when I asked you to come to college in St. Louis, I didn't think you'd go for it."

"Why not?" Sierra asked. "I was thinking about coming out here anyway."

"I just thought that maybe with you getting so close to your dad that you wouldn't want to leave him alone in Atlanta."

"Daddy knows I'm a big girl and that I don't actually have to be with him to *be with him*. You know what I mean?"

"Yeah," Corey said, "but I've been thinking. After you graduate, maybe we could make this move permanent. Maybe settle down."

Sierra looked up at him. "Are you serious? You mean settle like *settle* . . . as in get married and start a family?" she asked, fingering the ring he had given her after she promised to be celibate with him three years ago.

"Maybe." He smiled. "It's just a thought." Corey looked at the clouds and followed their movement.

"What's wrong?" Sierra asked when he suddenly stopped pushing her.

"Look over there," he said, pointing to a cloud.

Sierra laughed as she tried to look where he was pointing. They had been dating for almost four years and she still laughed every time his Midwestern twang changed the pronunciation of certain words. Although she would usually pick on him about it, his St. Louis accent was one of the things she loved about him.

"Sierra, this is not the time to be making fun of the way I talk," Corey said, still pointing. "Look."

Still laughing, Sierra saw what he was pointing at. There was a cloud in the sky that looked exactly like an angel; it seemed to be smiling at them. Its halo was centered perfectly on its head and its wings seemed to move in the breeze. Sierra smiled and said a thankful prayer to God. He knew she was happy to be alive and she took it as a message that she was one of His chosen angels.

"God must really love you," Corey said, as if reading her mind.

"I think He really loves all of us." Sierra smiled as he began to push her again.

LaToya sat on the picnic blanket and took small bites of her sandwich, while Jamal played with Jabari. She and Jamal had been dating, off and on, for three years and she felt like she never wanted to live without him, but she didn't know if he felt the same way. She reminisced on the first time she met Jamal.

Sierra and LaToya had arrived at Corey's new condo an hour after the party had begun. They had just gotten off of the plane and rented a car for the drive to Corey's house. After his old roommate allowed his girlfriend to move in, Corey decided it was time for him to get his own place. So after finding it the summer before he was to start his junior year, he threw a housewarming/birthday party for himself.

When they walked through the doors of the condominium, LaToya spotted Corey standing in the kitchen, surrounded by a group of guys. One particularly caught her eye. He seemed to look in LaToya's direction as soon as she walked through the door. Sierra dragged LaToya through the crowded living room and into the kitchen.

"Hey," Sierra said as she tapped Corey on the shoulder. "You lookin' real sexy, boo."

"Excuse me?" Corey asked as he turned around. When he saw Sierra, he broke into a huge grin.

"Hi," she laughed, hugging him. "Happy birthday."

Corey kissed her and saw his sister smiling behind them.

"Wassup?" he said, hugging LaToya. "I thought y'all weren't coming in until school started."

"We weren't, but when Sierra told me that you were having a party, I knew I couldn't miss it," LaToya said.

He looked down at Sierra. "I thought you said that you weren't going to be able to pay for a flight."

"I wasn't; Daddy said money was tight." Sierra shrugged. "But your dad said he had it covered."

"Dad paid for y'all to come up here?" he asked in disbelief.

LaToya laughed. "I don't know why you're so surprised. You know I can work him."

Corey smiled and turned around toward his friends who seemed to be staring intently at the two girls. "Fellas, this is Sierra, my girlfriend," he introduced, "and this is my sister, LaToya. Ladies, this is Dustin, William, Quentin, and Jamal."

"Hey," "Wassup?" "What's good?" and "How you doin'?" came from the guys who were still gawking at the two girls.

Jamal couldn't seem to take his eyes off of LaToya. His stare was so intense that she had to turn her head so he wouldn't see her blushing. She noticed that Corey and Sierra had left her standing in the midst of all the guys as they went to the middle of the floor to dance. Dustin seemed to be the only one not interested in approaching LaToya and she figured it was because of the girl attached to his arm.

William stepped forward and looked down at LaToya. "You wanna dance?"

LaToya looked at the rest of the guys who seemed to be disappointed that William had made the first move. She glanced at Jamal and wished he had asked her first. She looked back at the caramel gentleman who stood in front of her, patiently waiting for an answer.

"Sure," she said as he took her hand and led her to the dance floor.

She wrapped her arms around his neck and swayed to the music. Her four-inch heels allowed her to see past his shoulder. She spotted Jamal, who was looking directly at her, and made eye contact. They stared at each other as LaToya continued to slow dance with William. The intensity of the moment reminded her of a scene from Love and Basketball, her favorite movie. LaToya lowered her eyes when Jamal turned around to place his drink on the table.

Jamal walked toward the dance floor and tapped William on the shoulder. "You wouldn't mind if I cut in, would you?" he said, his accent as distinguished as her brother's.

William looked at LaToya, who shook her head. Although he seemed disappointed, he stepped aside, allowing Jamal take the lead. Jamal placed his arms around her waist as she laid her head on his shoulder. They slow danced to Alicia Keys's "Feelin' U, Feelin' Me." By the time the two-minute song had ended, Jamal was ready to make his next move.

"Come outside with me," he whispered into her ear, his voice deep and melodious.

LaToya wasn't sure if she should follow his command, but she didn't have time to think. She caught Sierra's eye, so someone would know who she was with if she didn't return. They walked outside and stood on the porch. LaToya played with the hem of her miniskirt as she stood against the door.

"So . . ." Jamal said, trying to think of something to say.

"So," Latoya replied as she waited for him to strike up a conversation.

"How old are you?"

"I just turned eighteen a few months ago," she replied. "What about you?"

"I'm nineteen. I'll be twenty in a few months." He gazed at her as if he was trying to memorize her every move. "Maybe you can come to my party."

LaToya smiled. "Maybe."

"You have a beautiful smile," Jamal complimented.

"Thank you," she blushed.

"How long are you planning to stay up here?"

She shrugged. "Probably just for a few days and then we have to go back to Atlanta."

"Well, while you're here, would you like to hang out with me? Maybe I can show you around."

LaToya smiled. "Well, Sierra and I already made plans," she said to his disappointment. "But I could give you my number. I'll be moving here in a few months to enroll in Missouri College, so maybe we could get together for a movie or something."

"Alright, that's where I go to school, so we can definitely hook up." Jamal pulled out his cell phone and handed it to her for her to program her number into it.

They went back to the party and became each other's dance partners for the rest of the night. Once the party ended and everyone had gone home, Corey settled the girls into the guest bedroom. Sierra had LaToya fill her in on her night with Jamal. And for some reason, LaToya knew she would be seeing more of him once she entered Missouri College.

LaToya had been right. Even before she settled into her dorm room, she and Jamal had spent time together talking on the phone for hours when she was at home. When she arrived on campus, they went out a few times before he finally asked her to be his girlfriend. They spent all of their spare time together. But ever since having Jabari, the spark in their relationship had died. LaToya wondered if Jamal was still with her because he was happy being with her, or because he felt as if he had to be with her in order to be a good father.

"You okay?" Jamal asked as he took a sandwich out of the basket.

She hesitated a moment before saying, "Jamal?"

"Yeah?"

"How do you feel about me?"

The question seemed to catch him off guard. "What do you mean?" he asked with his mouth full.

"Just what I said." LaToya repeated, "How do you feel about me? What do you feel when you look at me?"

He swallowed the food. "Why would you ask me that?"

"Because lately it seems like you are around just because of Jabari, and if you don't want to be with me, I don't want to be wasting your time."

Jamal turned so he would be looking into her light brown eyes. He noticed that she was on the verge of tears. "LaToya, when I look at you I see a beautiful, intelligent young woman who I love spending time with. I don't know why you would ask me how I feel about you because it seems like you are trying to see if I am happy. But if you can't see that just by looking at me, then something is wrong.

"Yes, at first the idea of you having Jabari scared me. I still had school to finish and I didn't have enough time or money to take care of a baby. But I love Jabari and if we had a chance to do things differently, I don't think I would. I love you and I love being with you."

He said exactly what LaToya wanted to hear. She knew he loved her, but today the words brought tears to her eyes. She leaned over and kissed him. "I love you, too," she whispered against his lips.

"Up, up," Jabari said, bouncing up and down on the blanket.

LaToya picked him up and placed him on her lap. "And Mama loves you, too," she said, kissing his forehead.

Chapter 6

"Mama, put this on," Ebony said, pulling a jean skirt from the dresser.

"I don't know," Shimone said. "I was thinking about this." She held up a pair of boot cut jeans.

"No." Ebony pulled the pants out of her mother's hands and handed her the skirt. "Daddy like this."

Ebony was right. Marques loved for Shimone to wear skirts, especially when she wore them with heels, and the one she held in her hand was his favorite. He'd said that they showed off her legs, which were thick, but shapely, due to her years of hip-hop, jazz, and ballet dancing.

Shimone loved to dance and had been doing so since before she was ten years old, prancing around in her mother's studio when it had first opened. Dancing on her high school drill team was the only extracurricular activity she took part in, but trying out for the college squad hadn't been an option. Her daughter always came first.

Shimone took the knee-length skirt from Ebony and placed it on the bed. "Find Mommy a top to wear," Shimone said as Ebony ran to the dresser and pulled out a lime green tube top.

"And this too," Ebony said, grabbing Shimone's jean half-jacket off the daybed.

"Wow, you are just Mommy's little fashion designer," Shimone said, impressed that everything her three-year-old had pulled out actually matched. "Now let's get you dressed before Daddy gets here."

Ebony ran out of her mother's room, across the living room, and into her bedroom. She pulled the Mickey Mouse jumper off of her bed and held it up for her mother to see.

"This is what you want to wear?" Shimone asked as Ebony nodded vigorously. "Okay, let's get dressed."

Shimone pulled Ebony's nightshirt off and put on a red shirt and placed the jumper over it. She put on Ebony's socks and shoes as she repeated a rhyme that would help her daughter learn to tie her shoes.

"Bunny boy, bunny boy. Around the ear to there. Step around the bunny hole and I'll show you a pair."

Ebony laughed as her mother tickled her stomach. "Mama, is Mama Ma okay?"

Shimone looked at her inquisitive child and smiled. "Mama Ma is fine. She's been out of the hospital for almost two weeks now and she is doing much better. Remember, you helped take care of her?" Ebony nodded.

Dr. Ingles had kept Misty in the hospital for almost a week. Shimone had to cancel her movie date with Marques because she visited the hospital everyday. She wanted to make sure her mother was doing as well as the doctor said she was.

"We just need to monitor her heart activity," Dr. Ingles had said when Shimone asked him why her mother was still in the hospital.

Shimone had also made the hospital waiting room her

temporary home just in case Tyler decided he wanted to show up again. Even after being asked to leave, Tyler showed up at the hospital the next day requesting to see Misty. Shimone was glad that she thought to give the receptionist a list of people who were permitted to see her mother. She had made sure Tyler Calhoun was not on that list. To take her precautionary measures a step further, Shimone repeatedly verbalized to the receptionist not to allow Tyler Calhoun anywhere near her mother.

After being released from the hospital, Misty practically had to push Shimone and Ebony out of the door to make them go home. Shimone was resistant because she didn't want Tyler to show up at her mother's house and cause her to return to Emory's hospital, but Misty assured her that she would be fine by herself.

Ebony followed her mother into her bedroom and sat on the bed as Shimone dressed. After donning her body in the clothes her daughter had chosen, Shimone walked into the bathroom to do her hair. She pinned her tresses into a bun at the nape of her neck, letting a few strands frame her face for elegance. Then, she applied mascara and eyeliner to her eyes and pink gloss to her lips. She moved back into the bedroom, smiling at Ebony who was playing with her Mickey Mouse doll, and grabbed a pair of hoop earrings and a pair of small diamond studs and put them in her twice pierced ears.

"Ebony, do you want some earrings?" Shimone asked as she held up a pair of silver studs.

"Yes," Ebony said as Shimone walked around the bed and put an earring in each of Ebony's ears, which had been pierced when she was just nine months old. "Daddy here," Ebony squealed when she saw Marques's car pull into the parking lot through the window.

"Okay, go into the den and when he comes in tell him that I am almost ready," Shimone said.

"Okay," Ebony said as she slid off of the bed.

As Ebony ran to the den to wait for her father, Shimone walked into her closet and grabbed a pair of three-inch-heel sandals with designs stitched in lime green. When she heard the door open, Shimone grabbed her purse and headed toward the front of the apartment.

"How is my baby girl?" Marques asked, lifting Ebony off of the floor. She laughed and kicked her feet as Marques planted kisses all over her face. "Where's your mother?"

Ebony pointed toward Shimone's room. Marques looked up to find Shimone standing by the sofa near her bedroom door with a smile gracing her lips. Marques had been struggling with the secret of Alexia's pregnancy for almost two weeks. When Shimone cancelled their movie date, he decided to take Alexia to a gynecologist to see if she was actually pregnant. When the test proved Alexia was telling the truth, Marques went home and released all the emotions that he had held in on the drive back to Alexia's house. He told Ronald about the situation and Ronald suggested that he tell Shimone before Alexia did. Ronald also took it upon himself to lecture Marques on his walk with Christ.

"If you woulda kept your eyes on Jesus instead of them girls, you wouldn't even be in this situation," Ronald had told his friend.

Shimone moved into the den and said, "Hi," and laughed as Ebony kicked her way out of her father's arms and ran to Shimone.

"Daddy, look." Ebony pointed to Shimone's outfit. "I pick it out."

"That's right," Shimone said, tugging at one of Ebony's ponytails. "You picked out Mommy's clothes today."

"Well, you both look nice," Marques said, admiring Shimone's skirt. "You know that's my favorite," he whispered in her ear.

"I know," Shimone said. "Your daughter thought you might like it."

"I do." He smiled as Shimone blushed.

After giving birth to Ebony, Shimone worked hard to get back to her inherited size fourteen, so she was glad that she could still fit into clothes that she had to pack away once she began to gain her pregnancy pounds.

They arrived at the mall that housed the theater ten minutes before the movie was to start. When they entered the building, Marques handed the attendant his prepaid tickets and they went into the theater and sat in the middle section as they waited for the movie to begin.

Throughout the entire movie, Marques's mind wandered to Alexia and their unborn child. He wanted her to get rid of it, but he couldn't even ask her to do that. It wasn't because he knew Alexia wouldn't agree to it, but he himself didn't believe in abortions. When he brought up the option of adoption, she quickly reminded him that he was not the only person involved in this situation.

"Think about when this baby grows up," Alexia had said when they arrived at her condo after the doctor's appointment. "What if he or she wants to find us when they get older? What are we going to say when it asks us why we gave it away? I don't want to have to answer that question. So you need to tell your girlfriend the deal and stop acting like you don't want to face up to your responsibilities."

Marques knew he needed to tell Shimone, and soon, because Alexia had already threatened to handle the situation if Marques was having difficulties doing it himself. That was the last thing he needed. He wanted to be the one to 'fess up to his mistakes and try to make everything right. He knew there was no way Shimone would stay with him once she knew the truth. If she did, it would be a miracle.

By the time the movie had ended, Ebony had gone through one soiled pull-up and had to use the restroom twice, letting her mother know by announcing it loudly to the entire theater. Throughout the movie, she'd asked for her cup and had commanded Shimone's attention by climbing on her lap and constantly moving around in her seat. Now, as the credits were running, Ebony's high-pitched voice made one last announcement, letting everyone know that she was hungry. So Shimone decided that they should visit the food court before leaving the mall.

"When did she get so loud? And needy?" Marques complained as they exited the theater.

"Well, Marq, she's just a toddler. Toddlers always need attention and your daughter has the worst case of it. You would know that if . . ." She left the sentence unfinished as she glanced at him out of the corner of her eye.

If I came around more often. Marques knew what she was about to say and he looked into her eyes and felt the urge to tell her the truth about his distance. "Shimone, I need to—"

Shimone stopped walking and faced him. Returning his gaze, she stood on the tips of her toes and placed a gentle kiss against his lips. "I'm sorry. I don't mean to call you out on your not being around like you used to, but I'm not going to pretend that it's not hard for me that you aren't. I love you and I'm willing to work with you on the situation." She smiled. "If you want to make it up to me and Ebony, though, some Chick-fil-A would be nice."

He breathed deeply. If only a meal from the fast food restaurant would remedy all the problems he'd brought into their relationship. He rubbed his head as they walked toward the food court.

They waited in line for almost five minutes before ordering their food. After receiving their orders, they looked for a table in the crowded area. It seemed as if every table was occupied. They finally found a table that someone had just vacated. Shimone put Ebony in her lap and tried to tear her chicken strips into smaller pieces so it would be easier for her to eat them. Marques bit into his chicken sandwich and laughed as Ebony made faces at him. He made faces in return, making her laugh.

"Daddy, you look funny," Ebony said.

"Eat your food, girl," Shimone said, handing her a piece of chicken. Ebony shoved the food into her mouth and continued to play with her father.

When Marques looked up, his heart began to beat at a rate faster than normal and his tongue swelled in his mouth, making it hard for him to moisten his parched throat. He prayed that what he saw was a ghost coming toward their table, but the closer she got, the more real she became. "Oh God," Marques muttered.

"Baby, what's wrong?" Shimone asked him when he began to pack his food away.

"Nothing," he said quickly. "I'm just ready to go. C'mon."

"What?" Shimone asked in confusion. "We *just* sat down."

"Just . . . just c'mon," he said, taking Ebony out of her lap and throwing food into the bag.

"Hi, Marques," Alexia said as she finally reached their table.

Marques tried to play it cool, but he knew beads of sweat were appearing on his forehead.

Shimone stood up next to him and took Ebony out of his arms. "Can she at least finish eating?" When she turned to sit back down, she noticed the unfamiliar girl standing with her hands on her hips and a wide smile on her face. "Oh . . . hi," Shimone greeted.

"Hi," Alexia replied politely. "Is this your little girl?"

"Yes, this is Ebony," Shimone said as she studied the girl's face. "I'm sorry. I don't think we've met. I'm Shimone."

"I'm Alexia." She held out her hand and Shimone shook it. "I'm a friend of Marques."

"Really?" Shimone raised an arched eyebrow. "He hasn't told me about you."

"*Really*?" Alexia said, smiling at Marques who seemed to be sweating profusely. "I've heard *a lot* about you."

"Shimone, let's go," Marques said, gently tugging at her elbow.

"How old are you?" Alexia asked Ebony, causing Shimone's attention to turn toward the young woman.

"Two," Ebony replied.

"Actually, she just turned three," Shimone corrected, making a mental note to teach her daughter her new age.

"I'm about three months now," Alexia said to Shimone as she touched her swollen stomach. "Was your pregnancy hard?"

"Not really. Marques was really helpful during my pregnancy and during my eight-and-a-half hours of labor." Shimone smiled.

"Well, I hope my pregnancy is just as easy," Alexia eyed Marques. "But my baby's father seems not to want to help. He took me to a doctor's appointment a few weeks ago, but that was just to see if I was being honest about being pregnant."

"Well, if you ask me, I think he is a jerk for not wanting to take care of his responsibilities," Shimone said.

"You know, I said the *same* thing," Alexia said, glancing in Marques's direction again.

"Shimone, let's go please," Marques said, rubbing his head.

"Why?" Shimone looked at him. "Baby, you are sweating like a pig. Are you okay?"

"I'm fine," he said, throwing away the uneaten food. "I have to go to work, so we really need to leave."

"I was wondering," Alexia asked, gaining Shimone's attention once again, "have you ever had to worry about Marques not being faithful to you?"

Shimone was slightly caught off guard by Alexia's question. Lately, she had been wondering if there was someone else Marques was spending his spare time with, but she didn't think it was any of this girl's business. "I really don't see why you would ask me something like that when you don't even know me."

Alexia shrugged. "I was just wondering . . . because if you don't, you should."

"Shimone, let's go," Marques said firmly.

"No, I want to see what she is getting at," Shimone said, stepping in the girl's face with Ebony still in her arms, seemingly unfazed by the fact that Alexia was significantly taller than her. "I really don't appreciate you telling me what I should be worried about in my relationship. If Marques was cheating on me . . . and I pray to God, for his sake, that he is not." She glanced at Marques and then turned her attention back to Alexia. "But if he was, I'm sure he would feel guilty enough to come and tell me so we could work things out," she said, unknowingly causing Marques's heart to sink.

"Maybe he doesn't feel as guilty as I thought he would by now," Alexia said with a smirk.

"Look, I don't know who you think you are," Shimone said, raising her voice, causing several people near them to look in their direction. "But I suggest you step out of my face before you make me lose all my religion up in here."

"Shimone, please," Marques nearly begged, but his voice went unheard.

"Look, I'm not trying to start nothing okay," Alexia

said, backing up with her palms in the air. "I just thought you'd want to know that my baby's father . . . is that *jerk* behind you." She watched tears immediately form in the corners of Shimone's eyes.

Shimone had known exactly where Alexia was going with her questioning, but didn't want to fully accept what she knew was the truth. Alexia hadn't wanted to hurt the girl, but she needed to know what type of guy she was in a relationship with.

Shimone glared at Marques, who looked like he had just finished an intense game of basketball. She stared into his eyes; he looked down at his feet and began to rub his head—a nervous habit. She knew that Alexia was telling the truth, but she didn't understand why Marques would do something like this and not even feel the need to tell her about it.

"Shimone—" Marques started, but Shimone's hand in the air cut him off.

"I really don't care to hear it," she said as she looked at him.

"Mama, I ready to go," Ebony whined.

"So am I," Shimone said, picking up her purse. She looked at Marques. "I want you to take me home, now," she said as calmly as she could. "We'll talk about this later, *if* we talk about it at all."

Marques rubbed his head and face as he followed Shimone, leaving Alexia standing in the middle of the food court, with people still staring and trying to figure out what had just happened. He knew when he dropped Shimone and Ebony off at home, that it would probably be the last time he'd ever see his family again.

Chapter 7

Angelica paced back and forth in front of her husband as she continued to yell at him, which she had been doing for almost fifteen minutes. It was after eleven o'clock and he had just walked through the door as if nothing was wrong. Angelica was close to tears as Malcolm sat on the couch, seemingly unfazed by her attitude.

"I don't know what is going on with you," Angelica continued. "I've been sitting here almost four hours waiting for you to walk through that door. The kids had taken their baths and been in bed and you still weren't here. It seems like you don't even stay here anymore. All you do is come home, shower, and change clothes before you leave again. To go where, I have no clue.

"Your son is running around with thugs doing who-knows-what when nobody's around to watch him. Your daughter went on her first date almost four weeks ago and you weren't even here to meet the guy. And me? Well, I'm just sitting around the house wondering where in the world my husband is. Since when does this family come second?" She finally took a breath and looked at him as she waited for an explanation.

"Angel, I told you, I have a company to run. Computers have been shutting down all day. I had to wait for the repair people to get there to upgrade the systems so they would be less venerable to viruses. And I had paperwork to file before tomorrow's presentation."

"And all of this took you past the usual eight hours?" Angelica interrogated, not believing a word that had just come out of her husband's mouth.

"No, I didn't go in to work until eleven," he said.

"Really?" Angelica said, crossing her arms over her chest. "Malcolm, you left the house at *eight o'clock*."

Malcolm seemed to become fidgety, but he didn't miss a beat. "I left at eight because I had an important business meeting to attend for our new clients and they wanted to meet for breakfast. We had our meeting and then I went to the office to work on the presentation for another company we have coming in. I didn't get to even leave the office for lunch, and when I finally finished it, I realized that it was late, so I came home."

Angelica knew better. He was a liar and he was also stupid if he thought she believed any part of the story he'd just fabricated. "Malcolm, I called the office around noon—you know, just to see how my husband was doing—but your secretary said you hadn't even been at the office and that you had called to tell her you'd be in around one o'clock. Then, when I called back around eight to see why you hadn't made it home, your secretary said that you had left around seven and told her to close up the office, which she was in the process of doing when I called." Angelica stopped pacing and looked at Malcolm who seemed to be muttering something. "What's that?" she questioned, placing her hand up to her ear. "You say that you got caught?" She stared at him as he sat on the couch, looking as if he was trying to think up another excuse. "Let me ask you something, Malcolm: Did you marry me because you loved me or was it because of Ronald?"

Malcolm looked at his wife with sorrowful eyes. "Angel, Ron was almost two when we got married. If I only wanted to marry you because of him, I would have done it sooner than that, but when we had him I didn't love you as much as I did when we actually got married."

"Well, your behavior isn't showing it!" she yelled.

"Angel, baby, just please lis–"

"No," Angelica screamed in his face. "Don't 'Angel, baby' me. I'm sick of it. I'm sick of you and all of your excuses. I wanna know why you weren't at work! I wanna know where you were, Malcolm! Who were you with?" She paused before asking the question she was afraid for him to answer. "Malcolm, are you having an affair?"

"Why would you ask me that?"

"I just want an honest answer, Malcolm, so *please* don't lie to me." She waited a moment before reiterating her question. "Are you . . . cheating on me?"

Malcolm breathed deeply and held his head down. Apparently, he wasn't going to lie, but he wasn't going to come out and tell the truth either, and that was all the proof Angelica needed. She turned and went upstairs, leaving Malcolm sitting on the couch.

Trying to hold back tears, she opened the door to her son's bedroom. "Jeremy," she called his name as she tried to wake him up. "Jeremy."

"Huh?" her son moaned.

"Baby, wake up," Angelica said as tears began to form in her eyes. "Wake up and pack some clothes."

"Huh?" Jeremy questioned again, rubbing his eyes. "Why?"

"Don't ask questions. Just pack your suitcase. We're going to visit Grandma for a while, okay?"

Jeremy got out of his bed and began to pack clothes as he was told. Angelica went to her daughter's room and was surprised to find that Nicole was sitting in her bed crying silently. Angelica sat next to her daughter and tried to comfort her.

"You're leaving him aren't you?" Nicole spoke knowingly as she wiped her face.

"I'm sorry, baby, I just can't take it anymore." Angelica wiped her own face. "I love your father. I do, really. It's just that when I was young, I promised your granddaddy that I would never let any man run around on me and I intend to keep that promise. So, go ahead and pack your suitcase. We are going to go to Grandma Rose's."

"I love you, Mama," Nicole said, hugging her mother.

Angelica held her daughter tight. "I love you, too, Nikki."

Once Angelica had left the room to pack her own luggage, Nicole went into her closet and began to pull her clothes off of the rack. She blindly packed her suitcase as tears flooded her eyes. She'd known that it would only be a matter of time before one of her parents got fed up with the situation that hung like heavy clouds over their household. Now that something was actually being done about it, Nicole felt as if her life was ending. She reached for the telephone and silently dialed her brother's number.

"Hello," Ronald answered, groggily.

Nicole cried into the phone.

"Hello? Who is this?" Ronald asked.

"It's Nikki," she cried as she looked at her clock and noticed it was almost midnight.

"Nicole, what's wrong?" Ronald asked, more alert now.

"Mama's leaving Daddy," she sobbed into the phone.

"Okay, Nikki, I need you to be strong for me, okay?" he said, trying to remain calm, but Nicole could hear the disappointment in his tone. "I'll be at the house in about thirty minutes. Do you think that you could try to keep Mama from leaving until I get there?"

Nicole loved that while Ronald was away at college, he was still close enough to get home if needed, but she knew he wouldn't arrive before their parents totally lost their sanity. "I don't think so. She and Daddy are downstairs arguing really loud. She said we are going to Grandma's," she cried. "That's all the way in Savannah. I don't wanna go to Savannah."

"Do you think you can convince her to come to my apartment?"

"I can try," Nicole sniffled.

"Okay, you do that, and I'll take care of the rest," Ronald said just before Nicole became hysterical. "Nikki, you have to calm down. I know this is hard, but I need for you to get Mama over here so we can take care of this."

"I can't believe she is leaving. I don't wanna leave. I have friends here," she cried.

Ronald tried to keep his voice steady so he wouldn't upset Nicole any more than she already was, but he was very close to screaming into the phone. "Nicole, please calm down. I want you to hang up the phone and go tell Mom to come to my apartment so you guys can get some rest and solve this, rationally, in the morning."

"Okay, okay," Nicole said, calming a bit. "I can do it."

"Now hang up the phone and do what I just said."

"Okay, bye," She placed the phone on the hook and finished packing as tears continued to run down her face.

* * *

"Mama, don't you think you should have at least let him explain before you jumped to conclusions?" Ronald asked as he poured another cup of tea for his mother.

"I didn't need any of his explanations. It was plain as day; it just took me three years to realize the truth," Angelica said as she took the cup from her son. She allowed the steam to infiltrate her nostrils before sipping the hot liquid. "I just don't see why he would do something like this to me, to our family. I've been good to him and I've always supported him. I've been a good wife and mother, right?" She looked at Ronald for confirmation.

The look in his mother's eyes was so upsetting that it made Ronald want to beat just a smidgen of sense into his father's head, but he wasn't sure if he could. After years of looking up to "the man of the house," his heart held a mixture of feelings for his father. He remembered when Malcolm reprimanded him when he had messed things up with Nevaeh almost four years ago. He recalled his father telling him that a real man has nothing to prove. Ronald wondered if his father was hypocritically trying to prove something by having an affair.

Ronald sat on the sofa next to his mother and wiped the tears from her eyes. "Mom, you are a wonderful wife and an even better mother," he assured, hoping to get rid of the question in her eyes. "I don't know why Dad would feel the need to cheat on you, but I'll certainly find out."

Angelica looked at her oldest son and hoped he wouldn't do anything stupid. "And just how do you plan to do that? I don't want you going to that house trying to fight your father. I know we've been close, and I know you'd kill anyone who would dare to hurt me, but, Ron, I don't need you ending up in a hospital because of me. And that is what is going to happen if you try to jump on Malcolm. I know you are big, but he is much bigger, so I don't want you getting involved in this at all, do you understand?" She looked at him and noticed his hesitation. "Ronald Jaheem McAfee, do you understand me?" she asked firmly.

Ronald looked back toward Marques's closed bedroom door and hoped that his roommate was so deep in his sleep that he couldn't hear Ronald being reprimanded like a young child. "Yes, ma'am," Ronald relented, knowing that his mother was nothing less than serious when she called him by his full name. He sighed as he arose from the sofa. "So, which is it? The couch or my room with the wild sleepers?"

"I'll take the couch, thank you," Angelica said as she took the pillows off of the sofa and placed them by the television. Ronald helped her pull out the bed and cover it with sheets. "Thank you," she said again, hugging Ronald, who didn't resist the embrace.

He turned out the lights as Angelica got situated in the bed. As he walked back to his room to join his siblings, he heard his mother sniffle. Soon she was sobbing softly. Ronald wanted to respect his mother's request, but he was going to find out what was going on with his father if it was the last thing he did.

Chapter 8

Shimone sat on the sofa with Ebony as she waited for Marques to arrive. It had been about three weeks since they last spoke to each other and the guilt that came with keeping her daughter from her father for so long was beginning to eat at her conscience. So she decided to give Marques a call to let him know he could spend time with Ebony this weekend. He had tried to convince Shimone to join them, but she wanted nothing to do with him.

After finding out Marques was Alexia's unborn baby's father, Shimone had him take her home and return the key she had given him to the apartment. She didn't even argue with him or listen to any of the excuses he was trying to offer. She took Ebony out of her car seat, let her kiss her daddy good-bye, and walked into the apartment, closing the door in his face. Shimone had waited until Ebony had eaten, taken her bath, and gotten into bed before she went to her room to cry herself to sleep.

She and Marques had been dating for almost four years, nothing in comparison to their best friends' six-year relationship, but there had been special times. Marques had been a player before he met Shimone. Nevaeh used to refer to him as a "bona fide dog", but after he declared his love for Shimone, Nevaeh's view quickly shifted and she began to treat Marques as if he was her brother. He became a new person before even finding out Shimone was pregnant and had stayed that way throughout their relationship, but it seemed that being a faithful boyfriend didn't fit into his definition of college fun.

"Daddy's here," Shimone said, releasing her thoughts upon seeing Marques driving into the complex. She pulled Ebony's bag from off of the sofa and helped her daughter to a standing position.

"You come?" Ebony said as she looked at Shimone with pleading eyes.

Shimone kneeled next to her daughter. "I'm sorry, baby, but I can't. Your daddy and I are not really speaking to each other right now," she explained as she had done several times in the last few weeks.

"Why?"

Shimone smiled slightly. Ebony's habit of asking "why" had come from Shimone's side of the family. Even Misty had declared that Ebony was just as inquisitive as Shimone had been when she was a baby. She pulled at her daughter's jean skirt and said, "There are some things that you don't understand right now because you are young, but I promise that even though your dad and I may not be speaking, we will always be family. You remember that, okay?"

"Yes, Mama," Ebony said as Shimone kissed her forehead.

Shimone stood and wiped away tears. Hearing a soft knock against the door, she walked toward the door and opened it. Marques stood there with his hands in his pockets, looking extremely handsome in his Sean John gear. He stared at Shimone as she stood in the doorway and glared at him. She could feel his eyes roaming over her body and hated that she had to fight off the flatter she felt from his appreciation.

"Hi," Shimone finally said.

"Hey," Marques breathed.

"Come in, she's almost ready," Shimone said. She walked from the door and back toward her daughter, who, she noticed, was now crying. "Ebony, what's wrong?"

"You come, too," Ebony said, trying to wipe her eyes.

Shimone closed her eyes to keep tears from escaping. "Sweetie, didn't we just have this talk? I can't go with you."

Ebony looked up at Marques, who was gazing at Shimone, wanting to say something, but it was apparent he couldn't find the words. "Daddy, Mama come, too?" Ebony asked, thinking that Marques would use his firm fatherly tone, like he did with her, to make Shimone spend the day with them.

Marques looked at his daughter, and then back at Shimone who was busying herself with making sure that everything necessary was in Ebony's bag. He walked over to her and gently pulled her off of the floor. Shimone stood in front of him as she tried with all her might to keep her tears from showing themselves.

Marques searched her eyes pleadingly. "Please come with us. Look at her; she wants you to come." He paused. "And so do I."

Shimone stooped down and picked up the backpack and handed it to Marques. "I can't. I told Mama that I would help her out at the studio today," she lied, knowing her mother had, for some unknown reason, decided not to attend any of her dance classes today, leaving her assistants over all rehearsals. "And besides, you wouldn't want us to bump into any more of your *friends*, now would you?"

"How many times do I have to apologize to you?" Marques asked, refusing to take the bag. "I made a mistake and I am sorry. I love you. Why can't you forgive me so we can get past all of this?"

Shimone's glare intensified as she shook her head, and then turned toward her daughter who still had tears streaming down her face. "Mommy can't go this time, but I promise we will spend time together." She kissed Ebony's cheeks.

"Okay," Ebony said as Shimone placed her backpack on Ebony's back.

"Come on Ebony," Marques sighed, holding his hand out for his daughter to take. "I'll have her back tomorrow morning," he mumbled as Ebony took his hand and looked back at her mother as they walked toward the door.

Shimone watched Marques and Ebony walk out of the front door. She closed the door when she saw them get in the car and pull out of the apartment complex. She walked back into the living room and picked up a few of Ebony's toys. She placed her stuffed animals in her room and put the car that Marques had gotten her in the corner of the living room. She then went to her room, picked up the phone and dialed her mother's number. She hadn't really spoken to her mother since she found out that Marques had been with Alexia. She had told her mother about Marques's affair. Misty had clearly voiced her disappointment, but hadn't said much else about it.

Shimone remembered back when she'd told Misty that she was pregnant with Ebony. At first Misty cried, and then she sat Shimone down and shared the hardships she'd dealt with as a single teen mother, practically living out on the street.

"You wanna know how I survived?" Shimone remembered her mother saying the night she revealed that she was pregnant. "I prostituted."

Those words stuck with Shimone because she knew she never wanted to be in that position. That was why she had been thankful that Marques would be around to help care for Ebony.

"Hello?" Misty answered the phone after the second ring.

"Hey, Mama," Shimone said into the phone. "How are you doing?"

"Good, I was just about to call you," Misty said. "I have a visitor over here and the person would like to see you, if it's okay." Misty seemed anxious.

"Who is it?" Shimone asked.

"Just an old friend of mine," Misty said, not giving any information on the unknown person. "Just come on over."

"Okay," Shimone said apprehensively as she wondered who the guest might be. "Ebony is with Marques, so it will just be me."

"That's great," Misty said before hanging up the phone.

Shimone replaced her pajama pants with a pair of jeans and her wife beater shirt with a yellow spaghetti strapped shirt. She finger-combed her hair and slipped into a pair of tennis shoes. She picked up her purse and keys and headed toward the door. She hopped into her used Kia that she had bought, with Marques's parents' help, during her sophomore year after refusing to take the bus to and from Ebony's daycare center and her classes for another year.

She raised the volume of her album that she had recorded after her high school graduation. It was a mixture of gospel and R&B love songs written by her, Nevaeh, and some of the recording company's writers. When Marques's dad first got in contact with Shimone and said that he had set up a meeting for her with a record producer, she thought he was kidding. But when she found herself sitting across from Vincent Gardiner, president of Power Records, Shimone couldn't help but give thanks to God for all of the blessings He had given her. After having Ebony, though, Shimone couldn't see herself on the road promoting her album, so she had her lawyer, who just happened to be Marques's father, call off all contracts with the record company so she could take care of her daughter. However, Vincent assured Shimone that when she was ready, there would be a job waiting for her at Power Records.

She sang along with the track, which she and Nevaeh recorded together, as she drove down the interstate toward her mother's house. She turned onto her mother's street three tracks later. She pulled up next to an unfamiliar black Escalade that sat in the driveway of the two-story home. Shimone turned off the car and opened the door. She saw Misty looking out of the window and wondered why her mother was so eager.

"Hey, Ma," Shimone said when her mother opened the door before she could even reach the porch.

"Hi, baby," Misty said, hugging Shimone and ushering her into the house.

"Who's this visitor that you want me to meet?" Shimone questioned as she walked into the kitchen. She froze when she saw Tyler sitting at the kitchen table sipping coffee. What was he doing in her mother's house, sitting at her mother's table, and drinking her mother's coffee from her mother's cup as if his being in the house was a normal, everyday thing?

Upon Shimone's entrance, Tyler placed the mug on the table and stood up. "Hi."

Shimone looked at him and then at her mother, who seemed disappointed at Shimone's reaction to Tyler's presence. "Why is he here? Is this supposed to be some type of reunion that I'm 'posed to be jumping up and down for? Mama, you know how much pain this man has put you through, but yet, he is in your house like nothing ever happened." Shimone glared at Tyler as if he were a lethal creature that should be put to sleep.

"Shimone, now you know I didn't raise you to be disrespectful," Misty said. "Now you need to apologize to Tyler."

Shimone glared at her mother as if she had just lost her mind and needed her help finding it. "What for? Tell me, has he apologized to you? I know how you raised me, but *this*"—she pointed at Tyler—"hasn't been there from day one and you expect me to give him respect he doesn't deserve. Why should I apologize to someone who has caused you so much pain and misery and made you raise me by yourself?" she said as she began to cry. "Why do I need to be respectful to someone who didn't even want me or you? What has he done that deserves the respect that you want me to give him?"

"Maybe we should do this another time," Tyler finally said as he began to move toward the door.

"No, we need to take care of this today," Misty said, stopping him as she looked at Shimone. "Shimone, Tyler came here because he was concerned about me . . . about us."

"He wasn't concerned twenty-two years ago," Shimone said with her arms defiantly crossed over her chest.

Misty gave Shimone a warning look and continued. "He has apologized to me and he had some things to say to me and I listened; now he has something to tell you and you are going to sit here and listen to what your *father* has to say."

Shimone's head reeled back when Misty referred to

Tyler as her father, but suppressed the comment that threatened to fly from her mouth as she sat on the couch.

Tyler remained standing and looked very uneasy. Misty gently pushed him toward the couch opposite the one Shimone was sitting on, and then sat in the chair adjacent to the couches. The three of them were engulfed in silence as Tyler searched for the words to say.

Shimone sat on the couch, not believing that she was sitting across from her father, a man that she had longed to see for the past twenty-two years. A man that she wanted to hug and forgive, but at the same time wanted to hate for all that he had put her and her mother through.

Misty sat and watched the man she once, and still, loved struggle with the words to say to his daughter. She had been surprised when Tyler called a few days after she was released from the hospital. He said he had gotten her number from the phone book and he wanted to see if all was well with her. When he asked to see her, Misty was resistant at first, but after several long conversations over the phone, she finally agreed to meet him at a coffee shop. They had spent time together over the past weeks and had gotten to know each other so much better. She'd learned that he had just moved to Atlanta from North Carolina a couple of years ago for career purposes. She'd filled him on her struggle with life after leaving their high school and, though it was hard, she attentively listened as he told her of his life since they'd last seen each other. Misty could tell from their conversations that Tyler was regretful about all that happened between them and she assured him that he was forgiven. Now she wished she could convince her daughter to do the same.

"Tyler," Misty said, gaining his attention, "you have something to say to Shimone."

Tyler looked back at his daughter and pulled at his left

ear. Shimone noticed that they had the same nervous habit. "Umm, Shimone"—his voice was a deep baritone—"I just want to apologize. I know I should have been there for you and your mother, but I wasn't and for that I am truly sorry." The words began to flow from his mouth with ease. "I'm not going to make excuses. I just didn't want nor did I have time to take care of a baby. I was only sixteen, but now I realize that if I thought I was man enough to make you, I should have been man enough to help take care of you." He fastened his gaze onto hers. "When I was younger, I'll admit that I was stupid for not being responsible on so many levels. But I want you to really believe me when I tell you that I did love your mother and if I would have just stuck it out, I know I would have grown to love you too. Looking at you now, I'm glad that Misty didn't listen to me and went ahead and had you.

"I'm not asking you to forgive me, although it would be nice." He tried to offer a slight smile, but Shimone kept an unemotional face. "I just want you to know that I am sorry, and if you need anything, I am here now and I hope that counts for something." Tyler sat back and rested his hands on his knees.

Shimone gave him a cold stare. "Tyler," she said, not fazed at all that she was calling her father by his first name, "I am a grown woman with a family of my own. Tell me, what do I need from you? What can you offer me that I don't already have?"

"A father's love," Tyler immediately replied.

Love your father as I love you.

Shimone ignored the voice she heard whisper in her ear. She stared into Tyler's light brown eyes and felt herself drawing closer to him, but she refused to let it show. "It's a little too late for that," she said as she looked out of the window and watched as kids ran around outside, savoring every moment of their summer freedom before having to return to school in a few weeks.

"Shimone, baby, it's never too late," Misty said as she looked at her daughter.

Love him with the love that I have stored in your heart, just for him.

God's voice always had a way of moving her in a way she'd never been moved before. It calmed her and usually made her realize that she needed to be more receptive in a particular situation. She knew God wanted her to accept her father in spite of her reservations.

Shimone turned to face her parents with wet eyes. She watched as Tyler slowly arose from his seat and walked toward her. He opened his arms, pleading with his eyes for a second chance. Shimone hesitated, but got up and wrapped her arms around Tyler's waist as she released all of her tears onto his chest. She had been waiting twenty-two years to receive a hug that only a father could give. Today, her wait was over.

Chapter 9

The Madison household was as quiet as it could get on a Saturday afternoon. James was at the dealership trying to reach his summer sales goal. Michelle was out with Nicole's mother and a few of their girlfriends, and Nevaeh was at Ronald's apartment. Imani was at home, all alone, and she was bored out of her mind. It was the weekend before school was to start and she had nothing to do. Her boyfriend, Eddie, had said he'd come over and keep her company, but she knew that wouldn't be a good idea. Even if he was a Christian, she knew he was a human first and there was always a chance that they could make a mistake that they would end up regretting for the rest of their lives.

She and Eddie had been going out since they had gotten out of school for the summer. They spent a lot of their time together and she loved it. He was sweet, gentle, and caring. When she was in the eighth grade, Imani had the biggest crush on her older sister's boyfriend. She and Nicole had always said that when they got older, they wanted to have a relationship just like the one their siblings shared. Now, since she was going out with Eddie, Imani didn't have to wish anymore. Eddie was everything she had ever wanted in a boyfriend. The only downside was that she had been spending so much time with him that she hadn't been talking to Nicole much.

The last time Imani spoke to her friend, which was easily three weeks ago, Nicole had told her that she had officially started going out with Shawn and that her parents were splitting up. Nicole's dad remained in their house, while she, her mother, and her brother were staying at Ronald's apartment until they could find a permanent home. Imani thought Marques would have an issue with sharing such a small apartment with Ronald and his mother and siblings, but Nicole explained that Ronald had convinced Marques that the living arrangements would only last for a few weeks while Angelica searched for a house. Ronald had given his bedroom to his mother and sister, while he and his brother shared the sofa bed. Imani had been praying that things would work out for them.

She decided she needed to check on her friend, so she picked up her phone and dialed Ronald's number.

"Hello," Ronald answered, talking over the loud noise coming from his apartment.

"Wassup? It's Imani," she said.

"Hey, Mani, what's going on?"

"Nothing much," she answered. "What's going on over there? Sounds like you got the whole football team at your house," Imani kidded.

"Actually, some of them and some of Marq's basketball teammates are over here watching the game," Ronald explained. "Oh, and Nikki's so-called boyfriend is over here, too," he said snidely as Imani laughed.

"Shoot, I'm 'bout to come over there," Imani said, and

then remembered why she had called in the first place. "Can I speak to Nikki?"

"Yeah, hold on a sec," she heard Ronald place the phone down.

She could hear several male voices cheering from Ronald's end of the phone line. A few moments later, Nicole came to the phone.

"Hi, Imani," Nicole greeted.

"Hey," Imani said just before another round of screaming and hollering erupted from the guys.

"Hold on, Imani," Nicole said. "Y'all need to shut up while I'm on the phone," she yelled to her brother's guests.

"Yeah, yeah, whatever," one of the boys yelled back at her followed by rude agreements from the other guys.

"Okay, I'm back," Nicole said. "What's going on?"

"Nothing, except me being bored with nothing to do," Imani replied. "If I would've known that all y'all were at Ron's apartment, I would have come with Nevaeh."

"Why don't you come?" Nicole suggested. "Just call Eddie and tell him that you want to come over here. I'm sure he'll drive you."

"But you know if Nev sees me with Eddie and no adult, she is going to flip," Imani said, knowing how overprotective her sister could be.

"Eddie is eighteen," Nicole said, "and he has a license. It's not like he and Nevaeh haven't met before. She should know him pretty well by now. What is she going to flip about?"

"Nikki, Nevaeh has only met Eddie a couple of times. As my mama says, 'She don't know him from Adam.' " Imani laughed. "But I guess I'll come anyway. I'll be over there in about forty-five minutes."

"Great, I'll see you when you get here." Nicole hung up the phone.

Imani placed the phone back on its hook and decided to get ready before calling Eddie. The forecaster had predicted high temperatures, so she decided to wear a pair of shorts and a baby-blue spaghetti-strapped shirt with a pair of sandals. She put her hair into a ponytail at the top of her head and adorned her ears with a pair of silver heart hoops. When she felt like she was ready, she called her boyfriend.

"Hello?" Eddie answered on the fourth ring. His voice was deep and mellow.

"Hey, it's me," Imani said, her tone suddenly soft and caressing.

"Wassup? You bored, ain't you?" He laughed.

"Yeah, that's why I'm calling," Imani said. "Nikki is at her brother's apartment and there's a bunch of people over there watching the game—"

"I'll be right over," he said without letting her finish.

"Great, I'm already ready, so you don't have to complain about me taking so long to get dressed," she said.

"I may complain," Eddie said, "but it is always worth the wait."

Imani was sure he could see her blushing through the phone. "Thank you. I try my best."

"Well, you do a great job," he complimented. "I'll be there in a few," he told her before hanging up.

Imani smiled as she hung up the phone. She could feel herself falling hard for Eddie and she didn't know if that was a good thing. What if he ended up hurting her? What if he didn't feel the same way about her as she did about him? Imani had never thought she'd have such strong feelings for a guy, but when she met Eddie everything changed.

Imani stepped off of her bus, placed her iPod in her backpack, and walked toward the school building. The first day she walked through the doors of Frederick Douglass High School she felt like her life was going to change. She was finally in high school. She walked into the gym, as directed by the administrators in the hall, and found a seat at the top of the bleachers.

"Mani!" She heard someone scream her name.

Imani looked to her right and saw Nicole sitting by herself near a group of what looked to be freshmen. Nicole got up and Imani laughed when she noticed that they both were wearing the same top and similar blue jean skirts.

"Hey," Imani said as Nicole sat next to her. "People are going to think we planned this."

Nicole dismissed her friend's comment with a wave of her hand. "Who cares? As long as I look . . . Oh my goodness," Nicole whispered frantically, grabbing onto Imani's forearm.

"Who are you looking at?" Imani asked, knowing Nicole had spotted a cute boy.

"That fine thing over there," Nicole said, "and he is looking right at you," she informed excitedly.

"Who?" Imani asked, trying to fix her hair discreetly.

"Right there," Nicole said, without pointing. "The one with braids sitting with that group of boys, four steps down. With the red and black on."

"Oh my, he is gorgeous," Imani observed once she caught sight of him. "But he looks like an upperclassman, which means he's too old for me." She turned away.

"Well, he is coming over here." Nicole sat back on the bleachers and straightened her skirt.

"Hey," the guy greeted when he reached them.

"Hi," the girls responded as he sat down next to Imani.

"We ride the same bus and I heard you singing along with your iPod," he told Imani. "You sounded real good," he admired.

"Oh," Imani said, not realizing she had been singing loud enough for someone to actually hear her. "Thanks."

"I'm supposed to be helping the music teacher recruit stu-

dents for the gospel choir and I was wondering if you would be interested."

"Umm . . . excuse me," Nicole interrupted. "How do we really know that you are really a part of this 'gospel choir' and that you are not just using that as a line?"

"Nikki," Imani admonished her outspoken friend.

"No, it's cool," the guy said, laughing. "Maybe it would help if I introduced myself." He extended his hand. "My name is Eddie Fulton and I'm a sophomore," he said as Imani took his hand. "Mrs. Wright, the music director, has been trying to get people to join the choir since last year, but there are only a few people who have tried out for it. She asked me to help out this year and I thought I'd get a head start on recruiting people. I just heard you singing on the bus and I thought the choir could use someone with your talent."

"Umm . . . I don't know," Imani said. "I have already been recruited for the dance team and I don't know if I could juggle all of it in my first year. Ouch," she winced when Nicole elbowed her in the side. Unlike her friend, Imani could care less if people knew of her status as a freshman. She was proud of her class and planned on representing them to the best of her ability.

"Oh . . . you're a freshman. You don't look like it," Eddie stated with a crooked grin. "Well, I'm sure you could handle it if you tried. I would be more than happy to help," he offered with a smile.

"I don't know. Ouch!" Imani grimaced again and gave Nicole a warning look. "I guess I could at least give it a try first," she said, turning her attention back to him.

"Great." Eddie pulled a piece of paper and a pen from his pocket. "What's your name?"

"Imani Madison," she said as he wrote it down.

He smiled. "Faith—I like that," he said as Imani blushed at the sound of this unfamiliar gentleman's voice speaking the

English version of her Swahili name. "Our first meeting is next Thursday right after school. Hope you are there."

Imani remembered going to the meeting. The first person she'd noticed was Eddie. He'd offered her the seat next to him and she graciously accepted. The meeting lasted about forty-five minutes and afterwards Eddie joined her outside while she waited for her father to pick her up. From that day, they were instant friends. But as their friendship developed, Imani noticed that her feelings for him were growing. The fact that he was a Christian made him even more attractive. They helped each other with problems and tried to be there for each other. They'd even gone on a few casual dates. She had introduced him to her family as her friend and vice-versa. She never thought he'd ask her to be his girlfriend a few weeks before her junior year ended, especially since he was about to graduate, but when he did, she eagerly accepted.

Imani looked out of her bedroom window as Eddie pulled his blue Mustang, a graduation gift from his father, into her driveway. She grabbed her purse, headed down stairs, and set the alarm before heading out of the door.

"Dang, can I ring the doorbell first?" Eddie laughed as he got out of the car and walked Imani to the passenger's side. He helped her into the car before returning to the driver's seat. He cranked up Fred Hammond's "You are My Daily Bread" and sang along as he backed out of Imani's driveway.

"Eddie, how are you going to listen to directions and sing extra loud at the same time?" Imani asked.

Eddie laughed. "Sorry, Faith," he said as he lowered the volume of the music.

Eddie hardly ever called Imani by her given name.

From the day they'd met, he'd called her Faith. At first Imani thought it was a little weird. When she'd asked him about it, Eddie simply shrugged and said, " 'Cause that's what Imani means in Swahili," as if Imani should've known the answer to her own question. But after more prying she found out that he thought of it as a pet name for her and hoped she didn't mind him calling her by it. Little did he know, Imani loved that he called her Faith. It made her feel special.

Turning his attention back toward the road, Eddie asked. "Where do I go now?"

A few minutes later they pulled into Ronald's apartment complex. The parking lot only had a few cars in it, but as they walked up to Ronald's apartment, the noise level let Imani know that all the guys were still sitting in the living room yelling at the television screen. She had to bang hard on the door to make sure someone would hear her knocking. Ronald answered the door a few moments later and smiled at his unexpected guests.

"What are you doin' here?" he asked.

"Nikki said I could come," Imani told him as she walked past him and into the house. "Oh . . . this is Eddie. Eddie, this is Nikki's brother, Ronald."

"Wassup man?" Ronald said.

"Nothin' but you," Eddie praised, recognizing Ronald from Clark Atlanta's televised football games. "You be killin' 'em out on the field."

Ronald laughed. "Thanks."

Imani pulled Eddie into the house. "Don't make his head bigger than it already is." She glanced around the living room and counted nearly fifteen people sitting on the sofa and floor around the television. "How do you fit so many people in this little apartment?"

Ronald shrugged. "Hey guys," he yelled to get his

company's attention. "These are Nikki's friends, Imani and Eddie."

"Hey," they greeted without looking back.

"Wow, I really feel welcomed," Imani laughed.

"Wassup, Mani, Ed?" Shawn said from his position on the floor in front of the sofa.

"Hey Shawn." Imani smiled. "Where's Nikki?"

"In that back room with your sister," he said, pointing toward Ronald's bedroom. "Hey, Ed, come watch the game, man. Atlanta is up by six."

Eddie looked at Imani, almost as if asking if she would be okay with him joining the rest of the guys. Imani laughed inwardly. She knew they were spending too much time together, but she loved every minute.

"Go ahead. I'll be in the back," she said before kissing him lightly on the lips.

"Okay," Ronald said, "not all of that in my house." He pushed Imani toward the back.

Eddie sat next to one of Ronald's teammates as Imani went to the back room. When she walked in, she saw Nicole lying on the bed crying with Nevaeh sitting next to her praying. Imani had no idea what was going on, but she joined in hopes that her prayers would heal whatever pain her friend had.

"Lord, just heal her heart right now," Nevaeh said, with her hand on Nicole's back. "Just heal whatever it is that may be hurting her. If it's her parents, Lord, just let everything work out for the good. If your will is not what she wants, let her understand that your decision is what's best for all. Lord, keep her and hold her. Let her know that she is your child and that you will never leave or forsake her," Nevaeh paused and Imani continued.

"Lord, I don't know the circumstances that are surrounding Nicole's hurt right now," Imani began, "and I know I haven't been there for her like a best friend should be, but I'm here now and I just come to you hoping that you can heal her pain. Take it all away so she can be happy like she should be. I don't know how this situation between her parents will work out, but let her know that, like Nevaeh said, your will be done and all things will work out for the good. Keep her under your wings, Lord. Show your loving kindness to her and let her know that you are here. In your name I pray, amen," she said as she opened her eyes. Imani looked at Nevaeh and mouthed, "What's wrong with her?"

Nevaeh shook her head and shrugged her shoulders. Imani looked down at Nicole who was crying so hard that the whole bed seemed to be shaking. When Imani had spoken with Nicole on the phone earlier, she'd seemed normal. She couldn't understand what could've happened in the course of an hour.

"Nikki," Imani called her name softly. "Nikki, what's wrong?" Nicole continued to sob into the pillow.

"Nicole, sweetheart," Nevaeh said, "just calm down and tell us what it is. We can help you. We just need for you to settle down so we can take care of it."

As Nicole continued to cry, Imani looked at her friend and she wondered why she had on long pants as hot as it was outside. Nicole was also wearing a long-sleeved shirt. Imani didn't know if it was a hunch or if she was just paranoid, but she quickly pulled up the sleeves to Nicole's shirt.

"No!" Nicole cried as she tried to pull her sleeves back down.

It was too late. "Nikki, who did this?" Imani asked incredulously as Nevaeh gasped at the sight of Nicole's scarred arm. It looked as if someone had punched her repeatedly. When Nicole didn't answer, Imani pulled up one of her pants legs.

"Oh my God!" Nevaeh screamed. She quickly ran and opened the room door. "Ronald!" she yelled. "Ronald, get back here, *now*!"

"No!" Nicole cried. "No! Why are you doing this? Please, no!"

"What is going on back here?" Ronald asked with everybody else in the house standing behind him.

"*This* is going on," Nevaeh said as she showed him what was on his sister's leg. Scars ran up and down Nicole's right arm and whip marks covered her legs.

"What in the . . . ?" Ronald caught himself before saying something that would surprise even his teammates. "Who did this? Did that punk, out there, do this to you?" he asked, referring to Shawn, not realizing the boy was standing with the group behind him.

"No, I ain't do nothin,' " Shawn said as he tried to examine Nicole's bruises from behind Eddie.

"No," Nicole cried. "Nobody did it! Just leave me alone, please!"

"No, we won't leave you alone," Nevaeh said, sternly. "Nicole, now you can tell us. Who did this to you?"

"I can't," she cried. "Just please leave me alone."

Imani stepped forward. "Nicole Tamia McAfee, you know whoever did this was wrong, so stop trying to cover for them. *Who* did this to you?"

Tell them, my child, and hurt no more.

Nicole heard God's voice and the fear in her heart began to dwindle. She glanced at Imani, Nevaeh, and then finally at Ronald who looked as if he was ready to carry out a murder. "Daddy," she whispered.

"What?" Ronald yelled as he began to back out of the room. "That's it. It's over now." He walked out of the room, grabbed his keys, and ran out of the apartment, slamming the door behind him.

"God, no!" Nicole screamed. "Don't do this, please."

A few of his teammates ran behind Ronald to try and get him to compose himself before he did something rash. Nicole went into hysterics as she screamed and kicked. The rest of the guys tried to keep her calm. Eddie stepped forward and immediately began to pray. Imani tightly held his hand, as she and Nevaeh joined him in praying over Nicole's body as tears ran out of their own eyes.

Chapter 10

Ronald had been heated since finding out about his father's abusive tendencies almost two weeks ago. He had just begun to calm down and think more clearly. Nevaeh had been worried about him because he had become distant from her. She was glad when he had called her a few days ago and apologized for being so isolated. Now she sat near the entrance of Copeland's restaurant as she sipped her lemonade and watched the door to see if Ronald had arrived yet. He had called her earlier and asked her to meet him for lunch, but he was almost thirty minutes late.

"Miss, are you sure that you don't want to go ahead and order while you wait for the rest of your party?" the waitress asked her for the second time.

"Well, here he is now," Nevaeh said, smiling when she noticed Ronald running up the stairs to the restaurant. "So I guess I could order now."

A grin spread across the waitress's face as Ronald walked through the door. "Wow, he is a cutie. How long have you guys been together?"

Nevaeh wasn't surprised that the waitress would just assume she and Ronald were a couple because she was sure that the gleam in her eyes had tipped the woman off. "Six years." She grinned wider as Ronald was led to her table.

"Sorry, I'm late," Ronald said before greeting her with a kiss. "Terrible traffic," he explained as he sat down and looked at Nevaeh. "You haven't ordered yet?"

"She wouldn't until you got here," the waitress said as Ronald for the first time seemed to notice that someone was standing by the table. "Hi, my name is Lana and I will be your sever. Could I get you a drink?"

"Yes, I'll have a Coke," Ronald said. "And we'll go ahead and order." He nodded in Nevaeh's direction.

"I'll have the seafood gumbo," she said without looking at the menu.

"And I'll have the catfish po'boy," Ronald said, handing both menus to the waitress.

"Your wait shouldn't be too long," Lana informed them, "but if you need anything before then, just call me."

Ronald looked at Nevaeh; she could see the remnants of anger in his eyes. "This is really bad, Nev. I can't even believe that my dad did something like this. What was he thinking? It just doesn't seem like him. I guess I really don't know who he is. I feel like beatin' him down for real." Ronald grew angrier with each statement. "I just can't believe he would do something like this," he repeated. "And I guess he waited until I moved out to really start tryna act the fool, 'cause he know if I was there I'd tear him up bad. Mama keeps saying that the trial is coming soon and he'll be in jail, but can't nobody in jail do what I feel like doing to him right now."

"Well, Ron, you see how big your dad is, and plus it wouldn't be very Christian-like for you to fight your father. No matter what he has done, he is still your dad and there's not much you can do," Nevaeh said, "except pray. I know how much your family probably needs all the prayers they can get right now. But don't you think it is best that your mother, Nikki, and Jeremy leave instead of staying and getting hurt even more?"

"Yeah, I guess," Ronald said. "But you should see Nikki. She's cried every night since she called me about Mom leaving Dad. And after we found out about the abuse, she stays shut up in my room. All she does at the apartment is sleep, cry, and she'll occasionally eat, but she barely gets in a meal a day. She won't go out with me to the store or nothing, and you know how much she loves to shop, especially if I'm buying."

"Maybe she just needs some time to get adjusted to things being like this," Nevaeh said. "She needs time to get over that fact that her dad would do something so terrible to her after she thought he loved her and cared for her as a father should."

"I don't know . . . I guess. But Jeremy is a whole 'nother story. It's like he is happy that Mama left. I guess that he was tired of hiding the effects the abuse was having on him. So with Mama leaving, he wouldn't have to endure it anymore. I can't even believe that he let Dad hit on him without telling somebody." He sighed. "Mama is kinda holding everything in. She was devastated to find out about the abuse, but she won't talk about it at all." He shook his head in dismay. "And then this thing with Marques and Shimone."

"I know, I thought he had changed," Nevaeh said, disappointed that Marques could do something as severe as cheating on Shimone. "I mean, I know he did change, but I thought it would last, especially after he got saved. I thought he would try to do better."

Lana came to the table with Ronald's drink and a refill for Nevaeh. "Your food should be out in a few minutes."

"Thank you," Ronald said. He waited until she left the table and then continued with their conversation. "He did try to do better at first. Then he just stopped coming to church with us. I guess he got tired of it. He kept saying that college was supposed to be fun, and he wanted to party. I invited him to some of the events that we went to, but even after going to a few, he still wasn't satisfied."

"And who is this girl that he was sleeping with?" Nevaeh asked. "I can't believe he got her pregnant."

"I've seen her around. Her name is Alex or Alexis or something like that. She graduated last year. She used to be all over Marq when we first started going to Clark. I think she likes athletes."

"Why would you just assume that?" Nevaeh asked.

" 'Cause she tried getting with me and several other guys on the football team." Ronald laughed when he saw Nevaeh's eyebrow twitch. "Don't worry. I told her that I had a girlfriend who I have loved since I was in middle school and no one is ever going to take her place in my life." Ronald smiled, showing his ocean deep dimples, as his dark eyes gazed into Nevaeh's brown ones, making her blush.

Lana came to the table with a steaming plate of gumbo and rice and another plate with a huge po'boy sandwich, overflowing with catfish, and fries on the side. She placed their plates in front of them and gave them extra napkins. "Do you need anything else?"

"No, thank you," Nevaeh said as Ronald shook his head.

As Lana walked off, they bowed their heads and Ronald blessed the food and asked God to watch over their families and friends, then they began to eat.

"You know," Nevaeh said, breaking the silence, "I've been thinking about something else, and it is really starting to weigh on my mind."

"What?" Ronald said, stuffing his face with fries.

"Tyler."

"Who?" Ronald asked with raised eyebrows. "Who is Tyler?" He began shaking his head. "I knew you should have gone to school with us. You being at Emory with all those wannabe doctors never did really set right with me. Who is Tyler?"

It was Nevaeh's turn to laugh, while Ronald wallowed in his jealousy. "Ron, calm down. I'm not trying to get with nobody at Emory. I'm talking about *Shimone's father*, Tyler."

Ronald's face relaxed and a slight smile replaced the grim look. "Oh . . . my bad. I thought you had somebody trying to talk to you and you know I can't be having that," he said, biting his sandwich. "Why are you worried about Shimone's dad?"

"I don't know." She shrugged. "It seems weird that he just shows up all of a sudden. Don't you wonder what he is doing here?"

"Not really, but if I had to take a guess, it would probably be that he regrets leaving Ms. Misty and he wants to make up for it. I just think his timing was bad. I don't think he intended on seeing her that night. I am pretty positive that he didn't mean to scare her into the hospital." He stopped to eat a couple of fries. "As a matter of fact, I wouldn't be surprised if he has actually been living here for a long time and has just gotten enough nerve to come and try to set things right with Ms. Misty and Shimone. And by Shimone's emotional breakdown, I'd say that she didn't totally hate the fact that her dad did come back. I think she was upset about him being the reason that her mother was in the hospital, but I think she wants to forgive him and I'm pretty sure she will."

"Maybe you are right," Nevaeh said. "It just seems like he wants more than to apologize. I think he wants to be a family. I just hope he doesn't hurt them again."

"He won't. I can just feel it," Ronald smiled. "I think he really wants to make things right." He looked at Nevaeh. "Can I have some of that?" he suddenly asked.

"My gumbo?" Nevaeh pointed at her still steaming plate.

"Yes, please." He tried to make a pleading face, but his wide smile ruined his attempts.

"I guess so." She dipped her spoon into the bowl and fed it to him.

He chewed, swallowed, and then leaned in for a light kiss. Their lips parted and they looked up when they heard the sound of someone clearing their throat.

"Hel-lo." Shimone smiled while Ebony laughed. "This is a public place you know. So try and keep it rated 'G'."

"Hi, Shimone," Nevaeh said as she got up to hug her. She was slightly surprised to see her friend, but remembered telling Shimone about her lunch date with Ronald and figured that she wanted to stop in and see her friends.

"Hey, Auntie's big girl." Ebony laughed as Nevaeh tickled her stomach.

"Hey, lil' bit." Ronald bent down to kiss Ebony, and then Shimone on the cheek. He looked up and noticed Tyler standing behind Shimone.

Shimone smiled as she made introductions. "Tyler, these are my best friends, Nevaeh and Ronald. Nev, Ron, this is Tyler Calhoun."

Tyler held out his hand toward Nevaeh. "Nice to meet you."

Nevaeh looked at his hand for a moment, and then joined hers with his. "You too."

Tyler shook Ronald's hand as Misty joined the group. She stood next to her daughter. "Hey, Nevaeh."

"Hi, Ms. Misty," Nevaeh said. "How are you?"

"Good, thank God," Misty said as she hugged Nevaeh

and then Ronald. "How's your family?" she asked Ronald.

"They're pulling through." He shrugged.

"I'll be praying for them," Misty said sympathetically. "Well, I guess we better head to our table," she said as she noticed the host standing next to them, waiting impatiently.

"Call me tonight," Nevaeh said to Shimone as they walked off with the host.

Ronald reclaimed his seat and put more fries into his mouth and glanced at his watch. "I think we are going to have to grab some take-out boxes. I have to go to work."

"Okay," Nevaeh replied mindlessly as if she hadn't even heard a word he had just said.

"What's wrong?" Ronald asked, searching her face.

"Nothing is wrong," Nevaeh said. "I just wish I knew what Tyler's motives for coming back were."

"I told you. He is trying to make amends," Ronald stated as if he knew it to be a fact. "So don't worry about it. Shimone and Ms. Misty can take care of themselves."

"Whatever you say," Nevaeh said.

Ronald smiled and reached for more of her gumbo. She smacked his hand playfully and laughed along with him as he motioned for the waitress and requested two carry-out boxes. Once they received them, they put their food into the boxes and Ronald paid the check, leaving a generous tip. Nevaeh looked back at Shimone's table and waved as she and Ronald headed out of the restaurant.

Shimone tucked a napkin in Ebony's shirt as she ate her chicken fingers. She looked up and saw Tyler making faces with Ebony, just like Marques used to do. She could tell Tyler was remorseful about his absence throughout her life; he'd told her that over and over when they talked for hours at her mother's house. All Shimone had ever wanted for the past twenty-two years were answers. Over the past two weeks, she had gotten them.

"I'm sorry if this seems like an inappropriate question," Tyler said, gaining Shimone's attention, "but how old were you when you got pregnant?"

Shimone looked at him. "Eighteen. I got pregnant in the beginning of my senior year. I was nineteen when I had her."

"And you finished high school?" Tyler asked.

Shimone stared at him and tried to determine the motive behind his questioning. She assumed he was just trying to find out as much about her as he could. "Yes, I graduated with honors."

Tyler's smile showed he was proud. "That's great."

Shimone returned the smile. "Thank you."

"So since the young man who was just here"—He gestured toward where Nevaeh and Ronald had been sitting—"appears to be in a relationship with your friend, I take it that the other gentleman who was at the hospital is your boyfriend."

Shimone looked down at Ebony who had ketchup all over her face. "Umm . . . he was. We broke up a few weeks ago, so the only time I see him is when he picks Ebony up on the weekends."

Tyler noticed that the entire time she spoke she avoided eye contact with him and busied herself with removing the ketchup from Ebony's face. He took that as a sign that the subject was a personal matter that she didn't feel comfortable discussing with him at the moment, so he decided not to pry.

He turned his brown eyes toward Misty and smiled. She returned the gesture and lowered her eyes. He took note of the unconscious habit that she'd developed back in high school anytime he made her blush. Although he did want to rectify his relationships with Misty and Shimone, Tyler also wanted another chance with his first love. Since she left the private school that they attended together back in North Carolina, he had not been the same. He'd felt guilty, lost, and lonely all through the remainder of his high school experience.

After high school, Tyler had attended a theological college in North Carolina and attained his ministerial license. In the process, he'd found love once again and married. After being married for two years, his wife died of cancer, leaving him to take care of his son alone. For ten years he spent his time as associate pastor of a well-established church within the state, but knew that God had called him for a higher purpose. Needing a change of scenery, he prayed and fasted before hearing the confirmation from God that he needed to take his son and relocate to Atlanta to start a church ministry.

In trying to establish his ministry and raise his son, Tyler had not known that single parenthood could be so hard. Now, when he thought back to the times when he had to change his nine-month-old son's diaper, feed him, take him to the doctor, or wake up in the middle of the night to tend to his cries, he thought of Misty and how his selfishness had put her out on the streets where she sold her body for money to take care of Shimone.

Tyler looked across the table at his daughter and his granddaughter, and prayed that God had forgiven him, and he thanked Him for this opportunity to make things right.

"How would you guys like to visit my church tomorrow?" Tyler asked.

"Really?" Misty asked, happy to be spending more time with Tyler.

"Sure, you can meet my son and . . ."

Tyler paused when Shimone's head popped up and

she gave him her full attention. Shimone had been shocked to hear that Tyler had a son he'd taken care of since the child came out of his mother's womb. When he'd shared that aspect of his life with her, during one of their conversations in the past weeks, Shimone had to fight off the unfamiliar twinge of jealously she'd felt within her heart. She wasn't sure how she felt about having a fifteen-year-old brother, but she didn't want to make Tyler feel any guiltier that he already did.

". . . He's wanted to meet you all for a while now," Tyler added hesitantly.

"I guess that would be cool," Shimone spoke softly, still unsure of the meeting.

"But how would you introduce us?" Misty asked.

"Well, Tim knows the whole story about us dating and Shimone being my daughter; he's fine with it. He's always wanted a sibling."

"No, I'm talking about your congregation," Misty clarified. She worried that Tyler's congregation wouldn't accept them as his family.

"If it is okay with you"—he looked at Shimone—"I'd like to introduce you as my daughter and her mother."

Shimone shrugged. "I guess that would be okay. But don't you think people in your congregation would say things about you being with a black woman?"

"My wife was black," Tyler said, causing Shimone's face to turn red instantly.

"I'm sorry," she said. "I didn't mean it in a derogatory way or anything like that. But don't you think they would say something about you having a child out of wedlock and then not taking care of that child?"

Tyler looked down at the half-eaten chicken on his plate and pulled at his left ear.

Shimone realized that she was making everyone at the table extremely uncomfortable. It was as if she couldn't control the questions that were coming from her mouth. "I'm sorry," she apologized once more. "I'm just saying all the wrong things. I'm not trying to make you feel guilty. I'm speaking from the view of the members of your church. I just don't want to go to the service and feel as if everyone there is talking about me, my mother, or you."

"I know." Tyler nodded in understanding. "But if it will make you feel better, I have a mixture of nationalities in my church, and there are interracial couples. There are also a few people with children out of wedlock and not all of them are black. Not that it's something I should be proud of, being that I am the presiding pastor, but it just shows that all Christians aren't perfect, including me." He smiled at Shimone, who returned the gesture.

"Well, I'd love to go," Shimone said, and then looked at her daughter. "What do you say, Ebony? Do you wanna go to church with Mr. Tyler tomorrow?"

Ebony nodded energetically. "Thank Jesus," she replied with her hands in the air as Misty laughed and Tyler smiled at his granddaughter.

"I think she's having church already," Tyler said as Ebony began to clap her hands and sing a song from her mother's album.

"I didn't even know she knew that song," Misty said, nearly shocked that her granddaughter was singing the song word-for-word.

Shimone smiled. "She sings it around the house a lot lately. I don't know where she hears it because I barely play that CD."

"Why not?" Misty asked as if the album was her own and she felt offended by her daughter's remark. "You should be proud. I still don't know why you won't call that man and let him put them on the market. You could use the money."

"Mama, I told you I don't have time to do that *and* take care of Ebony *and* go to school," Shimone stressed.

"Wait," Tyler interrupted in sudden realization. *"You* recorded a CD?" Shimone nodded. "Wow, I would love it if you performed a song tomorrow. Please?"

She looked at Tyler and burst into laughter. "You can't be serious."

"Why not? I'd love to hear you sing," Tyler said, genuinely.

Shimone thought about it for a moment. *Why not? It could be fun performing for another audience. And it would make Tyler happy.* She wondered why she was concerned with Tyler's happiness all of a sudden. "Sure, I'll do it," she said.

"Thank you," Tyler said as Ebony continued to sing.

Shimone turned her attention toward her daughter. "Ebony, where did you hear that song?"

Ebony stopped singing long enough to answer her mother's question. "Daddy play it . . . a lot."

Shimone's eyes glazed with tears as she continued to stare at her daughter while Ebony continued to sing. Misty gazed at Shimone with sadness in her eyes and then at Tyler who seemed to be just as compassionate without even knowing the details of his daughter's relationship with Marques. Tyler motioned for the waitress to bring the check as they got ready to leave.

Chapter 11

"You were always horrible at giving directions," Tyler said as Misty directed him toward Shimone's apartment. "I remember when you gave me directions to your house for our first date. You had me at every gas station asking for directions."

"Whatever," Misty laughed, pointing toward the next street for him to make a turn. "See, here it is," she gloated once they had pulled into the apartment complex.

"Yeah, and it took us ten minutes longer than you said it would," he chuckled as he parked in front of Shimone's building and turned off the car. He watched Misty as she fixed her hair in the mirror. "You look good," Tyler said as she lowered her eyes. "You always have."

"Thank you." She smiled.

Tyler exited the car and ran around to the passenger's side to open the door for Misty. After they had approached the apartment and knocked on the door, Shimone appeared at the door dressed in a pink two-piece suit.

"You look nice," Tyler said with Misty agreeing.

"Thanks." Shimone smiled. "I have to finish getting Ebony ready for church, so you guys can come in and wait in the living room if you want."

Tyler and Misty walked into the apartment, stepping over scattered toys.

"Sorry about the mess," Shimone said. "I have to start teaching her how to put away her toys when she's finished playing with them." She looked back at Tyler. "Where's your son?" she asked.

"Oh, Tim stayed with a friend from our church last night, so he is riding with them. You'll get to see him at the service."

Tyler and Misty sat on the sofa while Shimone went into Ebony's room to help her finish getting ready for the service. They had been sitting in silence for a few moments when Misty noticed that Tyler was steadily pulling at his ears.

"What's wrong?" Misty asked worriedly.

Tyler placed his hands on his knees, before saying, in a lowered voice, "I don't know, maybe the fact that I'm sitting in my daughter's house, surrounded by *her* daughter's toys. I should have been there, Misty. Everyday I ask myself why was I so stupid. I should have been there to hear you yell that your water broke. I should have been in the room, holding your hand while you gave birth to her. I should have been there to see Shimone's first steps and to see her start school. I should have been at her graduation and I should have been in the delivery room when she had my granddaughter. I should have been there, but I wasn't, and I hate it."

"Tyler, there is nothing that you can do to change the past," Misty said as she rubbed his back. "The fact that you are here now and that we are all about to go to church together, as a family, is progress. I mean, two weeks ago you were in my house apologizing, and today we are like a family. So you are doing just fine. We both have forgiven you. Now all you have to do is forgive yourself."

Shimone came out of the room with Ebony walking beside her. When Ebony saw Tyler, she ran toward him, not surprising Shimone at all. If Ebony liked someone, whether she had just met them are not, she would treat them as if she'd known them forever.

"Hey, Mr. Tyler," Ebony said.

"Hi darling," Tyler greeted, picking Ebony up and putting her on his lap. "Don't you look pretty?" he complimented, admiring her blue dress.

"Thank you," Ebony said.

Shimone went into the kitchen to fill one of Ebony's cups with juice just in case she became fidgety during the service. She walked back into the living room. "Umm . . . Tyler can Ebony's car seat be put in your truck?"

"Sure. Where is it?" Tyler questioned, sitting Ebony on the sofa and getting up.

"It's over by the TV," Shimone said.

Tyler headed out of the house with the car seat in hand. Shimone grabbed her purse, Bible, and Ebony's bag as she took Ebony's hand and headed toward the door.

"Nia," Misty's voice stopped her. Shimone turned around slowly. Misty always called her the shortened version of her middle name when she had something important to discuss with her. "Do you like him?"

Shimone broke into a smile, dispelling the worry she saw in her mother's eyes. "Yeah, I think I do."

They walked out to the car, Shimone locking the door behind them. As Tyler drove, he sang along to the songs on Praise 97.5 FM. Shimone noticed that he had a great singing voice. She always figured that she'd gotten her vocal talents from her father, since the only notes her mother could hit were the keys on a piano.

When they pulled into the parking lot of Unity Revival Church, Shimone noticed that the parking lot was nearly full. She tried to figure out how the small church could accommodate so many members. Her question was answered when she walked through the doors. The inside was very spacious. It held, at maximum, two-hundred people. People didn't appear to be crowded and they seemed to be enjoying the service. Several eyes were on Tyler as he led Misty, Shimone, and Ebony to the second row from the front of the church before taking his place in the pulpit.

As the praise service continued, Misty and Shimone joined in with the other worshippers. The worship service reminded Shimone of Greater Faith's praise and worship service. Despite age and ability, everyone participated in the service.

When praise and worship ended, Shimone saw Tyler slip through a door in the front of the church. She figured he was going to his office to get ready for his sermon. Just as he disappeared, a woman came to the front of the church with a folder in her hand. "Unity Revival would like to welcome all of our visitors. We hope that whether you are a first-time or a returning visitor, this will not be the last time we see your faces.

"Announcements are as follows: There will be a brief board of directors meeting following service today. Also, Sister Winsome would like to meet with all ushers to assign posts and duties for this month.

"Unity Revival would like to thank everyone who came out and participated on last weekend at Youth Quake. We just thank you for your time and efforts that made this year's Youth Quake a huge success. August twenty-seventh is our Youth's Praise Night. So, all youth

come out on Sunday night at six o'clock. Bring your
friends from school or from across the street. If you
would like to be a part of the service, please see one of
our youth leaders, Jasmine Jones or Felicia Downy. October thirty-first is our third annual Hallelujah Night. Instead of going out on the streets trick-or-treating, we are
going to have a fun-filled night here with games, talents,
and much more.

"Pastor Calhoun will be holding a baptismal ceremony for all of those who wish to be baptized on the fifth
Sunday in October. If you are interested, please see our
pastor's secretary, Sister Ceria Gillard, following today's
service. Also, on the Saturday before Thanksgiving we
are having a community outreach event. Pastor Calhoun
would appreciate it if everyone who can would come out
to Atlanta Community Center to help feed and witness
to the homeless. If you cannot make this event, come out
on December second to the Atlanta prison to help our
Prison Ministry witness to the incarcerated." She closed
the folder. "And now let's welcome our beloved Pastor
Calhoun."

Tyler came out of the office and walked up to the pulpit as he received a standing ovation from his church
members. He stood at the podium with his ministerial
robe over his suit and his hands lifted in praise along
with the congregation. "Come on and give Him praise.
Come on and give Him the praise. Praise Him. Lift your
hands and give God the glory."

Shimone thought her father looked much different now
than he had yesterday at lunch. With his hands raised
and eyes closed, giving honor to God, he reminded her of
a younger version of Rod Parsley.

She stopped observing her father and raised her hands
in praise, giving God thanks for all He had done in her
life thus far. She thanked God for His presence in her life

and for giving her the opportunity to get to know the man she'd always wished had been a part of her life, no matter how many times she denied it when her mother or friends questioned her feelings on the matter. She thanked God for being there when she needed Him the most. The times when Marques or Ebony would get on her nerves or the times when she just wanted to give up on life, He was there and she was thankful for it.

"Be seated if you can," Tyler said as he wiped his mouth with a handkerchief. He looked out over the congregation. "Once again, I would like to extend a welcome to all of our visitors. I see we have a few returning visitors and many new ones." He looked at Shimone and Misty. "I would just like to introduce a few. I have with me today members of my family that I haven't seen in a long, long time—Shimone Johnson, her mother, Misty Johnson, and little Ebony," he said as the members clapped.

"I haven't seen Misty since I was a sophomore in high school. Before I was saved, I was stupid and ended up losing someone who was very special to me all because I wasn't man enough to stand up and be responsible for someone I had created." He looked at Shimone lovingly. "Shimone is my first born," he said to his congregation's surprise. "She is my daughter and she looks just like her beautiful mother. I wasn't there for Shimone and Misty like I should have been, but, thankfully, God has forgiven me for my mistakes. I even have a granddaughter, Ebony."

Ebony squealed at the mention of her name as everyone laughed.

"I would just like to say that I love you all and I hope that you all can find it in your hearts to truly forgive me for abandoning you in your time of need."

Misty nodded as Shimone wiped a tear from her eye.

Tyler continued, "My daughter has agreed to share her

gift of music with us today." Applause erupted from the audience. "Shimone," he called out to her as he extended his hand.

Shimone stood up and placed Ebony in the vacant spot beside her mother. The congregation clapped as she made her way to the front of the church. She took her father's hand and Tyler pulled her into a hug as the congregation stood to their feet and the applause became thunderous. Shimone allowed her tears to dampen her father's robe and Tyler held her as tight as he could without hurting her. Misty stood with other members and continued to clap, wiping a few of her own tears. Shimone finally pulled back and accepted the microphone from Tyler. She stepped down from the pulpit and stood in front of the podium as seats were reoccupied and the applause began to decrease.

"You know, I've always wondered where I got my singing abilities. I knew God blessed me with a voice to sing His praises, but I always wondered how the talent was passed on to me. I knew it wasn't my mother because she can't stay on one key to save her life." Misty gave Shimone a warning look as she laughed along with the people of the church. "But on the drive here, my dad was singing every song that came on the radio and I realized that the talent was passed on to me from him." She smiled.

"I just thank God for being here, and furthermore, for being here with family." Shimone paused as applause, once again, broke out amongst the congregation. "Before a few months ago, I had never seen my dad. I had seen a few pictures of him and my mother together when they were still in high school, but I had never met him. And if you would have asked me a month ago if I cared, I would have told you 'no'. And if you would have seen me when I first saw him, you would have thought that I hated him." She turned toward Tyler who was sitting in the pulpit. "But all of my hitting and crying and screaming had nothing to do with me hating you. I never hated you. I may have said it on occasion, but that was never the case. All of my frustration was based on my confusion.

"When you came to the hospital to visit my mother, I didn't cause a scene because I didn't want you there. I caused that scene in front of all my friends and family because I *did* want you to come visit her. I wanted you at the hospital to comfort me and assure me that she was going to be okay, and I was confused as to why I wanted you to be there so badly.

"When we had that long talk a couple of weeks ago, I still couldn't figure out why I had this urge to hug you when I saw you sitting at my mother's kitchen table. I was so confused as to why I felt these things, so I covered my confusion with the anger that I truly wanted to feel toward you. But even as hard as I tried, I still couldn't hide the fact that I had developed a love for you. It was the love God had been storing away for the father that I never had, and I guess that when you came into our lives, that love decided it was time for it to be released. So I think I speak for my mother, and even Ebony, when I say, we love you," Shimone said as Tyler mouthed the words back to her. "I wrote this song for my heavenly Father, but today I dedicate it to you also. It is entitled *Beside My Father*."

She turned toward the congregation and closed her eyes and began to sing. Her soulful voice stirred the congregation and had everyone on their feet with their hands in the air. She held the last note of the song until she had no breath left to continue.

When she ended the song, Tyler and Misty were in tears. Before Misty could stop her, Ebony ran to the front of the church and into her mother's arms. Tyler and Misty came from their positions in the church and walked to join their daughter and granddaughter in a group hug as the congregation clapped. Tyler motioned for his son, who had been watching from his position on the drums, to join them. Timothy, who was the spitting image of Tyler, only slightly darker, moved from his seat and joined the rest of his family, who didn't hesitate in letting him into their circle.

When they released each other, there wasn't a dry eye in the church. Timothy looked at each one of his new family members with loving eyes. Ebony was continuously reaching for her new uncle, so Shimone handed her to him and Timothy kissed her cheeks. They walked back to their seats, with Timothy still holding his niece.

Tyler stood at the podium with his eyes closed as he said a gracious prayer, thanking God for giving him the opportunity to start over with his family. "You know," he said as he opened his eyes, "you never know when you are going to lose someone close to you and you never realize how important they are to you until it's too late. So right here, right now, just go to your family and friends and tell them how much they mean to you," he continued as members began to hug each other. "You never know what tomorrow may bring. If they were to go on tomorrow, would they know how much you really care for them? If your answer to that question is not yes, you need to let them know right now." Tyler reached out to his family and they came back to the front.

He handed Shimone the microphone and she began to sing *I Need You to Survive* by Hezekiah Walker as the people continued to hug each other.

Chapter 12

Sierra rushed into the den to answer the ringing phone. "Hello?"

"Hey, girl, it's Nevaeh. How are you doing?"

"Hey. I'm doing good. Actually, I've been doing really well lately," Sierra said. "I figure it's because I go running every morning."

"Well, that's good to hear," Nevaeh said. "How are Corey, LaToya, and Jabari?"

"They're all good. Today is Jabari's birthday, so La-Toya is throwing him a party at Chuck E. Cheese's, with a bunch of lil' rugrats that are going to send my head into pounding mode." Sierra laughed. "And Corey keeps bringing up marriage, so don't be surprised if I call you singing "Here Comes the Bride"." She laughed again.

"Well, go 'head, girl," Nevaeh said. "I'm happy for you."

"Yeah." Sierra sighed. "But I'm a little worried 'cause being married means being intimate and that will expose Corey to my disease."

"I'm sure he's well aware of that, Sierra," Nevaeh said. "You can always use protection. I know he wouldn't mind, since he knows your situation."

"Yeah, but that only makes the reality of me ever having kids less real."

"Sierra, haven't you talked about this with Corey?" Nevaeh asked.

Sierra was quiet for a moment before admitting, "Well, no. Why give him a reason not to give me a ring?"

"First of all, I'm sure he realizes by now that you all won't be able to engage in certain things because of your status. Second, by knowing this, he apparently hasn't changed his mind about marrying you, so don't sweat it. Talking about kids and things that relate to your marriage are things you do before getting married, so please don't wait until your wedding night to ask about using protection or the children issue."

"You're right." Sierra was grateful for Nevaeh's call because it gave her a chance to vent, something she hadn't had the chance to do. "Thanks Nev."

"You're welcome. Well, I just called to make sure you are doing well. I actually have a class in an hour. I can't believe I signed up for Saturday classes. Man, it's already September, almost three weeks since we got back to school, and I'm still not used to this schedule."

"Tell me about it," Sierra sighed. "Corey worries about me like he's my daddy. First he was trippin' about my course load, and then he was trying to get me to join this health group at Missouri College. I told him he had better get out of my face with that mess," she said, causing Nevaeh to burst into laughter. "First of all, I've already taken classes that have told me everything I need to know about what I'm dealing with. I think he's still worried that I'm struggling with the fact that I have HIV, but that's why I go to counseling. I really don't wanna sit in a class where all I can do is talk about it for two straight hours."

"Well, at least you know he cares about what you're going through. Ronald can get overprotective of me sometimes, but it's mostly because he can't keep watch over what guy is trying to talk to me," Nevaeh laughed. "But I told him that all of my focus is on becoming a licensed nurse." There was silence for several moments before Nevaeh spoke again. "Well, I was just calling to check on you. Tell everyone hello for me. I'll talk to you later, okay?"

"Hold up," Sierra said. "You didn't call only to check up one me. I know you, something is wrong. What is it?"

"Nothing, really—"

"Look, I know we've never been the best of friends. And, up until the last few years, I know I wasn't as nice as I should have been," Sierra said, remembering when she and Nevaeh despised each other. "But ever since you stood up for me when everybody else turned their backs on me, I see you as a true friend, so you can tell me anything. What's going on?"

Nevaeh sighed and lowered her voice as if someone might be listening. "A few weeks ago, right before school started, we found out that Ronald's sister, Nicole, was being abused by their dad."

"What?" Sierra shrieked.

"Yeah, we were at Ronald's apartment when we found out." Nevaeh began to recap all that had happened almost a month ago. "So when Imani lifted Nicole's sleeves and pants legs, we found whip marks and bruises all on her body."

"Are you serious?" Sierra said. "My God."

"I know," Nevaeh continued. "But this is the first time Malcolm has ever abused Nicole to this extent. But, apparently, he had been abusing Jeremy, Ronald's little, brother, for a while. Jeremy never told anyone though, so none of us knew.

"When Ronald found out, he drove to his dad's house and tried to fight Malcolm. They caused so much noise that the neighbors called the police and had them both arrested. So we got called down to the precinct. By the time we all got there, Ronald had already told the police what the fight was about. Nicole wouldn't say anything, but Jeremy told them that Malcolm had beaten him on several occasions for no apparent reason." Nevaeh paused to catch her breath.

"So was he convicted or anything?" Sierra asked.

"Well, they got a statement from Jeremy, but they also needed one from Nicole to get him on both counts. Ronald was upset with her because she was just sitting there not saying anything. So Ronald tells Nicole to show the police the marks on her body, but she pretended that she didn't know what he was talking about. Imani and I spoke up and said something about the bruises, too. Then a female officer took Nicole into a private room and asked her to remove everything except for her underwear so they could get pictures, but they said that they still needed a statement saying that Malcolm did this. Ronald went ballistic when they asked that. He was saying that his father did it and should be thrown in jail."

"Well, he should," Sierra said, remembering how her father used to abuse her, but had turned his life around for the better. "I mean, unless he is planning on changing or going to counseling or something like that, he should be locked up."

"That's what Ronald was saying. But the police still wanted a statement from Nicole. So she finally spoke up and let the police record the statement. From what I could tell from her story, she had her boyfriend take her to see Malcolm, the day before we found out, so she could ask him some questions about his affair—her parents are divorcing and his infidelity is the reason behind it," Nevaeh backtracked. "She said that she told her boyfriend to leave her there and she'd get her dad to take her back home. So the boy left, but when she went into the house, her dad was sitting on the couch drinking a beer and watching TV. She said she sat down with him and tried to get him to talk to her, but while they were talking, he was still drinking, and he would touch her arm or her knee, which made her feel uneasy. She said that he started to fondle and touch her while trying to get on top of her. Apparently, she pushed him away one too many times and he went off and began to hit her repeatedly. Now, Malcolm is like Ronald's size times two, so although he was drunk, he was still much stronger than she was.

"She managed to get from under his hold, but he caught her again and started beating her with his belt, which is what caused all of the whip marks. She did manage to get out of the house, but instead of calling the police or going to a neighbor, she called her boyfriend and told him to come pick her up. He noticed her disassembled clothes and tears. When he asked her about it, she basically ignored him.

"The officers got her boyfriend's statement, too, and he confirmed that he had dropped Nicole off at her dad's that night and when he'd picked her up she seemed upset, but said she didn't want to talk about it. So when the cops got both their stories, they put Malcolm in jail and he is going to trial for sexual assault and physical abuse."

"Thank God," Sierra said. "I can't believe that he would do something like that. I mean, I don't know the man, but I figure anyone with enough sense to raise good children like Ronald and Nicole should have some type of care and love for his family, you know," she said, trying to imagine the kind of effect that this was having on Ronald. "Did they keep Ronald at the jail overnight?" she asked.

"No, but Ronald wouldn't leave until he knew for sure that his dad would be locked up. And, apparently, Malcolm had been dealing with some personal issues concerning his computer company and he took all the stress he was harboring from that out on his family. I just don't understand why the kids wouldn't want to tell somebody something like that was going on. Even if Jeremy had told Nicole, it would've been better than keeping it in and enduring the abuse. Maybe Malcolm threatened them or something, I don't know." She sighed. "But things have kinda settled down now," she continued. "Ronald has cooled down. Ms. Angel moved Nicole and Jeremy into their new house and she is also filing for divorce. They are supposed to appear in court for Malcolm's case in a few weeks. I just really needed to talk to someone, you know? Because it was having a major effect on all of us."

"Well, I'm glad you called me," Sierra said. "I'll be praying for them, big time. But I have to go now. It's almost time to celebrate Jabari's second year of life."

"Okay," Nevaeh said. "I have to get to my own class before I'm late. Give Jabari a big kiss for me and make sure you tell everybody else I said 'hi'," she reminded. "Oh, and Sierra, take care of yourself, okay?"

"I will." Sierra smiled. "Bye."

"Bye bye," Nevaeh said.

Sierra hung up the phone and immediately knelt in front of the sofa. "Lord, I pray for Ronald's family right now. They all need you. I just pray that they can find it in their hearts to forgive Malcolm for all that he has done.

Also let Malcolm hear you calling for him to come back home to you. I pray for their well being. I love you and I lift you up. Amen," she said as she got up off of the floor.

She went into her bedroom and glanced at her digital clock. She realized that Corey would be knocking on her door any minute, so she found a pair of heels that matched her pink outfit, grabbed her purse, and sat on the couch as she waited for Corey to arrive. As soon as she got comfortable, the sound of light rapping against the front door teased her ears. She sighed as she went to answer the door.

"Hey," Corey greeted. "Mmm," he moaned as they shared a lingering kiss. "Are you ready?"

"Yes," she answered. "Oh . . . wait. Let me get my migraine pills."

"Are you okay?" he asked in concern as he followed her into her bedroom.

"Yeah," she assured. "I just know that it is going to be loud at this restaurant and I really don't want to be miserable the entire time."

Corey laughed as she rummaged through her drawer for her pills. "Did you get enough sleep last night?"

"Yeah, I went to bed around midnight," she informed. "I had a design to finish."

"Well, what time did you get up this morning?" he asked, worried.

"I didn't have a class today, so I got up around ten," Sierra said, locating her pills. "I got enough sleep," she assured him.

"Have you eaten?" Corey asked.

"Yes, I had a bowl of corn flakes this morning and I took all of my morning medication afterwards." She placed the pills in her purse and turned around to face him. "Any more questions, *Father*?"

"Actually, there is one more, but it ain't a question your *father* would ask." Corey's smile was mischievous. "I can't ask you until I think you are ready to answer, anyway. So it really doesn't matter, now does it?" he teased.

Sierra looked at him suspiciously, hoping he was finally going to pop the question that he had been hinting at for almost three months. Although she still had a couple of years of schooling left, the option of marriage, before graduation, wasn't totally out of the question. If they did get married before she graduated, she was sure that she would be able to balance marriage and school. She would just have to hold off on the kids until she had a steady job. Again the issue of intimacy and kids flooded her mind, but she refused to let that dissipate the happiness she felt when she was with Corey. It was something she'd have to deal with sooner or later, though. *But not today*, she thought to herself.

Corey continued to hold Sierra's stare, prompting her to ask him what his question was, but instead of asking him to reveal his secret question, she wrapped her arms around him and offered him a sensual kiss. Once she released him, she walked out of the room, leaving him standing in the middle of her bedroom rubbing his goatee.

"Maybe you are ready to answer," he said to himself as he followed her out of the apartment.

Jabari continued to kick and scream while Chuck E. Cheese made his way through the maze of children. The closer the character got, the louder Jabari would scream. LaToya was sitting with him in her lap, trying to calm him down.

"Why don't you just take him over there?" Jamal

pointed to the other side of the restaurant where arcade games filled the space. "Or better yet, outside?" he snapped.

"This is *his* party," LaToya defended. "I can't just take him out. And why are you just sitting there like you can't do anything? If you are tired of him crying, you take him outside."

"I would," Jamal said mockingly, "but it seems to me like *you* are the one holding him."

Sierra looked from Jamal to LaToya. "Both of you are being stubborn," she said as she got up from her seat next to Corey. "Come on, Bari." She lifted Jabari out of LaToya's arms and walked out of the restaurant. As soon as she was outside, Jabari's cries began to cease. "Yeah, that's better. I bet you were just tired of your parents arguing. I know."

Sierra smiled at a few patrons as they entered the restaurant. As Jabari began to rest on her shoulder, she walked back and forth in front of the building. She turned around to see LaToya standing behind her. Since they had been best friends since elementary school, Sierra knew when something was wrong with her friend and it had nothing to do with Jabari or his ruined birthday party.

"What's the matter?" Sierra asked, still bouncing Jabari in her arms.

LaToya began to cry softly. "It's just so hard. I love Jabari and I don't regret having him. I also love Jamal, but he is starting to get on my nerves and I feel like I'm raising Jabari alone."

Sierra searched her friend's eyes. "I think it's much deeper than that."

LaToya allowed the warm tears to trail down her cheeks before wiping them away. "Jamal is changing. He tells me that he loves me, but he is not acting like it. I don't know what or *who* has gotten into him in the last few months, but it's making us drift apart. He was supposed to take me and Jabari to the store last weekend to get Jabari some birthday clothes. I sat at the apartment for an hour and a half waiting for him, and when he showed up, he asked me for something to eat before we left to go to the store. He gave no explanation as to why he was so late. By the time he had decided he was ready to go, I had given Jabari a bath and put him to bed, so we ended up not even going anywhere.

"Then, I don't see or hear from him until last night when he called asking me what time the party was and if we needed a ride. Well, of course we need a ride. My car is in the shop, so how else am I supposed to get there? And he knew that my car wasn't working because he was the one who took it to the mechanic's. When I asked him if he sent out the invitations to Jabari's playgroup, he says no, like it's not a big deal. Hel-lo!" She waved her hand in the air. "How are we supposed to have a party without party guests? So that's why no one is at this stupid party. Jamal is just so dumb, but I love him and I can't stay mad at him. I just don't know what's going on with him." She took Jabari from Sierra.

"Why don't you just ask him?" Sierra suggested.

" 'Cause I don't want him getting all mad just 'cause I asked him a question," LaToya said. "He's been snapping at any and everything I do or say lately. It's been like that for the past year, at least. I'm just not up for another argument."

"Well, at least let's go back inside so little man can have *some* fun," Sierra suggested as she led her best friend back inside.

When they walked back around to the side of the restaurant where the party was, LaToya found Jamal talking and laughing with another girl at their table. It

was the first time in a few months that she had seen him
so happy and it made her angry to see that it wasn't her
face he was grinning in. She immediately walked up to
him and used her free hand to tap him on the shoulder.
Jamal turned around to find LaToya and Sierra standing
behind him, looking like they wanted to tear him to
pieces.

"Man, I don't have time for this drama," Jamal declared, knowing the predicament he'd just gotten himself
into.

"Oh, you haven't seen drama," LaToya said as she
glanced in the girl's direction and noticed that it was
Jamal's ex-girlfriend, Kim Hodges. "What is *she* doing
here?"

"We were just talking," Jamal said.

"I'm here for him to see his—"

"Kim!" Jamal cut her off. "It's time for you to leave."

"Excuse me?" Kim's voice level rose.

Jamal moved so she could exit the booth she was sitting in. "You heard me. You gotta go, *now*."

"So you gon' keep lying?" Kim asked rhetorically.
"Fine," she said. She stood and faced LaToya. "You don't
know how bad you've got it until you can't even see that
the one you love is playin' you like it's nothin'."

"What?" LaToya questioned in mounting anger.
"Jamal, you better tell this hoodrat to get out my face!"

Kim stepped closer to LaToya. "You might want to
watch who you callin' a hoodrat 'cause you *don't* know
me like that."

LaToya glared at Kim as if she wanted to take her by
the hair and drag her outside. "I know you well enough
to call 'em like I see 'em."

LaToya barely paid attention to Corey, who had come
from the restroom and stepped in front of her, blocking

her view of Kim. "What's goin' on out here?" he asked as he took a frightened Jabari from his mother.

"Nothin' that can't be handled." Jamal pulled LaToya toward him and away from Kim. "Now, Kim, I'ma tell you for the last time. You need to leave. I'll handle my business and you handle yours."

Kim's glare was so cold the temperature seemed to drop in the restaurant. "Fine, but this is gonna catch up to you." She looked at LaToya once again and struggled not to reveal the secret that had lain dormant between her and Jamal for the last two years.

LaToya placed her arm around Jamal's waist as Kim walked off. When he saw Kim headed toward the playpen, Jamal moved to gain everyone's attention.

"Alright let's get back to this party," he said, almost in exaggerated excitement.

"Bye Daddy," a small voice spoke, causing everyone to look past Jamal.

A young boy around four years old was holding Kim's hand as they walked past the booth and toward the exit door. LaToya's heart rate began to quicken and her breathing became uneven. She could find no moisture for her suddenly parched throat. She tried to steady herself after a fleeting feeling of lightheadedness passed through her body. The little boy had Jamal's eyes, wide nose, and big full lips. He even had the same perfect shade of dark chocolate skin. He was waving in their direction and LaToya instinctively knew whose attention he was trying to get. *I know this child doesn't belong to my boyfriend*, LaToya thought, but the rapid beating of her heart told her otherwise.

As Kim and the young child left the restaurant, LaToya moved out of Jamal's grasp.

"Baby, just let me explain," Jamal said slowly as if he

felt speaking too quickly would cause LaToya to lose all of her cool.

LaToya took Jabari from her brother to keep her hands from going upside Jamal's head. Corey and Sierra stood by looking extremely confused as they waited for Jamal to explain what had just happened. But LaToya didn't want to hear it. Before Jamal could say another word, LaToya grabbed her purse and walked out of the restaurant with Sierra on her tail. They had reached the Navigator by the time Jamal had caught up with them.

"LaToya, wait," he said as he ran toward the vehicle with Corey rushing behind him. "LaToya!" Jamal called again.

"What?" LaToya snapped.

Jamal stopped in front of her and paused to even his breathing. "Please let me . . . explain," he said between breaths.

"Explain what?" LaToya said with tears in her eyes as Corey climbed into the driver's seat. "You want to explain to me why you have a child, who's obviously *older* than Jabari, who I had *no* knowledge about? You want to try to hand me a bunch of tired excuses as to why you never told me this? We've been going out for four years, and, granted, we've probably spent a quarter of that time broken up or arguing, and, yes, we do have a rocky relationship, but you have a child that I've never met or even heard about! So is that what you want to explain to me? About why I never knew about this child?" she asked as Sierra climbed into the passenger's side seat. "Well, don't waste your breath 'cause that's something I should've known from day one, but now I couldn't care less," she said as she strapped Jabari in and shut the door. She walked around to the other side and opened the door to climb in.

"Will you listen to me for a minute?" Jamal held the

door open, but wouldn't let her shut it after she had gotten into the car. "The child is my son and his name is Jayson. Kim had him when we were freshmen. But instead of telling me about him, she withdrew from school, had the baby, and let her mother keep him while she came back and finished school. She just showed up with him right when we had Jabari. She must have thought that if I would take care of Jabari that I wouldn't have a problem taking care of Jayson. I swear, I didn't know about him until after Jabari was born," he explained as LaToya sat in the car as if everything he was saying was going in one ear and out the other. Jamal pleaded with his eyes for her to understand.

"Like I said, Jamal, I couldn't care less," LaToya said and then closed the door as Corey began to back out of the parking lot, leaving Jamal standing in the middle of the lot . . . alone

Chapter 13

Ebony had been attending Love Joy Childcare Center since she was born. Usually it would take the first weeks of every new school year for Ebony to get reacquainted with the arrangement because she knew she wouldn't be able to spend as much time with her mother as she had been during the summer. But despite the tears, Shimone would get up at eight o'clock every morning, drive Ebony to the center, and leave her there until her last class ended. It was all a routine. But now, a month and a half into the new school year, Ebony decided that she was not going to cooperate.

"Shimone, just leave her with me," Anya, one of the daycare workers, said. "She'll be fine."

"I can't," Shimone said as she looked at her watch. She had thirty minutes to drive to campus and be in her seat for her nine o'clock voice class. "Ebony, stop all this crying now," she said, placing Ebony on the mat next to Anya's daughter, Tammy. "Look, Tammy wants to play with you," she said as Tammy tried to hand Ebony a doll.

Ebony took the doll and threw it across the room, causing Tammy to cry.

"Tammy, she didn't mean it," Anya said, retrieving the doll.

Shimone looked back at Ebony who was still screaming at the top of her lungs. "You better hush before you get a whippin.' " Ebony immediately began to soften her cries at the sound of her mother's firm tone. "Now what is the problem?"

"Where Daddy?" Ebony asked, still crying. "Why he not here?"

Anya gave Shimone a sympathetic look. Shimone gazed at her daughter and softened her eyes. Marques usually came to the center in the mornings to spend time with her before going to his early morning class, but today he was missing in action and Shimone didn't know why.

"Sweetie, I don't know where Daddy is or why he's not here, but Mommy has to go to school. So I need for you to be a big girl and play nice with Tammy," she said.

Tammy tried, once again, to cheer Ebony up by tempting her with a bag full of blocks with various Disney characters on them. "Wanna play blocks?"

Ebony's eyes were still sad, but she sat on the floor and began to stack blocks as Tammy pulled them out of the bag.

"Bye, sweetie," Shimone said.

Ebony got up and kissed her mother on the forehead. "Bye bye, Mama," she said softly and then sat back on the mat and began to play with her friend.

Shimone watched her daughter for a moment longer, said goodbye to Anya, and then walked out of the daycare center. She got into her car and drove toward campus.

Ebony was just a toddler, but she knew what was

going on. She didn't have the same happy family that she used to have a few months ago. Although Marques still came by the apartment every weekend to take Ebony out, he had stopped inviting Shimone to come along. And now he wasn't even showing up to play with his daughter in the mornings. Shimone vowed to find out what kept Marques from coming to the center. If it had anything to do with Alexia, she was going to snap.

She pulled up to the music building with five minutes left to get to class. She walked swiftly, making it to class with three minutes to spare and took her seat in the second row next to one of her friends.

"Hey Shimone," Terrell smiled. "I thought you weren't going to make it for a second."

Shimone looked at him and sighed. "Ebony decided she wanted to act up this morning, so it took me a long time to leave the center," she replied.

"Is everything okay?" Terrell asked with genuine concern etched across his face.

"Yeah, everything is fine now," she said.

He smiled as the instructor walked through the door. "Well, at least you made it before Ms. Boland did, 'cause you know she be trippin' if somebody is late to her class," he whispered as Ms. Boland called for the students' full attention.

"Today we are going to work on range," Ms. Boland said. "I am going to have each of you come up to show me your vocal range so I'll know what we need to work on this semester and how to place you for class. Who wants to go first?"

Shimone looked around the classroom; no hands were up. Although it had been a trying morning, she felt like singing just to release some of the stress she was feeling, so she raised her hand. Ms. Boland called her to the front.

"Go 'head, girl," Terrell said as Shimone got out of her seat.

Ms. Boland took a seat at the piano and began to play each key as Shimone performed the warm-up routine that the class practiced on a daily basis. She started as low as she could and sang each set over and over until her vocal cords could go no higher.

When she finished, Ms. Boland recorded her range. "That was very good, Shimone. You went from tenor all the way to second soprano," she informed as Shimone went back to her seat. "Who wants to go next?" Ms. Boland asked just before a knock came at the door.

Marques burst into the classroom, out of breath, like he had just finished a ten-mile marathon.

"Excuse me, may I help you?" Ms. Boland asked, looking at Marques like he was a stray animal.

"I need . . . to see . . . Shimone Johnson," he said between breaths.

Shimone got up from her seat. "I'll be right back," she told Ms. Boland. She followed Marques out of the classroom and shut the door. Marques was sweating almost as hard as he had when Shimone found out about Alexia's pregnancy. "What is wrong?"

"Alexia is in labor," Marques said.

Shimone couldn't help, but laugh. "Marques, baby, I don't think you know what you are talking about. Alexia is only six months pregnant, she can't be in labor," Shimone said, slowly as if he were a mentally challenged child.

"Shimone, she is at Grady. She's had an asthma attack and something's wrong with the baby," he said. "The doctors are inducing her labor."

She stared at him and crossed her arms over her chest. "Okay, well what do you want me to do?"

Marques looked at her like she should not have even had to ask the question. "I need you to come to the hospital with me."

"What?" Shimone shouted, her attitude immediately flaring. "You must have lost your natural born mind if you think I'm going to the hospital to see about another woman that got pregnant by my boyfriend, who I *thought* loved me. You didn't even come see your daughter this morning at the daycare center. She was up there crying and throwing tantrums because her daddy wasn't there to play with her. She's not stupid, Marques. She can see that things are not right. And for you to not be there, at least for her, like you are supposed to, *is not right*. So, if *you* want to go to the hospital to see about some chick that is having *your* baby, *not* mine, then go! But I'll be dead and buried before I go see about somebody who slept with my boyfriend and then got pregnant by him."

"What type of Christian are you?" Marques asked harshly. "You are supposed to care about everybody and not hold grudges. I've apologized and I'm not even seeing her anymore. How can you stand here and say that you are not going to see about a woman in premature labor just because you are upset that it's my baby she's in labor with?"

Shimone rolled her eyes. "What type of Christian am *I*?" she reiterated the question. "I think you should have asked *yourself* that question before you laid in bed with someone who was not me." She paused. "No, I take that back. You should've asked yourself that before you laid up with anybody, period, knowing that we were supposed to be practicing celibacy. And the fact that you're not with her now doesn't even matter since we're not together anymore," she said with her hands on her hips.

"Fine," he conceded, "I'll go by myself."

"Now, you're getting the picture," Shimone said sardonically.

"Look, I'm sorry about cheating on you and I'm sorry about getting her pregnant, and I'm sorry about not being there for Ebony like I'm supposed to lately," Marques said. "But I really, *really* need for you to be here for me, as a friend. I'm about to have a premature baby and it is highly likely that it's not going to make it. So would you *please* come with me?"

Shimone could tell this was really hard for him, but she just couldn't find the compassion in her heart. "I'm sorry. I can't." Marques sighed heavily as she continued, "Maybe you would understand if *I* was the one who broke a commitment to stay celibate and faithful. Maybe you'd see it from my point of view if *I* were lying in the hospital going into labor with another man's baby. Maybe you'd understand how I feel if that was the case, but it's not, and you don't. And if I go to that hospital with you, I'd be lying to myself and to you and Alexia by making you think I care, because truthfully, I don't," she said as she walked back into the classroom, unconsciously slamming the door behind her.

"Is everything okay?" Ms. Boland asked as Shimone walked back to her desk.

"Yes," Shimone said with a forced smile.

No it's not.

Shimone turned a fiery gaze toward Terrell, ready to go off if he had made an inappropriate comment. Terrell gave her a sympathetic smile and then turned his attention toward the gentleman who was testing his ranges in the front of the class. Shimone looked around her and noticed that everyone's attention was focused to the front.

Shimone, My child, you have forgotten who you are.

Shimone's eyes darted around the classroom once

more and found no one looking in her direction as if they were speaking to her. She held her head in her hands and tried to hold back tears. She knew God was trying to speak to her heart, but she wasn't in the mood to receive His words. She didn't need to. Shimone knew she was not the same Christian she was a few months ago. She once used Marques as her motivation, thinking if she kept her focus on God, then maybe she could get him to come back to Him also. But, ever since finding out about Alexia's pregnancy, she had lost her drive to please God. Shimone stopped reading her Bible, she hadn't been to church since going with her father a month ago, and her daughter had to remind her at dinnertime that they were supposed to give God thanks before enjoying their meals. She held her head down as tears began to fall from her eyes.

"Shimone, are you okay?" Ms. Boland asked when she noticed that she was not paying attention.

Shimone lifted her tear-streaked face. "No. I don't feel so well. Could I be excused?"

Ms. Boland studied her face. "Sure."

Shimone gathered her books and walked out of the classroom. She didn't bother to wipe her face as she walked toward her car. When she got into her car, she looked at herself in the mirror. She looked gorgeous on the outside. Her outfit was amazing, her hair was intact, and, except for a few tear streaks, her makeup was flawless. But Shimone felt as if someone was tearing her insides apart. She started her car and headed for Grady Hospital.

She prayed as she drove down the interstate. *Lord, please forgive me for my selfishness. I know that what Marques did was wrong, but what I said to him was even worse. A baby's life is at risk here and I just hope that my attitude doesn't cause unnecessary stress. I pray that this baby makes it through and becomes a miracle child that will grow up and do your good works. I pray that Alexia is doing well and I hope that she makes it through this also.*

I pray that I will start to do what I am supposed to do for you. I want to praise and live for you and I pray that I never let a guy come between my relationship with you ever again. Lord, I love you and I pray that you forgive me for losing sight of what is important.

Shimone prayed the entire drive. She prayed as she parked her car, and she prayed on her way through the hospital doors. She walked to the nurses's station and asked for the room of Alexia Harrison.

"Are you a family member?" the nurse asked.

"No, I'm umm . . . a friend of hers," Shimone lied as she shook the guilt from her heart.

The nurse told her where Alexia's room was, but told her that she would have to wait in the waiting room because the doctors were tending to her at the moment.

"Thank you," Shimone said as she walked down the hall and got on the elevator.

When the elevator reached the right floor and its doors opened, Shimone noticed that the waiting room only had a few patrons in it. She saw Marques sitting with Ebony in his lap. *He must have picked her up in an effort to make up for not seeing her this morning,* Shimone thought. She walked over to them and tapped Marques on the shoulder. He turned around and she gave him a slight smile.

"Mama," Ebony said, smiling.

Shimone walked around the chairs and picked Ebony up. "Hey, I see that you are doing better," she said, kissing Ebony's cheek and then placing her back in the chair.

Marques stood up, his five feet and eleven inches towering over her five-foot-two frame.

She looked up at him. "I'm sorry," she said.

He pulled her into his chest and hugged her tightly. "Me too," he said. "This is all my fault. I should have been faithful. I'm so sorry," he said, looking into her eyes. "I do love you."

Shimone stared at him without saying a word. She wanted to tell him that he had a funny way of showing it. She wanted to ask him how many times he said those same words to Alexia. She wanted to understand his reason for cheating. But instead, she allowed him to pull her back into a loving embrace.

While they were hugging, a nurse came out into the waiting room. "Is there a Marques Anderson here?" she asked.

"That's me," Marques said, pulling away from Shimone.

"Ms. Harrison is asking for you," the nurse said, gazing peculiarly at Shimone.

Marques began following the nurse to Alexia's room when Ebony's tiny voice stopped him.

"Daddy, can I go?" Ebony asked.

Marques turned around and walked toward his daughter. "Sweetie, I need for you to stay out here with Mommy, okay? And be good."

"Okay," Ebony said with her thumb in her mouth, a habit that had just begun to develop.

"And take that out of your mouth," he said, pulling at her arm. He stood up and kissed Shimone on the forehead. "I'll be back." He walked back toward the waiting nurse, who looked puzzled.

"Mama, I got a broder?" Ebony asked after her father and the nurse had left the waiting room.

"Do you have *what*?" Shimone said, looking at her daughter in perplexity.

"A bro-der?" Ebony said as if her mother should have understood the first time.

"Do you have a *brother*?" Shimone asked for clarification. Ebony nodded. "Where did you get that from?"

"Daddy," Ebony said.

Shimone gazed at Ebony who continued to look to her for an answer. "I don't know, sweetie," Shimone said as she sat back in the chair and closed her eyes. She could feel a huge headache coming on.

When she had been pregnant with Ebony, Marques had claimed that Shimone was going to have a boy, but she always retorted and said that she would give birth to a girl. So it was no surprise to her that he would be claiming a boy now, but it disturbed Shimone that Marques would tell their daughter something like that.

Although she was there for support, she still wasn't over the fact that he cheated on her. And with him proclaiming the child to be a boy, Shimone wondered if Marques had impregnated Alexia on purpose so he could have another shot at having the baby boy he'd wanted since he found out Shimone was pregnant with Ebony. She knew that the thought shouldn't even cross her mind, but Marques had been full of surprises lately and the possibility that he could've deliberately impregnated Alexia wouldn't leave her mind. She continued to pray that Alexia and the baby would be alright, but the thought of her producing a baby boy for Marques made Shimone's stomach cringe.

"Mama," Ebony called, "you sleepy?"

Shimone smiled at her daughter who was sitting in her lap, holding Shimone's eyelids open to see if she had fallen asleep. "Yes, I'm a little tired."

"Me too," Ebony said, laying her head to rest on Shimone's chest.

Shimone smiled and rested her head back on the arm of the chair she was sitting in. She closed her eyes and wondered how this baby would change their lives.

Chapter 14

"They're gone," the doctor informed. "There was nothing we could do."

Alexia lay in the hospital bed as tears streamed down her face. Marques held his head down so no one would see the grief in his eyes. Although this wasn't a planned pregnancy for them—they definitely hadn't been expecting the possibility of having twins until the doctor had informed her of the growing problems within her uterus—Alexia had been looking forward to having the baby. Even Marques had seemed happy about having it. But through all of their planning, they failed to notice that something might be wrong.

After providing Alexia with oxygen, the doctors ran some tests on her. They found something terribly wrong with the way her babies were developing and quickly induced her labor, which had brought forth premature twins, a boy and a girl—both small enough to fit in the palms of Marques's hands—who died after only an hour and a half of life.

"I'm sorry," the doctor said, "but the fact that you were

in your sixth month of pregnancy with twins and your uterus was growing like you were only carrying one baby, and that you, yourself, have severe asthma were major problems. Your babies weren't getting enough oxygen nor were their organs developing at a normal rate." The doctor looked at Marques who was still sitting in the chair with his head in his hands. "How many times have you been to see a gynecologist to receive prenatal care?"

Alexia glanced at Marques, and then back at the doctor. "Only twice; once in my second month, and then again in my third."

"That's it?" the doctor looked incredulously at Alexia as she nodded. "Well, I'm sure if you would have gone more often, your doctor could have sighted the problem and given you a heads up so it could have been taken care of. But I'm sorry."

"Could we still name them?" Marques asked, surprising Alexia and the doctor.

"Umm . . . sure if you want," the doctor said as he motioned for the nurse to retrieve two birth certificates while pulling out the babies' charts.

Marques looked at Alexia for her to give the doctor the names that they had came up with a week earlier. They hadn't been aware of the gender of the child, so they'd come up with boy and girl names for the possible outcomes. "We said that if we had a girl we'd name her Andrea Monique Anderson and if we had a boy, his name would be—"

"Malik Andre Anderson," Marques said quietly as the doctor recorded the names on the chart.

"Okay," the doctor said. "I'll be back to check on you in a few minutes. We'll run some tests to make sure you suffered no internal damage or anything like that from the surgery."

Alexia nodded her head and the doctor left them in the room and silence enveloped them. She looked at Marques who still had his head in his hands. "Are you okay?"

"Yeah," Marques said as he lifted his head. "Yeah, I'm cool. What about you?"

Alexia looked down at her stomach. "I'm a little sad. I mean, I was looking forward to having a baby, and although having twins would've been some work, I know that we would have been able to take care of them." She sighed. "I shouldn't have been yelling at my boss like that. She had just made me so mad when she fired me for no valid reason. I went off. Before I could catch myself, I was short on breath. I'm sorry."

"No, it's not even your fault. I should have taken you back to your doctor."

She studied his face. "Are you sure you are okay?"

"Yeah, I was just looking forward to having a little boy, you know. I wanted to show him how to grow up and be a responsible man. I wanted to teach him to never be undependable like I am," Marques said.

"Marques, you *are* dependable," Alexia said as she sat up slightly. "You were there for me. You take care of Ebony and Shimone, and you were willing to support me and these babies. Now making these babies makes *all* of us irresponsible, but having them and taking care of them makes us reliable parents who don't want our children to grow up without the guidance that we have to give them," Alexia said.

"It's not just making the babies, Alexia," Marques said as he got up and began to pace the room. "It's breaking commitments that I made to God and to Shimone. It's neglecting my daughter because her mother wants nothing to do with me. It's having sex with you when I *had* a girlfriend that I love and who loves me. It's not being the

Christian that I became years ago," he said as he stopped pacing and looked at Alexia.

"So what are you trying to say?" she asked. "You regret being with me?"

He looked at her and nodded without hesitation. "Actually, I do. And it's not because I don't like you or I don't care about you or that I didn't enjoy the time we spent together. It's because my heart won't allow anyone to take Shimone's place. There is no one like her and no one else in the world that I would rather spend my life with. Yes, I let temptation take over for a while, but now I'm taking control and making things right. I want to be with Shimone and Shimone only."

Tears began to stream down Alexia's face. "So you don't love me at all?" Marques silently shook his head. "Well, I just hope that one day I can find someone who will love me like you love her," she said as she wiped the tears.

"Me too. I'll come in and check on you later," Marques said as he backed out of the door. "I'm sorry."

When Marques walked into the waiting room, he found Shimone sleeping in a chair with Ebony lying on her chest. He stood above them and wished he could make everything right. He'd been tormented night and day ever since he and Shimone had broken up and he wanted nothing more than to be able to call her his lady again. And only being able to see his daughter on the weekend was an arrangement he had yet to get used to, even when he'd done it voluntarily, and now he'd spend every spare minute he had with his daughter if he could. Knowing he could never reverse the events that had happened, Marques prayed that things would somehow go back to being normal.

Shimone looked so beautiful with Ebony peacefully

sleeping in her chest, that part of him didn't want to disturb them, but the urge to touch Shimone became almost
overbearing. Marques reached down and tucked a stray
hair behind her ear, caressing her smooth skin in the
process. The intimate gesture stirred her awake. Her
light brown eyes fluttered open and she saw Marques
standing over her, smiling. She sat up and looked at her
watch; she had been at the hospital for over four hours.
She placed Ebony gently on the sofa next to her.

"How'd it go?" Shimone asked as she rubbed her eyes.

"We lost the babies," Marques said.

Shimone stood and pulled him into a warm embrace.
"I'm so sorry. I am really sorry." Suddenly, she pulled
back. "Did you say *babies*?"

Marques nodded. "We found out after she was admit-
ted that she was pregnant with twins, a girl and . . . a
boy." He had to force the word "boy" out of his mouth.

He watched as Shimone sank back down in her seat.
He was almost positive that she'd been worried about
the effect the baby would have on all of their lives, but he
wondered how she would have felt if Alexia had given
birth to a healthy baby boy.

"So, are you okay?" she questioned, rescuing him from
his thoughts.

He took a deep breath. "Yeah, I'm good. I'm just kind
of tired," he said, rubbing his head. "It's been a long
day." He sat in the chair next to her and looked at Ebony.
"I can't believe that you stayed here this whole time."

"Yeah, well, I felt bad. I'm sorry about what I said. I
was just so angry that you would do something like that,
but I guess I can't expect for you to be perfect." Shimone
looked at Marques. "Why did you do it?"

Marques shook his head and looked across the room
toward the nurses's station. "Honestly, I don't know. I
mean, it was just so much going on with us." He looked

back at her. "I'm going to be truthful. Every time you got on my nerves, I'd go see Alexia. Every time you would turn me down for sex, I'd go see Alexia. I guess I did it because I felt like I was being neglected and Alexia was just . . . there."

Shimone looked away from him. "But I thought that you wanted to do this whole celibacy thing together. I mean, we talked about it that night when I told you that I was pregnant. I said that I didn't want to get pregnant again and we agreed that it was for the best that we not have sex anymore. You said that it would be hard, but you promised me that you would never cheat on me and that you wanted to be with only me. I just don't understand what I did to push you so far that you had to turn to someone else."

"It wasn't you, Shimone," Marques said, turning her face toward his. "I was the one who fell into temptation. It was me who couldn't control my own hormones and emotions. I wanted to be with you, but I couldn't, so I went to someone else. I did this to myself and to you and to Ebony. And I am so sorry."

Shimone looked into his eyes. "Did you get her pregnant on purpose?"

"What?" He dropped his hand from her face.

"Did you get Alexia pregnant on purpose?" she asked again.

Marques searched her eyes. "Why would you ask me something like that?"

"Because when I was pregnant, you wished over and over that I'd have a boy, but when we had Ebony, you seemed content with the way things were." She averted her gaze. "Then Ebony said that you told her she was going to have a baby brother and I was just wondering if you got Alexia pregnant just so you could have a second chance at having the son that you wanted the first time."

Marques stared at Shimone and wondered what had happened to the confident, vibrant woman he fell in love with. Maybe when he decided to be unfaithful, her confidence level dropped. He wished he could turn back the hands of time, but he knew he needed to stop wishing that the past would change and start working on the future. "Baby, I would never do something like that. I know I messed up by sleeping with her, but I never intended for her to get pregnant," he explained. "Yeah, I did really want you to have a boy when I first found out you were pregnant. And when I found out that Alexia was pregnant, I hoped she'd have a boy too. Even when the doctor told us that the twins didn't make it, I was upset because I was looking forward to having a little boy to teach things to. But I *didn't* get Alexia pregnant on purpose; I would *never* ever do that to you. I love you and I love Ebony. That's my little princess and you . . . you are my queen," he said as he looked deep into her eyes before leaning in to kiss her.

Right before his lips touched hers, Shimone pulled away. He'd always been a smooth talker and she had to force herself not to fall for his words when he continued to disappoint her with his actions. "I'm sorry, Marques, but I can't . . . I can't do this. I do love you, but I'm not sure if you love me like you say you do."

"Shimone, I do—"

"But the fact that you needed Alexia to fill that part of our relationship, just because I wasn't with it, contradicts everything you just said. If you loved me, you would have never gone to her. And even though you say that you didn't get her pregnant on purpose and that you regret having a relationship with her, that doesn't change that fact that you slept with her while you were still with me. I'm sorry, but for now, until you can prove to me that this type of thing will never ever happen again, our relationship has to be strictly platonic. Honestly, if it wasn't for Ebony, I'd probably never want to have any type of relationship with you again, but I'm doing this for our little girl." She searched his eyes for a reaction.

Marques pulled back and rubbed his hand over his head, taking a deep breath. He hadn't expected her to give him an ultimatum: friends or nothing. He wanted to be in a romantic relationship with Shimone and just being friends was nowhere near close to romantic. But when Marques thought about it, even when they'd first begun dating, they'd done so without being friends first and he wondered if that had anything to do with the problems they were having now. He vacated his seat and continued to massage his head, thoughts swimming around in his mind. Maybe being friends would lead to a better relationship in the future. Even if it didn't, he couldn't risk losing Shimone completely.

Finally, he faced her. "I guess having you as a friend is better than not having you at all. Besides, friends always make the best lovers." He smiled as she rolled her eyes.

Their attention was drawn to the sofa, where Ebony had awakened from her sleep. Her eyes darted around the room as if she was trying to figure out where she was. She looked at Marques and Shimone with a smile. "Daddy," she said as she sat up on the sofa, "my broder here?" she asked, her big, light brown eyes sparkling with anticipation.

Marques looked at Shimone before getting up and kneeling in front of his daughter. "No, baby, your brother didn't come. He was here for a while, but then he had to go to heaven to be with God," Marques explained as if he had practiced the speech in his head, knowing his daughter would have questions. "You had a sister too, but she had to go with God too. One day, you'll get to see them because God will decide that He needs you and He will take you to heaven to be with Him also."

Ebony listened intently, with her thumb in her mouth, as her father explained why she didn't have the siblings she had been looking forward to meeting. "Daddy see 'em 'gain?" Ebony asked.

Marques glanced back at Shimone as he rubbed his head once again. On the path that his life was taking, Marques didn't know if he'd ever get to see his children in heaven. He desperately wanted to tell his little girl that he would be able to, but he was not sure himself and didn't want to lie—he'd done enough of that for one lifetime. Marques looked back at Ebony. "I don't know, sweetheart," he said quietly. "I truly don't know."

Ebony searched her father's eyes and, as if she knew he needed it, she wrapped her arms around his neck and hugged him tight. Marques stood up with Ebony in his arms and let his first tear escape without trying to hide it.

Shimone watched Ebony and Marques before silently heading in the direction of the nurses' station. There was something she had to do if she were to be totally free from the bondage her troubles had kept her in for the last few months. When she approached the desk, she asked for Alexia's room number and was directed down the hall. She paused in front of the room, took a deep breath and opened the door gently so she wouldn't wake Alexia if she was sleeping or scare her if she wasn't alert. When she stepped inside of the room, Alexia's red eyes met hers.

"Hi," Shimone greeted as she stepped closer to the bed. "I'm sorry about the babies. How are you feeling?"

Alexia managed a weak smile. "Okay, considering. I didn't know you were here."

Shimone shrugged. "I wasn't going to come, but I

thought I should at least be here to support Marques."
She looked down at Alexia's matted hair and tired face
and noted that the girl still looked like a runway super-
model. *No wonder he went to her. She is gorgeous even in
these conditions.*

"He loves you, you know," Alexia stated, interrupting
Shimone's thoughts.

"What?" Shimone asked.

Alexia turned her head so she would be looking into
Shimone's eyes. "I said Marques loves you. He loves you
and Ebony. He wants you guys to be a family."

"We'll always be family," Shimone said.

"No, he wants you to be a real family. Not a broken
one. He doesn't like the weekend visits and he doesn't
like going out with Ebony without you. He wants to be
in a committed relationship with you," Alexia explained.

Shimone looked away. "If he wanted a committed relationship he shouldn't have cheated," she muttered before looking back at Alexia. "And who could blame him?
You're gorgeous, even after surgery. You look like a model."
Shimone looked down at herself. "Me? I'm just . . . *me*.
I'm just *big* ol' me. I used to think I was beautiful, but if
he has to run to you, then maybe I was wrong."

Alexia shook her head. "Girl, you *are* beautiful. I wish
I had the curves that you do. I've always wanted to be
full-figured like Queen Latifa or that girl, Tocarra, from
America's Next Top Model. I don't have curves like that."
She pointed at Shimone's hips. "You're not even fat. You
are just curvaceous, something I wish I could say about
myself. I'm so skinny. I've always been told that I was
pretty. That I had a model figure and that I could grace
the covers of magazines, but no one knows that I've
wanted to get breast implants or some kind of butt
surgery to make myself look more like a woman. I struggle with my image everyday. You would think that be-

cause I get so much attention from guys that I would be happy with myself, but I'm not. I wish I could say that my measurements were 38, 30, 42."

Shimone's eyes became wide and Alexia laughed softly. "Oh, you think that he never talked about you when we were together. Girl, I can go buy you an entire wardrobe. That's how much Marques talked about you. He's called me your name so many times while we were . . . you know," Alexia said in a lowered voice, "that I just let it go in one ear and out of the other. When we first got together, he would say things like how much you could get on his nerves and how you were constantly nagging him about something, but every time he spoke of you I could see the love in his eyes and it made me jealous of you.

"When he told me that you guys were practicing celibacy and he was getting tired of it, I figured maybe that could be the one area that you wouldn't have an advantage in. He wouldn't be able to compare you to me in that area, since you guys weren't doing it. So I guess I took advantage of his vulnerability and also ruined something special in the process." She gave Shimone an apologetic look. "And I am so sorry."

"Did he ever tell you that he loved you?" Shimone asked, not really wanting to hear the answer.

"No," Alexia said to Shimone's relief. "I think he never said it because he knew he wouldn't mean it. And I don't think he would have wanted that on his conscience."

"Do you love him?" Shimone asked.

Alexia looked toward the ceiling and breathed deeply. "I thought I did. When I told him that I loved him, he just looked at me and I felt *so* stupid. But now that we don't have anything to connect us"—she touched her stomach—"I realize that I fell for what we shared and not him. I do still care about him and I hope that one day I can meet someone who will love me like he loves you, but until then, I'm through hooking up with every guy I meet."

Show her Me.

Shimone felt the opportunity to present Christ to Alexia and she didn't want to pass it up. "Alexia, are you a Christian?" she asked.

"Do you mean am I a saved Christian?" Alexia asked. Shimone nodded. "I used to be. I remember when my grandmother was alive. She would drag me out of bed every Sunday morning, make me put on my best dress, then drag me to church and any other service that went on during the week. When I was sixteen, she led me to the altar to be saved. After that, we would have our own little Bible studies at home. We'd pray and worship together." She smiled at the memory. "I'd even have devotional times with God by myself. But when my grandmother died, right before my high school graduation, I lost all of my faith. Being an only child, I had no one left, except my mom, and she was out on the streets somewhere. I stopped going to church. I stopped reading my Bible. My times with God were replaced with parties that my friends would invite me to.

"When I got in college, it got worse. I'd go to every party on and off campus. Sometimes I'd leave one party early to go to another one. I'd get drunk and then wake up the next morning next to a guy whose name I didn't remember getting. My grades were slipping and, because I was in college on a full academic scholarship, I was placed on academic probation. After my sophomore year, my mom got sick, so I kinda slowed down. I don't drink anymore, besides the occasional wine on special occasions. I stopped partying so much and got into the books, but I'd still find myself in bed with a guy who I'd probably only gone on one date with. It would seem like someone with a bachelor's degree would have better sense, but I guess after both my mother and grandmother died, I had nothing to live for, so I strayed from my religion and did my own thing."

Shimone placed her hand on Alexia's shoulder. "You know it's not too late to come back home," she said.

Alexia wiped a tear from the corner of her eye. "I don't know. God probably wouldn't want me now anyway."

Yes, I do.

Shimone heard His voice again and she knew she hadn't been the only one when Alexia looked around the room as if she were waiting for someone to appear out of thin air. "He wants you now," Shimone told her. "Don't you want to see your grandmother again someday?"

"Of course I do," Alexia said, wiping her tears.

"And don't you want a better life for yourself?"

"Yeah." Alexia nodded.

"The only thing stopping you is you," Shimone said. "So how about coming back home?"

Alexia shrugged. "I could use a change." She smiled.

"Then close your eyes and repeat after me," Shimone said as she began to lead Alexia in the sinner's prayer.

As Shimone began to pray, tears flowed from Alexia's eyes. She repeated the words that Shimone spoke softly, "Lord, I am a sinner . . . I confess my sins to You . . . and ask that You wash me clean . . . I believe that Jesus died on the cross for my sins . . . and that He rose from the dead . . . I know that Jesus is Lord . . . I open my heart to You . . . Accept me as Your child, Lord . . . I give my life to You . . . so that I may live my life according to Your will . . . I love You, Lord . . . In Your name . . . Amen."

Alexia opened her eyes and smiled. She felt calm and peaceful. She looked at Shimone who was smiling over her.

"Welcome to the family." Shimone smiled as she held Alexia's hand.

Chapter 15

Sierra had spent the last month trying to convince La-Toya to work things out with Jamal, but she refused to even speak to him over the phone. LaToya's day consisted of her taking Jabari to daycare, going to classes, picking up Jabari, and coming home. When Jamal wanted to spend time with Jabari, he would have to call Corey and ask him to call LaToya. Then Corey would have to pick Jabari up and drive him to and from his father's apartment. Although she missed Jamal, LaToya refused to admit it, and it was nearly killing her. The whole situation was starting to work Sierra's nerves also, so she decided that a Saturday night would be a perfect time for LaToya and Jamal to sit down and talk things out.

"Girl, are you ready yet?" Sierra yelled toward La-Toya's room.

"Almost," LaToya yelled back. "If you would tell me where we are going, I'd probably be able to find something to wear."

"I told you we are going out to eat," Sierra replied. "Dress is dressy casual or dressy, whichever you prefer."

"Wow, that tells me a lot," LaToya responded sarcastically.

"Just wear something nice."

"And what about Jabari?" LaToya asked. "Where is he supposed to go?"

"How many times do I have to tell you?" Sierra sighed, walking toward LaToya's room. "He's going to come with us. So put him on a nice pair of pants and a good shirt and he'll fit right in," she said as she walked into the room. She paused as she studied her friend's attire. "Wow! For someone who didn't know what to wear, your outfit is perfect," Sierra said, admiring her friend's fire red dress.

"Thanks," LaToya said. She looked at Sierra's ensemble. "Are we going out alone? Just me, you, and Jabari?"

"Yeah," Sierra said softly, hoping her friend hadn't caught onto her plan. "Why?"

"Are you tired of my brother or something? 'Cause dressed like that, you are liable to pick up another brotha." LaToya smiled as she studied Sierra's clingy black dress that flared out just above her ankles.

Sierra was relieved and smiled to hide her brief anxiety. "Whatever," she said, dismissing LaToya's comment with a wave of her hand. "Are you ready?"

"I will be as soon as I put Jabari's shoes on," LaToya said, turning around toward her son who was examining the several different pairs of heels on his mother's bed. "No Jabari, please don't play with those." She took the shoes from him.

"What? Are you afraid he's going to ruin them?" Sierra laughed playfully.

"No, I'm afraid he may poke his eye out or something," LaToya said seriously.

Ever since having Jabari, LaToya had become much

more motherly. Not that it surprised Sierra that she would, but just seeing her interact with Jabari made it seem so real. It seemed like just yesterday they were in high school discussing the names they would give their children years later.

After having an abortion at age fifteen and a miscarriage at sixteen, Sierra had felt empty inside, so she couldn't wait to have kids. But the fact that she hadn't discussed that with Corey still haunted her mind and she worried that her heart's greatest desire would never come to pass. She watched as LaToya sat Jabari on the bed and placed a shoe on both of his feet. She slowly tied his shoes as he studied her every move. When LaToya finished, she kissed his forehead. Sierra tried her hardest to hold back tears. *Oh, I need to talk to Corey before he proposes*, she thought. She was tired of crying about this, and she wanted to be truly happy once she and Corey united.

"Okay," LaToya said, "we're ready."

Jabari climbed off of the bed and ran to Sierra. "Up, up," he said as he held his hands up.

Sierra bent down and scooped him into her arms. She kissed his cheek and he laid his head on her shoulder. This is what she wanted—someone she could hold and take care of. She smiled at LaToya.

"You are going to make a great mother someday," LaToya said as she returned the gesture.

"Thanks," Sierra said. "I can't wait," she added, placing a kiss on Jabari's head.

"Translation: My brother needs to hurry and pop that question," LaToya said as she picked up her purse.

"Exactly," Sierra laughed as they headed out of the apartment and toward her car.

Jamal sat nervously at a secluded table in Truffles restaurant along with Corey as they waited for Sierra and LaToya to show up. When Corey called him last night and told him that Sierra had come up with an idea to get him and LaToya alone so they could talk, Jamal didn't hesitate in joining in on the planning. After trying to talk to LaToya for the past month, he was getting tired of trying. But he held on to his hope that she would somehow have to at least look into his sorrowful eyes and forgive him.

"Man, would you stop shaking," Corey said.

"I can't," Jamal said. "I ain't been this nervous since my prom. I mean, I love this girl, for real. But what if she don't even come and we're just sitting here for no reason," he panicked.

"Look," Corey said, placing his menu on the table, "she is going to come. Trust me, if Sierra is as convincing as she can be, Toya will be here. Everything is gonna work out fine, so stop stressing." Corey looked at his distressed friend. "You know, if you had been honest from the beginning, maybe you wouldn't be in this position. I just can't believe you didn't tell *me*. Man, we been cool for years and I'm just finding out you have a four-year-old son." He shook his head. "You are so lucky I'm a forgiving person, because the way I was feeling about this whole situation would've had you sittin' at this table by yourself."

Jamal ran his hand across his head. "I know, and I appreciate everything you've done. You didn't have to go out of your way to bring Jabari to my house just so I could see him, but you did."

"I'm still confused about this," Corey said. "How could you keep something like this a secret?"

Jamal shrugged. "Man, I didn't even know about him until he was two. A few months after LaToya had Jabari, Kim comes runnin' me down on campus talking about she had something to tell me. At first I didn't even believe her. Then I saw the boy; he was still young, but he had my big nose and he was dark like me. I still wasn't gonna take care of him if I didn't even know if he really belonged to me, so we got a DNA test. Two days later, I found out that I was Jayson's father."

"Well, when you found out, why didn't you just tell us then?" Corey asked, still not believing that his friend could be so irresponsible.

"I thought about it," Jamal said, "but I was just so scared. I mean, I didn't even want Toya to have Jabari, and then I'ma run up on her talking 'bout I got another child, one older than Jabari. She would have flipped before letting me explain, just like she did at the party." Jamal glanced toward the front of the restaurant, thinking he had seen LaToya and Sierra walk through the doors, but realized that it was just the *maître d'* leading another couple to their table. He turned his attention back toward Corey. "I thought about telling you too, but I knew you would just try to get me to tell her. Plus, I thought you were going to beat me down for doing something like that, especially since that is your little sister. You see how you acted when I didn't want her to have Jabari. It's not that I wanted to keep it a secret; I really wanted to tell her, but I just didn't know how.

"That day at the park, she asked me if I was with her because I wanted to be with her or if I was just sticking around for Jabari. It really hurt me that she would think something like that because I do love her and I told her that. But the reason it seemed like I was acting that way was probably because I was still struggling with the truth that was inside of me." He paused and inhaled deeply. "Then Kim was putting so much pressure on me to tell LaToya. She kept saying that she didn't think that LaToya and I could have a good relationship unless everything was out in the open."

"Well, here's your chance to do that now," Corey said, " 'cause they're here."

Corey and Jamal stood as the hostess led Sierra, La-Toya, and Jabari to their table. Jamal's eyes were fixed on LaToya the entire time. She was definitely *wearing* that red dress. By the way her steps slowed as she neared the table, he knew she wasn't expecting him to be there. Jamal continued to stare at LaToya as she slowly approached the table. Her gaze was set on him, and he looked past the anger in her eyes and saw that there was still love there for him.

Sierra walked up to the table and Corey took her hands and spun her around as he admired her dress. "Girl, you look good."

"Thank you," Sierra smiled. "I do try." She turned around to see LaToya standing behind her staring angrily at Jamal. Sierra looked at Jamal, who looked like he want to say something, but didn't know what would come out of his mouth if he opened it.

Jabari moved toward his father. "Daddy," he said.

LaToya tightened her grip on his hand and pulled him away from Jamal's open arms before glaring in Sierra's direction. "What are they doing here? Specifically *him?*" She pointed at Jamal. "You told me that it was just me, you, and Jabari."

Sierra hadn't thought about how she would tell her best friend that this was all a ploy to get her to talk to her baby's father. She just assumed that she and Corey would leave Jamal and LaToya to work things out on their own. "Umm . . . I . . . we just thought that it was time for you to hear Jamal out on this whole situation."

"Really? *You* thought that *I* would want to hear what *he* had to say?" she asked. "You thought wrong. I want to go home," she stated decisively, waiting for Sierra to accompany her out of the restaurant.

"Unless you are going to walk, I don't know how you plan to get there," Sierra retorted with a bit of an attitude, but then softened her voice. "Now this is getting ridiculous. You need to at least let him apologize."

LaToya looked around at the people at the nearby tables and the host who was patiently waiting to seat them so he could return to his post. Then her gaze moved to Jamal, who was looking extremely handsome in his Sunday best. Then, she looked down at her son who had no clue as to what was going on, but seemed to sense that something wasn't right. "Fine," she said as she sat in the chair that Corey had vacated and placed Jabari in her lap.

Jamal sat back in his seat as the waiter approached the table.

"Would you all like to be moved to a table for four?" the host asked when he noticed that Jamal and LaToya were seated at a table for only two people.

"No thank you," Sierra said too quickly. "We would like a separate table and a high chair for Little Man," she said, taking Jabari out of LaToya's arms and placing his bag over her shoulder. Jabari began to reach for LaToya. "Don't worry, you'll get to see Mommy later," Sierra said as the host led them to a table not too far from the one their friends were sitting at.

The host waited as Sierra sat Jabari in the high chair and Corey pulled out Sierra's chair and then sat in his own before placing their menus in front of them. "Your server should be out momentarily," he said, and then walked away from the table.

Sierra opened and scanned her menu. She was in the mood for seafood and the salmon sounded pretty good. She looked up and saw Corey staring at her. "What?" she asked, thinking that maybe a strand of hair was out of place or something was on her face.

Corey smiled and picked up his menu. "Nothing," he

said, causing Sierra to think that something was really wrong with her appearance and he just wasn't telling her.

"Corey, don't play with me." She pulled a mirror out of her purse. "Is there something on my face?" She touched her face, careful not to smear her makeup.

"No, your face is fine." He took the mirror from her. "It's perfect." He placed his menu down on the table and rested his hands under his chin as he continued to gaze at her. "You are so beautiful," he said, causing her face to flush.

She looked down at her menu. "Thank you," she said. Although Sierra knew she was attractive and had been told so throughout her life, it seemed different coming from someone who truly loved her for who she was.

The waiter approached their table, introduced himself, and asked for their drink orders. After giving them, Corey told the man that they were ready to order their food. He waited for Sierra to speak first. "I would like the grilled Atlantic salmon," she said. "Would it be a problem to get a child's size bowl of bouillabaisse for him?" she asked, pointing toward Jabari.

"It wouldn't be a problem at all," the waiter said, scribbling on his notepad.

"And I would like the sautéed calves liver." Corey smiled at the disgusted look on his girlfriend's face as he handed both menus to the waiter.

"I'll have your drinks out soon and your food should be ready momentarily," the waiter said before walking away from the table.

"Why did you look at me like that when I ordered my food?" Corey asked.

Sierra looked at him and scrunched her nose. "Why is it that no one in your family can eat anything normal? You are always eating an unusual part of an animal."

"I guess I like to eat every part of the animal," Corey shrugged as Sierra smiled.

She leaned forward and looked into his eyes. "Have I ever told you that I love your accent?" she asked him.

He smiled. "No, you are usually teasing me about it."

"Well, I think that it is very sexy." She smiled when he blushed.

Jabari grabbed a fork and began to bang it on the table. Sierra gently took the fork from him and explained that he could hurt himself by playing with sharp objects. Although he probably didn't understand, she was sure that he knew not to play with the fork again. When she noticed that his shoe was untied, she leaned over and tied it. As she sat up, Jabari placed his hands on her face. She took his hands and kissed them. Then she kissed his forehead. She sat up straight and faced Corey who was smiling.

"You are going to make a great mother," he said.

It was like déjà vu. LaToya had said the same thing only an hour ago. Sierra looked at Corey and reached across the table and grabbed his hands. She looked into his eyes so he could see how serious she was being at the moment. "I know this may sound kind of awkward and I really don't know where it's coming from, but it's been on my mind for a while and I really have to ask you this." She paused to gather her thoughts. "Do you want to have children with me?" she asked him.

Corey gave her a strange look before answering. "Of course I want to have children with you. What type of question is that?"

"The kind you ask when you have a sexually transmitted disease," she said.

"Are you saying that you don't want to go through the sexual process to get the children?" he asked her.

"That's what I'm trying to ask you," she clarified. "I know you've thought about it because it's been running through my mind nonstop. When we get married, are we going to be intimate with or without protection? Are we going to have children?" she questioned rhetorically. "I know you haven't been thinking about proposing to me without those same questions running through your mind."

He looked across the table at the woman he had loved since his teens. He'd always fantasized about marrying her and spending their honeymoon in a five-star hotel where the "do not disturb" sign would remain on the outside of the door for their entire stay. And, even after finding out that Sierra had HIV, his fantasy hadn't been completely altered. He knew that he wanted to have children with Sierra. That wasn't the problem, but he wasn't sure if he wanted to have them naturally.

The waiter delivered their drinks, giving Corey a moment to gather his thoughts and turn them into spoken words. "Your food should be out shortly," the waiter informed.

"Thank you," Corey said as the waiter left their table. He looked at Sierra and couldn't imagine being with anyone else. "I have thought about it." He sighed heavily before continuing. "Baby, I want to spend my life with you and I know for sure that I want to be intimate with you and have children with you, but I just don't know that if doing those things naturally would be our best option, considering your condition." He sighed again when Sierra slid her hands out of his.

"I understand," she said, placing her hands in her lap.

Corey searched her eyes. "Do you?"

"Yes," she responded. "I mean, you know that I want to have a sexual relationship with you and I know that the feeling is mutual . . . or it was before we found out about me. I don't want to give you something that you will have to live with for the rest of your life. Maybe we shouldn't have children of our own. I know that there are medications that could prevent our child from catching the disease, but it's still risky. Maybe we should just adopt or something. I definitely don't want our child to end up with it. That would be something that you would have to deal with once I'm gone."

Corey looked at her and breathed deeply. "Baby, please don't talk like that. You make it seem like you have the full-blown disease."

"I know. But I'm just coming to the realization that I'm not going to be here with you forever and I just don't want to leave you here without you understanding that."

He reached across the table and grabbed her hands again. "Sierra, I understand that you have this disease, and I'm not blind to the fact that I may someday lose you to it. But as long as I've got God and you, whether here physically or spiritually, my life is complete." He smiled before leaning in to kiss her. "And make no mistake, even if we don't have children, the sexual relationship is something I'm definitely looking forward to," he said, before he kissed her again.

They looked up when Jabari started to squeal and kick his feet, letting them know he wanted attention.

Sierra's eyes found her friends' table and Corey followed her gaze. "How do you think they are doing?" she asked.

"I don't know," Corey said. "I'm praying hard though."

"You're not hungry?" Jamal asked LaToya, who had received her filet mignon five minutes ago and had barely touched it.

She silently shook her head and continued to focus her gaze on the white linen tablecloth.

Jamal had been trying to get her to speak to him for the past twenty minutes, but she wouldn't utter a word. Tired of receiving the silent treatment, he placed his fork on his plate, leaned forward and stared intently at La-Toya, so much that his eyes began to hurt.

She raised her eyes and returned his gaze. "Why are you staring at me so hard?"

Jamal leaned back in his seat, picked up his fork and took another bit of his lobster ravioli. "Just to get you to say something to me." He placed his fork back on his plate and squinted in her direction. "Why aren't you speaking to me?"

LaToya's glare was so fierce that Jamal could feel her anger rising. She didn't even want to dignify his ignorant question with an answer. She just looked at him so he could see the anger in her eyes. After a while, her anger turned into sadness and tears formed in the corners of her eyes. Not wanting to break down in front of him, she lowered her head and placed her hands on her forehead to shield her eyes. Jamal slowly reached across the table and used his index finger to lift her head so that her eyes would meet his. Tears made a slow trail down her cheeks.

"I'm sorry," Jamal said, still holding her face up with his finger. "I'm really, really sorry," he said again.

LaToya shook his finger from under her chin and turned her head. "Why didn't you just tell me?" she asked, still not looking at him.

"I was scared," Jamal stated honestly. "I didn't know what your response would be. I didn't know if you would accept it and I didn't want to lose you."

She looked him straight in his eyes. "Well, look what happened because you decided to keep me in the dark for two years. You've lost me, Jamal."

"Baby, please don't say that," Jamal pleaded.

"No, it's true," LaToya insisted. "How can I be with someone I can't even trust? We've spent the last year or so at odds because you were struggling with this secret. This is the reason why you always got so defensive when I asked you simple questions. This is the reason you continued to push me away when I just wanted us to be closer. You acted like you were out messing around when, in reality, you were just trying to take care of your son without losing your family.

"It's not like Jayson was born after we had Jabari. You could have told me that, after our baby boy was born, your ex popped up, saying that you fathered her baby and wanted you to take care of him. You could have told me that and I would have gone through it with you. But instead, you decide to keep it from me for two years and expect me to just accept it. I'm not saying that I'm never going to accept Jayson, especially since it seems like I have no choice, but I just can't see myself dealing with the baby mama drama. I know Kim can't stand me and I don't want her to have more of a reason to hate me."

"LaToya, Kim doesn't hate you," Jamal defended. "It's just that she felt I was neglecting Jayson to preserve your feelings. And she was right. You are the best thing that's ever happened to me. I mean, before you, I had never thought about settling down or having a family, but you make me want to. I know I messed up by not telling you about Jayson and I do apologize for that, but I'm asking you to forgive me." He looked deeper into her eyes. "I do love you and I do want to be with you," he said. "And I know it may be hard for you to accept, but Jayson is going to be a part of our lives, and I'd really like for Jabari to get to know his older brother."

LaToya shrugged. "I don't mind Jayson and Jabari spending time together. It's me that is going to have to get used to this arrangement. This is a child we are talk-

ing about and I'm not going to get upset because you
want him around us, but I just have to get to a point
where I'm comfortable with him being around me."

Jamal nodded. "I understand that and I promise to
give you some time," he said. "I just need to know that
you believe that I am genuinely sorry and that you do
forgive me for this."

"I do believe you, and I forgive you," LaToya said.

Jamal searched her eyes. "Do you still love me?" he
asked.

She nodded with a smile. "Yes, Jamal, I do still love
you."

"Good, because I love you too," he said as he took her
hand and kissed it gently.

As they continued eating, LaToya hoped that she wasn't
falling for the type of guy who told one lie after another
and expected for her to stay with him every time. She
hoped that this was the last bump that would slow down
their relationship, but her heart told her not to even try to
live the fairytale life. She knew there were more speed
bumps to come.

Chapter 16

The hall was bustling with students who could have cared less about getting to their first period class on time. Imani joined them, walking down the hall toward her locker. As she turned the knob to the series of numbers that would grant her entry to her locker, she was distracted by someone tapping her on her shoulder. She turned around and her mouth dropped open in shock at the sight before her.

"What . . . did . . . you do?" Imani asked Nicole as she touched her friend's hair.

"I cut it all off," Nicole shrugged as she fingered her chin length curls.

"Why?" Imani asked, remembering Nicole's long, curly hair.

Nicole shrugged again. "I needed a change. You know after everything that's happened," she explained.

Imani nodded knowingly. "Well, it's cute," she said, smiling. "Has Shawn seen it yet?"

Nicole shook her head. "I don't know what he is going

to say. He really liked it long." She touched her hair self-consciously. "I don't know if he'll like it or not. But then again, it's my hair so who cares if he doesn't like it?"

Imani grabbed her books and she and Nicole headed to their class. They walked into the classroom just as the bell rang and made it to their seats before the teacher began the lesson. Imani took her regular notes. She noticed that Nicole's mind seemed to be elsewhere. Imani ripped a sheet of paper out of her notebook, scribbled a note, and passed it to Nicole. Nicole opened the note and read it, *Are you alright?* Nicole picked up her pencil and wrote back. *No, will you come with me to the counselor's office after this period?* She passed it to Imani. After reading her friend's answer, Imani turned toward Nicole and nodded.

An hour later, the bell rang for students to report to their second period class. Imani and Nicole walked down the hall to the counseling center. No one was at the front desk, so they headed toward their counselor's office. When they knocked on the door, Patricia Welling raised her head from the pile of work on her desk and welcomed her visitors with a warm smile.

"Hi, Nikki, Mani," she greeted as she motioned for them to sit. "Oh . . . Nikki, I love your hair."

"Thanks," Nicole said, fingering her curls again.

Patricia took off her reading glasses. "To what do I owe this lovely visit from two of my favorite students?"

"A listening ear," Nicole said.

Patricia became serious. "Is something wrong?"

Imani looked at Nicole, who began to fidget nervously. She had no idea why they were here. She was only there for support. Other than the fact the Nicole seemed upset, she was in the dark as to why they were sitting across from the most popular counselor at Douglass High. She sat and waited for Nicole to state her reason for coming.

"I just can't get over it," Nicole said as a few tears began to stream down her face.

"Get over what?" Patricia asked as she handed Nicole a tissue.

Nicole dabbed at her eyes. "My dad trying to rape me," she said as more tears began to flow. "I mean, what did I do that was so bad it would make him want to try to force himself on me? I've always been close to him. What did I do?"

Imani stared at Nicole as she tried to hold back her own tears. "Girl, you didn't do a thing," she said as she rubbed her friend's back.

"My thoughts exactly," Patricia said, handing Nicole more tissues. "Nothing about this situation is your fault. I don't know what happened in detail, but from the child services report and what you have told me, everything falls on your father. The only thing that you lie in fault of is not telling someone sooner."

"I know, but I just didn't want to get him in trouble," Nicole said, wiping her face. "I know that he was wrong, but I don't think he meant it. He was drunk and in a vulnerable position considering the separation. I . . . I shouldn't have forced him off of me. Maybe I should have tried to talk to him." She shrugged. "Maybe I should have tried to ease my way out of the situation by reminding him who I was to him. I shouldn't have pushed him and I definitely shouldn't have slapped him. That's what ticked him off. When I slapped him, he started beating me."

Imani stared at her friend in total disbelief. "Nikki, what are you talking about? Why are you trying to defend his actions? I don't understand this at all. You know when we talk we've always said that if we were being abused we'd definitely tell someone because that person should receive some sort of punishment for their actions.

We talk about that stuff, but now that something like that has actually happened, you want to blame things on yourself." Imani turned Nicole's face in her direction. "None of this is your fault. Stop blaming yourself and stop trying to justify your father's actions."

Patricia nodded. "She is right, Nikki. You have to let this go and stop placing the blame on the wrong person. Your father was wrong, not you. And you have to come to terms with that. I know it may be hard to even fathom that he would do something like that to you or your brother, but he did, and if he wasn't locked up, he'd definitely be capable of doing it again.

"You need to understand that when people go through things, they handle them in different ways. Some may take their anger out on someone they don't know, someone they do know, or even someone they love. If someone feels that they are being neglected at home, they will go somewhere else to get the attention that they want. I had a student who was in the graduating class with your brother. She felt like her father didn't love her or care about her, so she found the love and care that she wanted in various guys that could, temporarily, provide her with what she wanted. Now her actions have caused her to contract a lifetime disease. Although she is now in her senior year of college, has a boyfriend who loves her dearly, and is living for Christ, she is still carrying the repercussions of her actions, and she cannot get rid of it.

"I'm telling you this because you are handling what you went through by going around feeling sorry for and blaming yourself. Don't do that. You will end up with low self-esteem and no self-respect. You will walk around here with your head hanging so low that no one is going to even try to see what is wrong with you and people are going to stop trying to comfort you. Your friends are going to get tired of you not wanting to go anywhere with them. I mean, look at who you're dating. Shawn likes to have fun." Nicole smiled, in spite of her tears. "I know he is not going to sit around waiting for you to get over your pain.

"I'm not telling you that you need to just forget everything that happened. I'm telling you to not let it consume your mind. *Acknowledge* what happened. Take time for yourself and *realize* the pain it caused you," Patricia paused. "I'm really not supposed to say this, but because I know you believe in this method of healing, you need to *pray*. Ask God to heal you and take the pain away. Ask Him to help you not wallow in your hurt. After you do that, push all memories of this hardship out of your mind. Mind you, it may creep back in from time to time, but don't dwell on it or you will be back to where you started.

"If you don't get it together in due time, life will pass you by at the speed of light. You'll miss out on what God may have in store for you in the future. So all you have to do is focus on the positive side of things. You and your mother and brother are much happier in your new home and you have wonderful friends who are here to help you through these rough times," she said, nodding in Imani's direction. "You have got to get through this. I want you to get through this, and I know you want to as well.

"Now, we can schedule weekly counseling sessions with you and Imani, your mother, your brothers, or anyone you feel should be here to hear how you feel about this situation. But I'm telling you, the only way you are going to get over this is to do four things: Acknowledge the circumstance; realize the pain; pray that you will be healed; and then push it out of your mind." Patricia broke into a grin. "Can you do that for me?"

Nicole nodded. "Yes, ma'am. I think I can."

Patricia came from behind her desk with open arms, and Nicole welcomed the embrace. "You are a strong young woman. And God is going to carry you through this." She released Nicole and hugged Imani. "And you . . . you are a great friend. Remind Nikki of that sometimes."

Imani laughed as Patricia released her. "Thank you, Ms. Patricia."

"Thank you so much," Nicole said as she hugged the counselor again.

"Oh, you both are very welcome," Patricia said as she went back around to the other side of her desk. "Now let me write you all passes so your teachers won't think that you were skipping in my office, like everyone else tries to do."

They laughed as she pulled out her pen and two tardy excuse passes.

The last bell sounded as students rushed from their classrooms and out into the hallways. Imani and Nicole exited their British literature class and headed for their lockers before going to dance practice. As they stuffed their books in their lockers and backpacks, Nicole's thoughts were still on the meeting that she had with her counselor that morning. She knew she needed to get past everything that had happened if she wanted to move on with her life. She just didn't know when she'd be able to do that.

She sighed softly as Imani began to talk about how much she missed Eddie and was anticipating her date with him in the coming weekend. Nicole loved her best friend to death, but she was honestly tired of hearing about Eddie. Nicole knew she was jealous and wished she shared with Shawn what Imani and Eddie had, but Shawn was too busy trying to prove himself a lady's man to show Nicole hardly any attention. She liked him a lot, but hated the fact that he was so flirtatious, whether she was around or not. She was beginning to feel like she was in a relationship by herself, and the only reason she was in that relationship was because she was losing the relationship she shared with her best friend.

The girls retrieved their practice clothes and shut their lockers. As they exited the hallway, Nicole spotted a couple sharing a sensual embrace at the far end of the adjacent hallway. The closer she moved toward the hall, the more she hoped that her eyes were deceiving her, but she knew they weren't. She could clearly see Shawn pinned up against the wall with Sheila Rogers.

Imani hadn't noticed the couple as she continued to walk down the hall, but Nicole's movement in the direction opposite of the gym caught her attention. When she turned to see where her friend was headed, she caught sight of Shawn. Imani knew that a confrontation would only end in someone getting suspended. Although Imani knew for a fact that Nicole didn't fight over boys, she did know that her friend didn't mind fighting Shawn or Shelia just for being in the wrong.

Imani made her way to Nicole and grabbed her arm before she could get to the hall. "Don't do it," Imani said, still gripping Nicole's arm. "He's not even worth it."

Shawn looked up briefly, locking eyes with Nicole. Nicole's breathing was uneven and her eyes were full of rage. It was just like the look that had appeared in Ronald's eyes the day they found about Malcolm's abuse. As if he could sense her anger, he quickly grabbed Sheila's hand and left the building.

Imani's grip tightened on Nicole's arm as they watched Shawn and Sheila rush toward the nearest exit. As Nicole's heartbeat slowed to a normal rate and her eyes seemed to return to their sockets, Imani led her toward the girls' locker room so they could change for practice.

Nicole couldn't believe Shawn could do something like this to her, especially after he'd told her that he couldn't stand the sight of Sheila. It didn't make any sense. Though she was angry with him, she was more hurt by the fact that he didn't seem to care about her feelings. She couldn't understand why everything in her life seemed to be headed downhill. She couldn't find happiness anywhere and she was tired of searching for it. She'd just have to settle with the fact that she'd be miserable for the rest of her life.

When Nicole and Imani reached the locker room, they quickly changed their clothes. Imani pulled her hair back into a ponytail and waited for Nicole, who was still fuming over the sight of her boyfriend in another girl's arms. Nicole slammed her locker shut causing some of the other dancers to look in her direction. Seeing the challenging look she gave them, they didn't even dare to ask her what her problem was. They walked out of the locker room and into the commons to take their places for practice.

Coach Bullock scanned the girls' faces to see if all of them were there. Satisfied that everyone was accounted for, she started the music that they had been practicing to for the past week.

Normally, Nicole was full of energy when she danced. She always had a genuine smile on her face, not like the fake ones that seemed to be plastered across the faces of some of the other girls just because Coach Bullock required them to show some joy throughout the dance. Sometimes she'd get excited while dancing, causing the other girls to assume that she'd had an energy drink before coming to practice. But today, she lacked her authentic smile and didn't even bother to fake one. Her movements were not as sharp as they usually were. Today, they were lanky and lacked passion.

Imani turned to her friend, smile still in place and

keeping up with the dance steps. "Come on," she said through clenched teeth.

Nicole looked at her and rolled her eyes before turning her attention back toward the front.

Coach Bullock observed the girls as they danced and shouted out orders. "Head up, Charmaine. Donna, I don't see attitude. April, keep count. One, two, three, four, five, six, seven, eight. One, two, three, four . . ." Couch Bullock walked over to the stereo and turned off the music. She looked at Nicole. "What's going on with you?"

Nicole looked at the coach as if she was crazy. She wasn't in the mood to be reprimanded or lectured and was sure if Coach Bullock did either one, she'd take her attitude out on her elder.

As if assuming that Nicole hadn't realized to whom the question had been directed, Coach Bullock stepped closer to Nicole, looked her directly in the eyes, and repeated the question. "Nicole, I'm speaking to you. What's going on?"

Nicole stared at her coach with unyielding eyes. "Oh . . . I knew who you were speaking to, I just didn't think you really expected me to answer the question," she said, causing a few of the girls to snicker.

Coach Bullock was taken aback, but she refused to let her surprise take over her face. "You might want to put some of that attitude into your dance moves," she said before walking back to the stereo. "Start from the top." She started the song from the beginning.

Nicole continued to dance without attitude or passion and she couldn't have cared less. Her trials had already gotten the best of her and she was tired of trying to conquer them. There was nothing left for her to do other than allow life to get the best of her.

Coach Bullock stopped the music again after noticing

the lack of change in Nicole's movements. "Nicole, I'm going to have to ask you to sit out if you can't step it up."

Nicole shrugged. "Fine," she said as she walked out of the commons and toward the gym locker room to retrieve her belongings.

Imani watched as her friend left nonchalantly. "Coach, I have to go with her. I can't leave her like that. Plus, we are riding together," Imani pleaded.

"Go ahead, but if you don't have this dance down pat by competition date, I am not putting you in front of those judges," Coach said as she started the music again.

Imani ran toward the locker room. When she got there, Nicole was grabbing her belongings and stuffing them in her gym bag. She hadn't even bothered to change out of practice clothes. Although it was chilly outside, Imani decided not to change either. Without saying a word, they walked out of the locker room and to the gym where the basketball team was practicing. They walked past the sweating guys and out to the parking lot in the cool October air.

Since practice usually lasted until six o'clock and it was only a quarter until five, Imani's mother wouldn't be by to pick them up anytime soon. So Imani decided that she and Nicole would just sit on the bench and have one of their "girl talks," something they hadn't done in a while. Nicole followed Imani over to the bench and placed her bag beside her. They sat in silence for a moment as Imani tried to figure out how to approach the situation, but her time was cut short when Nicole began to violently shake.

"Nicole, what's wrong?" Imani asked as Nicole's body continued to shudder and angry tears began to stream down her face. "Nikki, please tell me what's going on."

Nicole tried to calm her anger. "I just can't take it anymore. I don't want to be here, Imani. I'm not happy. I haven't been happy for a while. I don't want to live like this. I just wish that I was never born. Everybody's life would be better if I wasn't here," she proclaimed, rocking back and forth, tears clouding her vision.

Imani felt as if everything Nicole had just said sounded a little too close to signs of depression and suicide. She held back her own tears as she tried to be strong for her friend. "Nikki, you don't mean that. You're just going through some things right now and you are letting them get the best of you," Imani said, hoping that Nicole would believe her. "You have a good life. Although your family is going through some changes, your life is still the best that you can make it. You are letting these things take over your judgment. You have people who love you so much that if something were to happen to you, all of our lives would change. And not for the better, please believe that."

Nicole looked at Imani. "Girl, nobody loves me. *Nobody!* My parents are divorcing without considering their children. My dad abused me. My oldest brother spends most of his time with your sister. My younger brother is so annoying that I would do just about anything to get away from him. My best friend spends all of her spare time with her boyfriend. And my boyfriend . . . well he definitely doesn't love me or else he wouldn't have been pushed up against a bunch of lockers with his ex-girlfriend."

She stood and stared Imani square in the eye. "So please, Imani, tell me who, in that list of people that I just named, loves me. You guys don't even spend any time with me. We hardly even talk anymore. Seriously, can you remember the last time we talked on the phone?" Nicole asked, throwing her hands up.

Imani was trying to hold back her anger, but Nicole

was pushing her. She knew her friend was upset. But why she was taking her anger out on other people, Imani didn't understand. "Last week. I called you last week."

"Yeah, but you didn't even call to really talk to me. You called me because you missed *Eddie*. And then just when we were starting to have a *real* conversation, he beeps in on your other line, and you just cut me off with whatever I was saying, and tell me you'll call me back," Nicole said as she paced. "When are you going to call back, Mani?

"The only reason I don't say anything is because I know how much you love Eddie and I understand that. He's a really nice guy who cares a lot about you. You'll end up with the dream guy we've always talked about wanting, while I'll get stuck with someone like that *thing*, who calls himself a good boyfriend. The only reason why I started going out with Shawn was to have someone to spend time with since you and Eddie are always together. Yeah, I liked him, but I never thought I'd really get caught up." Nicole sat back on the bench. "I just want someone to really care about Nicole for once. I don't want you to feel obligated to spend time with me just because we are best friends. I want you to truly want to go out to the mall or just chill at the house. I don't want you to feel like you are missing out on spending time with Eddie because you *have* to spend time with me."

Imani's anger faded as she realized that Nicole was right. She did spend all of her time with Eddie and she couldn't deny the fact that she did love being with him, but she missed spending time with Nicole. They'd been best friends since the eighth grade and she didn't want their four-year friendship to end because of her four-month relationship with a guy. "I'm sorry, Nikki. I didn't realize, until now, how much of my time is actually spent on Eddie, whether I'm actually with him or talking to him, or thinking about him. I know that sometimes I put

him before you and that's not right. I want you to understand that no guy, not even the one I marry, will ever come
between us. I love you. You are my girl, and girlfriends are
forever." Imani smiled. "So do you forgive me?"

Nicole wiped a few tears. "You know I do," she said as
they hugged.

"But I don't ever want to hear you talking like this
ever again. You scared me half to death when you stared
talking about life being better without you. It wouldn't
be the same without you here to keep everyone's spirits
up. Your mother needs you because she has been really
unstable since she found out about your father's affair
and him abusing you and Jeremy. She doesn't want you
guys to see her like that, so she spends most of her time
out with my mom and their friends. And Jeremy is acting
out because he has been thinking the same things you
have. And Ronald . . . well, Nevaeh tells me that when
they are together, she spends most of her time consoling
him on the whole situation. He was really upset about
your parents' separation, now he is angry about the
abuse and he thinks that it's his fault because it started
after he moved out."

"It's not his fault," Nicole said. "It's not like he could
have prevented it."

"Exactly," Imani said. "So why do you keep making
excuses for your dad?" Nicole shrugged. "I'm not
putting Mr. Malcolm down or anything because he *was* a
good father, but whatever drove him to do what he did
had a major effect on you guys and there is no valid excuse for him or his behavior. And there isn't one for
Shawn either," Imani said.

"Oh, girl, that boy is so cut. He is not even worth the
tears," Nicole said. "I just wish he could have at least had
the guts to tell me that he didn't want to be with me. I
would have told him off for wasting my time first, but at

least I wouldn't feel like he didn't want me because he wanted someone else."

Nicole and Imani talked for the next thirty minutes. When they saw that some of the dance members were coming out of the school, they gathered their things and waited for Imani's mother to come pick them up. Some of the girls stopped to see if Nicole was okay, while others stood around and talked as they waited for their ride home. Nicole spotted Coach Bullock speaking with another dancer, so she walked over to her.

"Coach," she said once the other girl left, "I want to apologize for my attitude today. I'm just going through some things and I wasn't focused on the routine."

"I know," Coach Bullock said. "I just hope that you will be fine by regionals because we are going to need you."

"I will." Nicole smiled. "Thank you," she said as she walked back over to Imani.

"My mom's here," Imani said.

The girls went to the car. Nicole prayed that she would be able to get over the burdens that had been weighing her down for the past few months. She knew God would never put more on her than she would be able to bear, but if He handed her another tribulation, she knew she would fall.

Chapter 17

Tyler sat nervously on the leather sofa in his living room as he awaited Shimone's arrival. He and his son had been cleaning their house all day in anticipation for this moment. This visit was important to Tyler for two reasons: Number one, this was Shimone's first visit to his home, and number two, he had a very important question that he wanted to ask her. Ensuring that everything was perfect was essential.

Over the past few months, he and Shimone had been spending a lot of time together, trying to make up for the years lost. Their relationship had grown stronger than Tyler ever thought it would. Needing to rebuild her relationship with Christ, Shimone had been found comfort within the walls of Tyler's church. Although she was not yet an official member, she and her mother had attended services for the last few Sundays and was even planning to attend the Hallelujah Night that was scheduled to take place in a couple of weeks.

Shimone had become dependent on him for things he thought he'd never get a chance to be involved in. She went to him for comfort when she was having trouble coming to terms with the fact that Marques had fathered another woman's baby. She went to him after the death of the premature twins and told him how she'd led Alexia to Christ despite their differences. Shimone shared everything with Tyler that he'd missed out on, and he was extremely grateful.

Hearing a car pulling up in his driveway, he got off the couch, pulled back the white curtains, and peeked out one of the bay windows. "Tim, they're here," Tyler yelled up the stairs to his son.

Seconds later, Timothy came sliding down the banister.

"What have I told you about doing that?" Tyler reprimanded.

"My bad." Timothy smiled, noticeably happy about seeing his sister and niece again.

Tyler opened the door while Shimone was getting Ebony out of her car seat. He stood in the entrance and a huge smile spread across his face when Shimone placed Ebony on her feet and the little girl ran toward him with open arms.

"Papa," Ebony squealed as Tyler scooped her up into his arms and gave her a kiss on the forehead. Ebony had just recently began to call him "Papa," but the odd thing about it was that no one had ever told her that Tyler was her grandfather. It was as if she instinctively knew. Tyler took it as another blessing from God.

Shimone walked up the cobblestone walkway. She stood up on her toes and kissed Tyler's cheek. "Hi," she said before being escorted into the elegant home.

"Wassup, Shimone?" Timothy greeted.

"Hey," she said, hugging her brother as if she'd known him all his life. "I brought you that copy of my CD you wanted." She reached in her purse and took out the CD.

"Oh, thanks," he said. "I'm gonna listen to it as soon as I get a chance."

Shimone's eyes scanned the black and white décor of the living room. She admired the art on the walls and the photos on the mantle above the fireplace. One, in particular, caught her eye. It was a black and white portrait of a woman and a man, seemingly no older than Timothy, holding on to each other as if their lives depended on it. She picked up the picture and took a closer look at it. The woman looked exactly like her, only darker, and she saw that the man had her eyes. She didn't need to ask who the couple was. She instinctively knew that they were her parents.

"We took that picture a couple months after we started dating," Tyler said, walking up behind her and looking at the picture from over her shoulder.

"You guys look like you are really in love," Shimone observed.

Tyler smiled. "We were."

Shimone placed the picture back on the mantle and made her way around the living room. "Your house is beautiful," she said. "How can you keep it so clean?"

"All the work of the master," Timothy boasted from his position on the floor as he played with Ebony.

"Don't let him fool you," Tyler said. "Before he found out that you were coming, this whole area was a mess." Shimone laughed. He motioned for her to join him on the couch.

"Well, I'm glad that I motivated you," Shimone said.

They all sat in silence for a few moments. Finally Tyler spoke. "Well, I didn't call you over here just for us to sit around in dead silence," he chucked. He got up from the couch and began to pace. "I have something very important that I want to ask you and Timothy," he said, gaining both of their attention. "I've been thinking about this for a while now, and I just want your blessings."

"What's up, Dad?" Timothy asked curiously as he sat on the love seat, opposite Shimone, and pulled Ebony into his lap.

Tyler rubbed his hands together and tried to gather his thoughts. He turned to Shimone and looked her directly in her eyes. "I really want your approval with this because I know I haven't been around long and it may seem like it's too soon for this, but I know that it's really something I want to do," he rambled as he pulled at his ear.

Shimone smiled. "Oh . . . there you go yanking those ears. What is it?"

"I don't really know how to ask it, but I just want you guys to be open minded and at least think about it before giving me a final answer," he said.

"Dad, would you just please say what you got to say before *I'm* old and gray," Timothy said as Ebony laughed at Timothy's contorted expression. Tyler gave him a stern look. "Ebony thought it was funny." Timothy shrugged.

Tyler stood in place and looked at both of his children, one whom he'd known for fifteen years and the other he'd only known for four months, but he loved each of them equally. Finally finding the words, he opened his mouth and asked the question that had been on his mind since Misty had come back into his life. "Well, Misty and I have been spending a lot of time together over the last few months. I've realized how much I love her and want her to remain a part of my life. And God has told me that if I go through with this, Misty will accept. So . . ." He paused. "I want to ask . . . Misty to . . . marry me," he said.

Shimone and Timothy stared at Tyler with no emotion on their faces. They both seemed to be speechless upon hearing the news. Neither of them would have guessed that this was why they had gathered today. Not knowing what was going on, Ebony followed the lead of her mother and uncle and stared blankly at Tyler. Timothy broke his stare from his father, who was gazing intently at Shimone, and locked it onto his sister. Once again, following the lead of her elders, Ebony looked at her mother with no emotion on her face. Noticing that everyone was now looking at her for a reaction, Shimone tried to find the words to express her feelings.

"Shimone," Tyler said her name slowly, "what do you think?"

Shimone sat there, her face still blank. Finally, she found her voice. "I . . . umm. Well . . . I . . . Tyler." She sighed heavily. "I don't think that is such a good idea," she said.

Tyler's face dropped. He had been working up the nerve to ask Shimone this question for the last few weeks. He thought that with her coming to him for advice and counseling on her problems that things were getting better between them. He thought for certain that she would be happy about his desire to fully commit to Misty. "You don't?" he said, softly.

Shimone shook her head. "No, I don't. It's not that I don't think you love my mother or that I don't think you deserve her or anything like that. It's just that I think it is too soon . . . much too soon," she said. "I mean, we're just really starting to get to know each other. It's only been four months." She sighed. "Don't get me wrong," she continued as she stared into Tyler's distressed eyes. "I love you. Ebony loves you. And I know Mama loves you—she never stopped. It's just that . . ." Shimone wanted to be honest, but she didn't want to hurt his feelings and his face seemed to be crumbling by the second. "I just don't think . . . I don't want my mother to get hurt again," she said as silent tears began to flow. "I . . . I don't want to get hurt again. I don't want to . . . I just don't think that I'd . . . we'd be able to take it," she said as she wiped her face.

Tyler used his thumb to wipe the tears before they even left his eyes. "I understand," he said, solemnly. "I'll wait until you are comfortable with it."

Shimone walked toward him and hugged him. "Thank you," she said.

Tyler tightened his embrace and let a few of his tears fall onto her head.

She released him and looked at her watch. "I have to go. Ebony is supposed to be spending time with Marques today. Thank you for inviting us over. Come on, Ebony," Shimone called to her daughter.

Ebony hugged her uncle and then ran over to Tyler. "Bye, Papa," she said as he picked her up and cradled her in his arms.

Shimone hugged Timothy, who seemed to be a little disappointed. "Family no matter what, right?" he asked.

"Yeah, no matter what," she said, releasing him. Shimone took Ebony's hand and led her out of the door.

Tyler and Timothy stood in the doorway until Shimone had pulled out of their driveway. Tyler closed the door, walked over to the sofa, and sank into its cushions.

"Dad, everything is going to work out," Timothy said as he squeezed his dad's shoulder.

Tyler patted his son's hand. "I hope so, son," he said before getting off of the couch and walking up the staircase toward his room to pray that what God had placed in his heart would be received by Shimone and she would come around soon so that they could really be a family.

Marques pulled into the parking lot of Greater Faith Tabernacle Church and shut off his vehicle's engine. He sat in the driver's seat to collect his thoughts. It had been almost a month since the death of his twins, and he couldn't seem to shake the feeling of guilt that hung over his head. He didn't even know why he was feeling guilty about something he had no control over. He knew he should have paid more attention to Alexia's condition, and he should have known that neglecting prenatal care would lead to undetected problems in childbirth. He just wished he would have done something to prevent the loss of his kids.

"Daddy, you okay?" Ebony said from her car seat.

Marques looked back at his daughter. "Yes, princess," he said. He climbed out of the car and went around the back to get his daughter. "Come on," he said, pulling her from the car seat and handing her a small bouquet of flowers. "We are going to see your brother and sister."

Ebony gave her father a confused look. "They're here?" she asked, looking around.

"No. We are not really going to *see* them," Marques said. "We are going to see their gravesites," he explained, knowing that Ebony didn't have a clue what a gravesite was, although she had visited the burial site before.

They walked hand in hand toward the graveyard that sat to the left side of the church. Many of the church members had their loved ones buried here. The day after the twins died, Marques went to his parents and explained everything about his break up with Shimone and the premature birth and death of the twins. After enduring a severe, reprehensive lecture, Marques's parents agreed to help pay for the small memorial service. Since Alexia had no family that she knew of, the only people in attendance were her, a couple of her close girlfriends, Marques, his parents, Shimone, Ebony, Nevaeh, and Ronald. Marques knew that asking Shimone to actively participate in the service would be a waste of time, but he had no idea that it would take him, Ronald, and finally, a reluctant Shimone to coax Nevaeh into singing "His Eye is on the Sparrow." Alexia reminded Marques that his friends' willingness simply to be in attendance revealed how blessed he was.

Marques led Ebony to the tombstone that the twins shared. He kneeled at the site and solemnly gazed at the small inscription that Alexia had wanted on the tomb: *Malik & Andrea Anderson, you will always be loved.*

"They're in there?" Ebony pointed down at the ground.

Marques nodded. "Their bodies are, but remember, I told you that their spirits are with God." He pointed to the heavens and Ebony looked up, smiling toward the sky.

Ebony stood next to her father and traced the inscription with her pointer finger. "Broder and sister," she said as Marques helped her place the flowers in the holder that was attached to the tombstone. "Daddy say heaven good. You'll like it there," she said, touching the stone.

Marques pulled her into his arms and hugged her as if his life depended on it. Without realizing it, he let a few tears escape into his daughter's hair.

Ebony pulled back and examined her father's face. She wiped his tears and gave him a smile. "God need them," she said, repeating what Marques had told her many times before.

Marques smiled at his daughter, who seemed to be his God-appointed angel. She was so smart for her age, and he wondered if her premature wisdom would follow her throughout life. She gave him her biggest smile and hugged him tight as if she knew he needed it. When she released him, he resumed looking at the tombstone. "I love you guys," he said before rising to his feet and leading Ebony back to the car. He knew that, in time, he'd get over their deaths and his guilt. He just hoped that the time would come soon.

Marques drove down the highway. Glancing at his watch, he noted that he had about an hour and a half to spare with his precious angel before he needed to get her home. He exited and made a right. Finding an available spot in the mall's parking lot was a living nightmare. Every time he thought he had found a good one, someone would appear out of nowhere and take it. Finally, he found a spot, even though it was not as close to the mall as he would have liked it to be; he was tired of circling the lot. He got out of the car and helped Ebony out of her car seat.

"Daddy, you buy me shoes?" she asked as they walked to the entrance of Sears.

"You want some shoes?" Marques asked as they entered the store. Ebony nodded enthusiastically, causing her ponytails to flop back and forth.

As they walked through Sears and into the open area of stores and the crowd of bustling shoppers, Marques held Ebony's hand tighter so she wouldn't get lost as he headed for the shoe store. They entered Footlocker and were immediately welcomed by a female employee.

"Hi," she welcomed, throwing her long braids over her shoulder and giving Marques a smile. "My name is Veronica," she said, pointing to the nametag on her chest. "How can I help *you* today?"

Marques tried to ignore the seductive look in her eyes and sultry sound of her voice. He had let temptation get him in enough trouble and he was not about to head down that road again. "I'm looking for a pair of shoes for my daughter," he said as Ebony clung to his arm.

Veronica looked down as if she was just noticing that the little girl in pigtails was beside Marques. "Oh . . ."

She smiled. She kneeled in front of Ebony. "What's your name?" she asked.

"Ebony," she said, briefly taking her thumb out of her mouth.

"And you need some shoes?" Veronica asked. Ebony, who was still holding onto her father, nodded. Veronica stood and looked at Marques. "Well, let's go find her some good ones." She walked toward the kids section, swaying her hips in the process.

When Marques saw Veronica cast a quick glance over her shoulder and catch him watching her walk, he knew he had let his stare linger much too long. Taking Ebony's hand, he followed Veronica. She pulled five of the newest styles of shoes off the shelf.

"Which ones do you like?" Veronica asked. Ebony pointed to the baby blue and white K-Swiss that were in the lineup. "Good choice. She seems to know exactly what she wants," Veronica said, looking up at Marques. "Most girls do." She winked at him.

Marques rubbed his head and tried to suppress the urge to laugh at her behavior. *Lord, these women*, he thought to himself. He remembered in high school when he had to be the aggressor. Now all he had to do was flash his captivating smile and he'd have a date the next night.

Marques told Veronica what size shoe Ebony wore and she went to the back to get them. When she returned, she allowed Ebony to try the shoes on. After walking in them and assuring Veronica and Marques that they fit perfectly, Ebony finally took the shoes off, and Veronica packed them into their box.

Veronica rang the shoes up, and Marques paid for them. Before handing him the receipt, Veronica turned it over and wrote her number on the back of it. "Call me," she said as she handed him the paper.

Marques took the slip of paper and the bag with the shoes in them. *Please, you are not even my type,* he thought as he returned her smile.

"Bye, sweetie," Veronica said to Ebony as she and Marques headed out of the store. Ebony turned back around and waved.

When they turned the corner, Marques took the receipt and threw it into the nearest trashcan.

Ebony looked up at Marques. "I no like her," she said matter-of-factly.

Marques looked down at his daughter and burst into laughter at the serious look on her face. "Me either, baby," he said. "I think I'll get you a couple of outfits," he added as if the brand new clothes were a way of awarding her for her good judgment.

"Yay!" Ebony squealed.

After purchasing her a few winter garments, they left the mall, reaching Shimone's apartment twenty minutes later. She answered the door and immediately Marques noticed that she had been crying. Her eyes were red and she looked flustered.

"Mama, look what I got!" Ebony exclaimed, not noticing that her mother seemed to be upset.

Marques looked at Shimone and wondered what could be wrong. "Ebony, go inside and get ready to go to bed," he told her.

Ebony gazed up at her mother and finally realized her eyes were red. "Mama, you okay?" she asked Shimone. Shimone's eyes filled with tears as she looked at her daughter.

"Ebony, do like I said," Marques said, sternly.

Ebony walked inside the house, past her mother and into her room, while Marques followed Shimone into the apartment and shut the door. She headed straight for her bedroom and, after placing the shopping bags on the sofa, Marques followed. She sat on the bed, but he continued standing by the closed door.

"What's wrong?" he asked her.

Shimone let more tears fall. "Tyler wants to ask Mama to marry him," she said.

Marques's face didn't show any surprise. "Okay . . . I don't understand the problem here," he replied, walking over to the bed and taking a seat.

"The problem is that we barely know him," Shimone said, wiping her face. "I mean, I love him, but I just don't want to get hurt again. What if he decides that he doesn't want to be here with us, and he runs out on us? Another heartbreak for me and Mama . . . and Ebony. And what about Tim?" she asked as Marques held her. "What if he doesn't want this? He may not want another woman taking his mother's place in Tyler's life. He loves Ebony though, and I know he loves me as his sister. I love him too," she rambled. "It's just going to be hard because there's something in the back of my mind telling me that I should shut Tyler out because he's twenty-two years too late, but then there's something else telling me I shouldn't have a problem with this at all because he has been there for me for the past few months. I've filled him in on everything that has gone on in my life. Everything I can remember from when I was smaller, up until now, I've told him. So it's not even that I don't feel comfortable talking to him. I really don't know what it is," Shimone said as Marques pulled his fingers through her hair.

"Maybe, you're just afraid," Marques said.

"Afraid of what?"

"Whatever the future may hold for you and Tyler," he said, "as father and daughter. I don't know what it's like not to have a father or even a mother, but I do feel for you. I know it's hard accepting the fact that Tyler is your dad and that he is here now after not being around for over two decades of your life. I know it's hard for you to realize that your mother still has feelings for a man who walked out of her life when he found out that you were about to enter it, but the fact that he is here now is a blessing in disguise. I don't know what he may be here to do. God may have sent him to you because He knew that you felt that emptiness inside of you and deep, deep down somewhere you wanted to know your father, you wanted to love your father, you wanted to have your father in your life. So maybe his being here has filled an emptiness that you've had to harbor your entire life."

Shimone wiped the tears. "I know all of that. I know that God is doing some kind of work in my life and I know that Tyler could be a part of that work. I just don't think that it's the right time for him to become a permanent fixture in our lives. I don't think that if he proposed tomorrow, my mother would readily accept. And I know it wouldn't be because she doesn't love him, but she might have the same reservations that I am having right now. Granted, she has spent much more time around him than I have—they go out to dinner or the movies like every other night—but she would still have that fear that he would run out on her again if a situation came up and he thought he couldn't handle it.

"I know that Tyler is not going to propose until I am comfortable with him doing so, but I also know that the longer I hold out, the more impatient he is going to get. I just don't want to say, 'It's fine with me,' when it really isn't."

"Well, Shimone, that's fine," Marques said as she shifted her head from his lap to her pillow. "You should take all the time that you need. Don't try to make yourself feel comfortable with something you really aren't comfortable with. And if you think that it may take you longer than Tyler would like for it to take, sit down and talk to him. Let him know how you're feeling and then continue to evaluate you decision." He leaned down and kissed her head.

"Thank you," she whispered.

"No problem," he said as he got up from the bed. "I'm going to put Ebony to bed and then I'm out." He walked out of the room and then walked back in. "What time do you head out for church in the morning? I haven't heard Pastor McKinley preach in a while, so maybe I'll swing by."

Shimone sat up and looked at him in surprise. "Well, I've been going to church with Tyler for the last few Sundays, but I don't mind going to Greater Faith if you wanna come. I get up at eight, if you can be here by ten, we can ride together."

"Thanks. I'll be here," he said, walking out of the room and shutting the door behind him.

He walked into Ebony's room and noticed that she was already kneeling on the floor, saying her bedtime prayers. When she finished he changed her into her nightgown and tucked her into bed, then headed out of the house. *Hopefully there's a message for us both tomorrow,* he thought as he got in his car and backed out of the apartment complex.

Chapter 18

Shimone stepped out of the shower and slipped into her bathrobe. She walked into her closet and pulled out the black suit that she had chosen to wear. She placed it on her bed and decided to wake up her sleeping angel before getting dressed. She walked into her daughter's bedroom and laughed as she picked up the comforter that her wild-sleeping child had kicked off of the bed during the night. She gently stepped toward the bed.

"Ebony." Shimone shook her daughter gently. "Ebony, wake up."

Ebony's eyes fluttered open. "Mornin,' Mama," she yawned.

"Get up so you can wash up and get some breakfast," Shimone said as Ebony sat up and rubbed her eyes.

She climbed out of bed and put on her Mickey Mouse house shoes. They walked across the hall toward the bathroom. Shimone helped Ebony wash her face and brush her teeth. They went into the kitchen and Shimone helped Ebony into her chair. She didn't feel like cooking anything so she scanned the few boxes of cereal Marques had just purchased that were on top of the refrigerator.

"What cereal do you want?" she asked her daughter. "Mickey's Magix, Cheerios, or Frosted Mini Wheats." She chuckled, knowing what her daughter would choose.

"Mickey Mouse," Ebony said, banging her fists on the table. "Mickey Mouse, Mickey Mouse," she said over and over.

Shimone laughed and shook her head as she grabbed the box of cereal. "Okay, okay, Mickey Mouse it is," she said, preparing a small bowl. She placed the bowl of cereal in front of Ebony. "Now, I'm going to go get dressed."

Shimone walked out of the kitchen and into the bathroom. After hot curling her hair so that it would hang just below her shoulders, she walked into her room and took off her robe. She moisturized her body, put on a pair of stockings, and stepped into the skirt of her suit. The long skirt fell past the bottom of her feet. *Good thing I'm wearing heels*, she thought as she slipped the jacket on. She walked back in the kitchen to find her daughter finished with her breakfast.

"You must have been really hungry." Shimone laughed. "You better slow down or you'll be fat like Mommy."

Ebony smiled. "Mama not fat. Mama thick." She nodded. "That what Daddy say."

Shimone blushed inwardly. "You are going to have to stop repeating things that Daddy says," she said, helping Ebony out of her chair and taking the bowl to the sink. "Come on, let's get you dressed," she said as she led Ebony back into her room.

"Mama, I wear this," Ebony said, walking over to her closet and pulling out an outfit similar to Shimone's.

Shimone smiled. "You wanna be dressed like Mama?"

Ebony nodded as she placed the skirt and jacket set on

her bed. Shimone cherished her daughter's innocence; soon these years would be over.

She helped Ebony out of her nightgown and into her church clothes. After restyling Ebony's ponytails, Shimone put black and white bows and ribbons on them. By the time she had helped Ebony into her shoes, it was 9:45. Marques should be on his way to pick them up, but knowing him, he probably wouldn't get there until eleven o'clock. *Maybe he'll surprise me and be on time today.*

She felt like Marques was trying to change back into the person she'd fallen in love with. He had been trying to get her to go out with him for the past several weeks, but she had turned him down every time. She'd go out occasionally when he came by to pick up Ebony, but she didn't trust herself to be alone with him. She could see him trying to be the old Marques; the fact that he was going to church with them this morning proved that theory to be true.

Shimone instructed Ebony to sit on the sofa. "Now when your daddy gets here, come get me, okay?"

Ebony nodded as Shimone went into her room to get her Bible and her purse. As she reached for her Bible, which rested on her nightstand, she began to hum a song that she couldn't seem to remember the name of. She began to hum the tune louder and she paused to see if she could figure out what song had just entered her soul. She finally got the words together and then began to sing them aloud. It was "Use Me" by the Truthettes. She began to sing the song louder and louder; singing out prayers for God to use her as He pleased as the Spirit began to sweep throughout her body. She was His child, His instrument, to do whatever He wanted. She felt as if the song was placed in her heart by God for a reason. Lately, she'd been feeling as if Power Records was where she belonged, so that her voice could be heard throughout the world as she sang about God's goodness. Not wanting to make any rash decisions, she concluded that if it was God's will, it would happen in His own time. In the meantime, she felt good just relishing in His presence in her bedroom as she continued to belt out the song.

"Mama," Ebony shouted. "Mama!"

Shimone stopped singing and turned around to see her three-year-old standing in her doorway with her hands on her hips. "Huh?"

"Daddy here," Ebony said, walking back into the living room.

Shimone laughed as she picked up her belongings and headed out front. She opened the door just before Marques was about to knock for a fifth time. He stood at the door with his hands in his suit pockets. Shimone suppressed the urge to tell him how good he looked.

Apparently, Marques didn't feel the need to hold back his thoughts. "You look great," he said as she invited him into the apartment. "What took you so long to answer the door?"

"Mama singin' loud, Daddy," Ebony said.

"Hey, pumpkin," Marques said, kneeling to hug his daughter. "You say Mommy was singing?"

Ebony nodded. "Loud, too," she added.

Marques looked up at Shimone and smiled. "Is that what took you so long to answer the door?" He shook his head. "You couldn't have been singing so loud that you couldn't hear me knocking."

Shimone smiled. "I plead the fifth," she said as Marques stood.

He walked closer to her. "You are . . . unbelievable."

She lowered her eyes from his intensifying gaze. Marques cupped his hand around her face and leaned in to kiss her. Shimone closed her eyes and fell into the feeling she'd missed having over the past months. The smell of his cologne and the softness of his touch engulfed her, but as quickly as she fell in, she opened her eyes and regrouped.

"Marques," she whispered, placing her hands against his chest and slightly pulling away from him.

Marques looked at her and smiled. Rubbing his head, he backed away from her. Shimone could see the flirtatious sparkle in his eyes, and she turned away so she wouldn't be tempted to push aside all of her reservations concerning their relationship.

She turned toward her daughter. "Ebony, let's go. Do you have your Bible?"

Ebony held up her children's Bible that was filled with Bible stories and pictures, then grabbed her mother's hand. Marques stood, still gazing at Shimone.

She tried not to allow his stare to have an effect on her, though they both knew that it was. "Are you coming?" she asked him.

Marques's grin was as wide as the ocean was deep. "After you," he said, making a sweeping motion with his arm. They walked out of the house and toward his car.

Nevaeh and Ronald moved down a couple of seats to make room for their friends. As they took their seats, Shimone waved at Nevaeh's family, seated on the row behind them. She didn't see her mother in her usual seat and guessed that she'd decided to attend church with Tyler this morning, even though her daughter wouldn't be joining her. Once again, she thought of her father's proposal. *Lord, please let there be a word for me today*, she prayed.

Ronald reached across Nevaeh and Shimone and slapped hands with Marques. "Good to see you guys, especially you, man," he spoke to Marques.

"Isn't it though?" Marques grinned. "How are you do-ing?"

"I woke up this morning." Ronald shrugged. "That's enough to keep me happy."

Nevaeh leaned in her best friend's direction. "We've missed you around here, girl." She smiled. "How'd you get him to come back to church," she whispered in Shi-mone's ear.

Shimone shrugged. "I didn't do a thing. Last night when he brought Ebony home he asked what time we leave. I told him ten and he was knockin' on my door at 9:50 this morning," she whispered back.

Nevaeh sat back in her seat and smiled. Shimone knew that the last thing her friend expected was to see Mar-ques back in church; it had been a surprise to her, but having Marques with her for Sunday service made everything seem normal.

Once praise and worship began, Nevaeh walked up to the choir stand, along with the rest of the young adult choir. When she started to lead one of the praise songs, every person in the building was on their feet, giving honor and glory to God for all He had done. After they finished the first three songs, Nevaeh walked up to the choir director and whispered in his ear.

She stepped back and spoke into the microphone. "For this next song, the choir would like for Sister Shimone Johnson to join us." Applause erupted from all angles of the sanctuary.

It had been awhile since Greater Faith had heard Shi-mone's melodious voice, and they considered it a treat to be able to hear her sing God's praises this morning. From her seat, Shimone glared at her friend with an "I know you didn't" look on her face and began shaking her head.

Marques pushed her to her feet as if telling her she had

no choice. "Gon,' girl," he said with everyone else around them cheering her on.

As Shimone walked to the front of the church, various members shouted words of encouragement: "Sang girl," "Alright now," "Do it for J.C."

When she took her place next to Nevaeh, she nudged her friend in the side as the director handed her a microphone. The pianist began to play the introduction to an old song, but one of the congregation's favorites, "Silver and Gold" by Kirk Franklin and the Family. The choir began with the chorus, and when Nevaeh began singing the first verse, the congregation applauded. But when Shimone began singing the second verse, her soulful voice stirred the crowd, causing some people to stand on their feet and join in the worship. By the time the choir began to sing the chorus over and over again, Nevaeh had stepped back, allowing Shimone ad-lib to the song. Many members were on their feet, hands raised, giving praises to God. The church was filled with so much of the Spirit that when the song was over, the pianist began to play "shouting music."

People moved from their positions in the church to the floor to dance and shout along to the music. Ushers came from their posts to help contain some of the members who had really gotten caught up in the Spirit. Even some of the choir members had started to do the "holy dance." Shimone stood with her hands in the air, shouting out holy tongues toward the heavens. Nevaeh had never had the type of connection with God where she was able to communicate with Him in a totally different language, so she just lifted her hands and shouted out her praises in the only language she knew. Ronald stood at his seat and continued to praise his Heavenly Father. Even Ebony was jumping up and down to the beat.

Marques stood at his seat, knowing he should join in giving God the praise He deserved, but not feeling comfortable doing so. He knew that many of the people were just giving God thanks for all He had done in their lives. He also knew that he had much to be thankful for, but he just didn't feel right after all he'd put his family and friends through. So he continued to clap along with the music, and he didn't feel too much out of place since he saw that he wasn't the only one not jumping up and down or speaking in different languages.

As Pastor McKinley walked up to the pulpit, more praises erupted from all sides of the building. He lifted his hands and offered up praises along with his congregation. The excitement began to die down and people walked back to their seats, still praising God. Nevaeh and Shimone found their way back to their seats and prepared themselves for the message that was about to come forth.

"Hallelujah," Pastor McKinley said into the microphone. "Oh yes, the Spirit is moving in here this morning," he said as "amens" came from all over the building. Apparently not satisfied with the response, he repeated himself. "I don't think y'all heard me. I said *the Spirit* is moving in here *this morning.*"

This time the organist tuned up the organ and people jumped up in praise once again.

When it became calm again, Pastor McKinley proceeded. "Glory be to God. Our young adult choir has been working overtime," he said as members shouted out in agreement. "And I'm told that this was an impromptu performance and Sister Johnson was not informed on the order of praise service this morning," Pastor McKinley said, looking at Shimone and Nevaeh. "Shouldn't you two be in a recording studio somewhere?" He laughed along with the members of his con-

gregation, but kept his eyes on Shimone as if he were trying to send her a spiritual message.

Shimone involuntarily inhaled deeply at the sudden
warmth she felt surging through her body. She continued
smiling, knowing that God was speaking to her heart,
but for extra emphasis, He'd used one of His most faithful servants to assure her of His words.

Breaking eye contact with her, Pastor McKinley opened
his Bible. "Let us bow our heads in a word of prayer. Our
most Righteous Father, we humble ourselves as we come
to you right now thanking you for another day of life, another day to serve you and give you honor and glory. We
magnify your name and we lift you up in all righteous-
ness. We ask that you open our hearts and our ears so that
we may hear the Word that will come forth this morning.
I don't know who needs to hear your voice this morning. I
am just the messenger. Only you know who this Word is
designed for and we pray to you right now that whoever
it is meant for, that they hear what you have to say and
that they live by your Word. In your Son's name we pray.
Amen."

"Amen," the congregation repeated.

"Open your Bibles to Romans 7:15," he said as the
sound of turning pages filled the building. When the noise
died down, he began his sermon. "Why is it, we know
what is right, but we continue to do what is wrong?" He
paused as if waiting for an answer. "Well, Romans 7:15
says, 'For what I am doing, I do not understand. For
what I will to do, that I do not practice; but what I hate,
that I do. If, then, I do what I will not to do, I agree with
the law that it is good. But now, it is no longer I who do
it, but sin that dwells in me. For I know that in me (that
is, in my flesh) nothing good dwells; for to will is present
with me, but how to perform what is good I do not find.
For the good that I will to do, that I practice. Now if I do

what I will not to do, it is no longer I who do it, but the sin that dwells in me.'

"Verse twenty-one goes on to say, 'I find then a law, that evil is present with me, the one who wills to do good. For I delight in the law of God according to the inward man. But I see another law in my members, warring against the law of my mind, and bringing me to captivity to the law of sin which is in my members. O wretched man that I am! Who will deliver me from this body of death? I thank God—through Jesus Christ our Lord! So then, with the mind I myself serve the law of God, but with the flesh the law of sin.'"

Pastor McKinley looked up from the scripture. "Now this tells us why we continue to sin, even though we know it's wrong. It's temptation. As long as we live we will struggle with sin. We will struggle with making righteous choices in our lives. But because Jesus died on the cross, we have a chance to repent.

"Romans 12:1 says, 'I beseech you therefore brethren, by the mercies of God, that you present your bodies a living sacrifice holy, acceptable to God, which is your reasonable service.' Verse two, 'And do not be conformed to this world, but be transformed by the renewing of your mind, that you may prove what is that good and acceptable and perfect will of God.'

"Now when you think of the word 'sacrifice' you may think of death because back in the Old Testament, when someone offered a sacrifice to God, it seemed to always involve the death of animals." Pastor McKinley smiled. "But this is a different type of sacrifice. Yes, it still involves dying, but not the type you may be thinking of. Becoming a *living* sacrifice means dying to *yourself* and living for Christ. You must rid yourself of your old worldly ways once you become born again.

"Romans 6:1 says, 'What shall we say, then? Shall we continue in sin that grace may abound? Certainly not!'" he shouted. "'How shall we who died to sin live any longer in it?'" He looked out into the congregation. "How can you?" he asked. "How can you come to church on Sunday, repent of the things you did during the week, and then go back out into the world and do it all over again? Once you are a part of this family, you are forever a member of this family. Yes, you may stray, but it is your responsibility to die to the worldly ways of sin and follow God's commandments for your life."

"Amen," several members shouted.

Marques listened intently. He knew that there would be a message for him today. That had been one of the main reasons he'd asked Shimone if he could join her. Pastor McKinley had a way of hitting the nail on the head for someone any time Marques heard the man speak. He was glad that he had come, if he hadn't, he would have missed out on his wake-up call.

"And once you have become born again, you have to start acting like a Christian. You have to become *Christlike*," Pastor McKinley continued. "You cannot go around doing the same things: partying, cheating, lying, sexual immorality, holding grudges against people who've done wrong to you. If you are born again, you become conscious of everything you do. You can't go on sinning with a clean conscious. If you have the love of Christ in your heart, you can't hold a grudge because love does not keep record of wrongs. If someone has done you wrong, forgive them and let it go. If you are afraid to let it go because you want to protect yourself from it ever happening again, just read Romans 8:14–16, 'For as many as are led by the Spirit of God, these are sons of God. For you did not receive the spirit of bondage again to fear, but you received the spirit of adoption by whom we cry out, 'Abba, Father. The Spirit Himself bears witness with our spirit that we are children of God.'

"So, if you are afraid and need help turning your back on the world, just call out 'Abba, Father!' Get on your knees . . ."

The crowd began to get wound up as Pastor McKinley kneeled on the floor and looked toward heaven with his Bible held in the air.

"Get on your knees and shout out, 'God help me! Take this fear away from me, Lord. Help me to do your will, not the will of man. Teach me your ways. Free me of this fear, Jesus.'"

"Hallelujah." The congregation shouted out praises as they stood to their feet.

"If you are afraid to let go of that lover you've been creeping around with, if you can't seem to put down that bottle of liquor or that cigarette, or if you are afraid to let someone into your life because they have done wrong against you in the past," Pastor McKinley said, still on his knees, "shout out to God, 'Take it, Lord!' "

"Take it, Lord!" several members repeated. "Take it, Jesus!"

"Oh, I'm talking to somebody today," Pastor McKinley said as he got up off of his knees and walked across the pulpit. "By not letting certain people in your life, you can ultimately change the path your life takes in the future. That person, who caused you hurt five, ten, twenty years ago, can cause you joy, happiness, and peace right now!"

Shimone nodded in agreement as she absorbed every word that came out of her pastor's mouth. She knew God would be looking out for her. He knew she needed assurance on her feelings for Tyler. This morning, Pastor McKinley's message said it all. She needed to let go of the past and grab on to whatever the future may hold for her and her family, her father included.

"Somebody's getting it, Lord," Pastor McKinley said, looking toward heaven as he began to jump in place. "Do not let your bitterness keep you from doing what God has set in your heart for you to do," he continued, wiping his forehead with a white handkerchief. "Do not let worldly desires get you off of the path that will lead you to the face of the Almighty."

As Pastor McKinley continued with his message, Shimone and Marques looked at each other. Their smiles let each other know that they had received the word they had come for. Fifteen minutes later, Pastor McKinley was holding an altar call. He called Shimone up to sing a soft melody as several members and visitors walked up to the front to receive or come back home to Christ. Marques didn't hesitate in walking toward the front of the church when Pastor McKinley called for those who wanted to renew their faith.

As Shimone continued to sing "We Fall Down" by Donnie McClurkin, tears fell from her eyes. Seeing Marques walk to the front of the church to rededicate his life to Christ made her want to drop the microphone and start shouting. She had been waiting a long time to see him make that walk again, and the day had finally come. When Marques saw her tear-filled eyes, he smiled and winked at her as she continued to sing.

Soft music played as more than thirty people accepted Jesus into their lives. Marques stood among them, lifting his hands in praise and thanks to God for giving him a second chance. This time he was going to do things right. And after getting right with God, he was going to try his luck with Shimone.

Chapter 19

Imani sat at the computer in her room, proofreading her report for her advanced biology class. She pressed the save button and exhaled when she knew she was finally finished. After printing her report, she sprawled across her bed and relaxed as she reflected on the events that had recently occurred in the lives of her friends.

After the finalization of her parents' divorce, Nicole released all of her anguish onto Imani's shoulder. And after hearing the verdict of his father's case, Ronald relished in the knowledge that Malcolm wouldn't be seeing the outside world for several years. Although Nicole didn't seem too happy about the sentence, Imani assured her it was for the best.

Imani was glad that things were starting to get back to normal in her friend's life. But over the past two weeks, she had been having some internal struggles of her own. Imani wasn't sure if she should turn to Nicole with her problems because she knew her friend would just go with whatever decision would make her happy, without really offering her own opinion. And she definitely couldn't go to her sister because she would only ridicule her for her thoughts. She'd considered going to her parents, but her mother would probably break down in tears and her father . . . no, she couldn't go to them either. She'd just have to solve this on her own.

Ever since Eddie had gone off to college, Imani had been feeling that something was missing in their relationship, but she couldn't quite put her finger on it. She took time out to evaluate her relationship with Eddie and she couldn't find anything wrong. That was until a few weeks ago, when she overheard a couple of her dance teammates talking about their relationships with their boyfriends.

"Yeah, girl," one girl had said to another. "Me and Bobby be tearin' it up when my parents ain't home," she'd said with a proud smile on her face.

"I know what you mean," the other girl said. "Ayin and me did it for the first time a couple of months ago, and now it's like we can't even stop. It's like our relationship is even better with sex in the mix."

"I know," the first girl agreed. "It's like expressing love on a whole 'nother level." She smiled with a gleam in her eyes. "And, girl, my man really loves me." They laughed.

That conversation had been on Imani's mind for the last couple of weeks. She'd tried to get it out of her head, but it wouldn't leave. It had been occupying all of her thoughts. She had been thinking about it so much that she'd had several dreams of what it would be like to actually be intimate with Eddie. She had expressed her feelings to him in a phone conversation last weekend after coming home from Malcolm's trial.

"Why are you so quiet?" he had asked her.

"I don't know," Imani replied. "Just thinking about some things."

"Hopefully, it's about me," he said.

She sighed. "If only you knew."

He became serious. "Faith, is something wrong?"

"I wish," she said quietly. "But everything is just perfect."

Eddie was confused. "Am I missing something here? What's wrong with perfection?"

"Nothing," she said, "but do you feel something is missing in our relationship?"

"Like . . . ?"

"Sex," Imani said softly.

Eddie became quiet and Imani knew he was pondering over her assumption. She was surprised at his response, though.

"Honestly, I've been thinking about that, too, but I don't necessarily think that it will enhance our relationship. And I don't want to put any pressure on you to do anything that you don't want to do. I also know that we both are Christians, but it seems like we are planning to compromise our relationship with God just to fill some empty spaces in our relationship."

"I'm not saying that I want to do anything now," Imani defended. "I'm just telling you that I've been thinking about it."

"Well, I'm just telling you," he replied, with softness in his voice, "I know that we know what's right and what's wrong, but there is a difference between what we *feel* is right and what we *know* is right."

"I know," she said quietly as if an adult were reprimanding her.

"But like I said before, I'm not putting any pressure on you to do anything. Just know that whatever happens in this relationship happens."

"Okay," she said, slightly amused by the seriousness in his voice. "I don't want to put any pressure on you either."

"Good. Well, I have to go," he said. "I have to study for a test on Monday."

"Okay, I'll let you go," Imani said.

"I love you, Faith." His voice was soft on her ears.

Imani smiled. That was the first time he'd said those words and it made the need to fill the gaps in their relationship more urgent. "I love you, Eddie," she said, her voice matching his.

That conversation replayed in her head, even in her dreams. She couldn't get over the fact that Eddie wasn't turning down the option of a sexual relationship, but he was also throwing in the realization that their actions would have consequences. She could tell that he wanted to explore that side of their relationship just as much as she did, but he didn't want to have to compromise his relationship with God as much as she didn't. Now she was more confused than ever. Maybe she should talk to someone.

Imani rolled off of her bed and walked across the hall toward her sister's room. She remembered a time when she couldn't wait for Nevaeh to get her own apartment, but at times like these, Imani appreciated the fact that her sister was within three feet of her on a daily basis. Imani hesitated before knocking, then opened the door slightly. Nevaeh was on the phone, but motioned for her sister to come in anyway.

"Well, just talk to them both, but at different times," Nevaeh was saying. "You should probably talk to your mom first. Don't tell her about his plans to ask, just see if she has been thinking about marriage or if she feels like she's ready to make that big step. Then you can take her feelings back to Tyler and tell him whether or not he should wait, or if he should pop the question." Nevaeh paused. "Okay, tell my niece I said hello and I love her . . . That's what friends are for . . . Love you, too, girl . . . Al-

right, bye," Nevaeh hung up the phone and smiled at
Imani. "What's up?"

"I need to talk to you about something," Imani said.
"Are you busy?"

"Nope," Nevaeh said, closing her poetry book that
Imani figured she had been working in before Shimone
called. "What's on your mind?"

"A lot of things." Imani sat on the edge of Nevaeh's
bed. "Eddie and I were talking the other day and I told
him that I had been thinking about taking our relationship to the next level—"

"What *next level*?" Nevaeh said, looking as if she was
ready to give a lecture.

"Please, let me finish before you start yelling at me,"
Imani said, rolling her eyes. "Like I was saying, we were
talking about it on the phone and he was saying that he
wasn't going to pressure me, but we as Christians should
think things through before acting on them. I was confused because it seemed like he wanted the same thing,
but then again he didn't want to do anything that would
make God upset with us."

Nevaeh shook her head and laughed. "Y'all children
are a mess."

"*Children*?" Imani said, sounding offended. "Don't forget you went though the same *exact* thing at this *exact*
same age."

"I know, I know," Nevaeh smiled. "But I'm grown now
and so is Ronald. We are both saved and we know that
when we are together, there are boundaries that should
never be crossed."

"Me and Eddie are saved too, and we also know that
there is a line that shouldn't be crossed, but what if it
feels right."

Nevaeh looked at her baby sister. "Mani, there's a difference in something that *feels right* and something that *is*

right. You have to figure out which it is. Something that *feels* right can be *very* wrong."

"But Nev, you just don't know how he makes me feel," Imani said, trying to be as convincing as she possibly could. "He is so gentle and loving. And his voice is so . . . so calming and . . . sexy. And he calls me '*Faith,*' " Imani said, falling, dramatically, across her sister's bed.

Nevaeh smiled. "Girl, that's just that English version of your name, but if it makes you feel special, then I guess it is kind of nice. But the only thing you are feeling is love. You don't have to sleep with someone to show them that you love or care for them. And you seem to be trying to find something to justify your thoughts, but there's nothing that you are going to be able to do to convince me or anyone else why you'd do something you think *feels* right, when you *know* it is wrong."

Imani sat up and looked at her sister. She knew Nevaeh was right, but she didn't feel any different than she had before. She still wanted to explore her sexuality and she wanted to experience it with Eddie. She felt like crawling into a ditch just to get away from all of the confusion her heart and head were feeling. Imani knew what was right, but she didn't know if she would do what was right or if she would do what felt right to her. For now, though, she'd let her sister believe that she'd changed her feelings on the issue.

"Thanks, sis," Imani said as she got off of the bed. "I think I know what to do now."

"Glad I could help," Nevaeh said as her phone rang. She picked it up. "Hello?"

The smile on her sister's face let Imani know that Ronald was on the phone and it was definitely time to leave before the conversation started to get too sappy. Imani walked out of the room and closed the door. She walked into her room and picked up her cell phone.

Scanning her contacts list, she found Eddie's number and pressed the button that would connect her to him. As the phone rang, she felt her heart pulling her in two different directions. She didn't know if she should hang up before it was too late or if she should set her mind on her goal.

"Hello?" Eddie's deep voice made her go for the goal.

"Hey, it's me," she said, her voice quiet and soft.

"What's goin' on?" he asked.

"I was just wondering . . ." Imani couldn't find the words.

"Yeah?" Eddie urged.

"Umm . . . I was just calling to ask . . ." Imani hated that she couldn't force the words out of her mouth. She had decided to do this, but now she was losing her confidence.

"Faith, what is it?" he asked softly, like he thought something was wrong.

"Oh . . . you are not making this easy," she groaned.

"What is it?" he asked again, seeming to grow impatient, but his voice not showing it.

"I wanna do it," she said softly, almost laughing at the way she'd said it.

"Do . . . what?" Eddie said, obviously confused.

Imani felt like an idiot. She couldn't believe she was actually doing this, over the phone at that. She took a deep breath. "You know . . . what we talked about last week . . . *it*," she said, hoping she wouldn't have to spell it out for him.

Eddie was silent for a moment and Imani didn't rush him to respond to her proposition. "Are you sure?" he finally asked quietly.

"Yeah . . . I think so," she spoke, following suit and lowering her voice.

Eddie seemed to be thinking it over. "I don't know if you are. I mean, I know what I want," he said suggestively. "But I'ma let you think it over some more and then we'll talk about it when you are positive."

"Eddie."

He laughed at the whine in her voice.

"I'm serious," she said. "I've been thinking about it for the longest. You see how hard it was for me to tell you."

"I know." He chuckled softly. "That's why I'm saying if it happens, it happens. I don't want to plan anything because anything planned can go wrong. If we do anything, I want it to be something that just happens because we know it's the right time, not something we sat down and mapped out, play by play. You feel what I'm sayin'?"

"Yeah, but I wish you would've said something sooner so I wouldn't have had to force myself to tell you that I wanted this."

Eddie laughed. "I knew what you were going to say before you even said your first word. It was just fun to hear you sweat it out like that. But I think that we should just stay where we are right now, and when the time is right, we'll *both* know."

"Okay," she said. "But what about the consequences you talked about last time?"

"I know this sounds kind of stupid, since we both know that what we are thinking about doing is wrong, but if we do take it to the next level, we will have to handle the consequences as they come."

Imani knew that they were compromising their religious convictions, but she knew that she wanted this and nothing could stop her. "Okay, Eddie," she said, softly, in a sing-song manner.

He laughed. "Why you say my name like that?"

"What . . . 'Eddie?'" she asked. "It's the same way you say 'Faith.' "

"No, you said, '*Eddie*." He mimicked her soft feminine

voice. "I say . . . '*Faith,*'" he said, his voice deeper and softer than ever before, causing her to blush.

"Eddie," she said seriously, but with gentleness still in her tone.

"Yes, *Faith,*" he teased.

"Okay, I'm getting off of the phone, now," Imani said, feeling as if she wanted to jump through the phone line and take him into her arms, then and there.

"Imani?" he said before she could hang up.

"Yes?" she said, surprised that he actually used her real name.

"I love you." Eddie could envision her face turning red.

She smiled. "I love you, too, Edward."

He laughed. "Now, you know I don't like that."

"Well, I do. It sounds strong . . . and sexy." She smiled.

Eddie could feel the heat rising to his face. "Just like my Faith," he said.

"I think it's time for me to get off of the phone now," she said, knowing that with each compliment, they were further pushing the limits of temptation. "Bye, Eddie."

He chuckled softly. "Bye, *Faith,*" he said before hanging up.

Imani hung up the phone with a huge grin on her face. *Faith.* She loved it. Every time he said it, his voice would become soft and melodious, causing her to experience emotions she'd never felt before. She hoped that if they did begin to have a sexual relationship, that they wouldn't regret it. She loved the Lord and wanted to please Him, but this was something that she wanted to do, and she didn't want to turn around now. No, she wanted to give her virginity to her first love and she was sure she'd do it soon.

Chapter 20

LaToya sat in the living room of her apartment with Jabari as they waited for Jamal to arrive with Jayson. Sierra had just left with Corey to give the family some time alone. This would be Jabari and Jayson's first official play date and LaToya felt like calling Jamal and telling him that she wanted to cancel. She had spent the last few weeks trying to convince herself that everything would be all right, but her attempts had been in vain. She didn't even know why the whole situation was bothering her as much as it was. She had nothing against Jayson and all of her anger toward Jamal for not telling her about his son sooner had dissolved. She didn't know if she was so apprehensive because Jayson was really not her son or if it was just the simple fact that she hadn't been Jamal's first.

The latter couldn't be the reason because Jamal had been sexually active before meeting her or Kim, so the fact that Kim had been with him before her wasn't an issue. Besides, Jamal had not been LaToya's first either. She had lost her virginity in her junior year of high school to a guy she had been dating for several months.

And the fact that Jayson wasn't her son wasn't bothering her either; she had her hands full with Jabari. She just couldn't put her finger on the reason behind her apprehension, and it was causing her to become more perturbed.

Jabari pulled himself up to a standing position and walked over to his mother. LaToya smiled at her son. He had become her reason for living, and if anything ever happened to him, she didn't know what she'd do. Maybe that was it. She didn't want her son to suffer any type of loss because of Jayson's entrance into their lives. She didn't want Jabari to have to share his father with someone else. She didn't want Jamal to show favoritism, especially if Jayson was the favorite. She didn't want her son to feel as if he was less important now that there was someone new in their lives. She prayed that Jamal would take that into consideration.

LaToya rose to her feet when she heard a knock at the door. She took a deep breath before answering it. *Lord, please let this work out*, she prayed. When she opened the door, she plastered a smile across her face as she greeted her guests. Jamal stood on the other side of the door with Jayson, who, as always, was clinging to his father's leg.

"Hey," Jamal said as he walked into the apartment, pulling Jayson in with him. He leaned down and kissed LaToya's cheek.

"Hey," she said with her smile still in place. *God please let this work.*

Jamal looked down at Jayson who looked like he wanted to run out of the house to get away from these strange people. "Jayson, this is Ms. LaToya," Jamal introduced. "Say hello," he said, nudging his son.

"Hi," Jayson said quietly as he lowered his eyes.

LaToya could sense the boy's uneasiness and it made

her feel better knowing that she wasn't alone. She knelt in front of him and smiled. "Hi, how are you?"

"Fine," he said with his eyes still lowered.

LaToya stood, looked at Jamal, and then at her son, who was standing by the sofa studying the boy who was still clinging to his father's leg. She walked over to Jabari and pulled him toward his brother. Both boys stood there staring at each other as if they knew that they were being set up for something.

Jamal gazed at LaToya, and she was sure he could see the nervous look in her eyes. But he resumed with the introductions. "Jayson," he said as he took hold of Jayson's hand. He looked at LaToya for reassurance. When she nodded, he continued, "This is your brother, Jabari." He nudged Jayson toward Jabari.

Jayson walked forward, looked at Jamal, back at Jabari, and then back at his father again. "*My* brother?" Jayson asked, pointing to himself as if he was trying to get the information right.

When Jamal nodded, Jayson looked at LaToya for confirmation. LaToya probably would have almost laughed at the expression on the child's face if she weren't so anxious. After she nodded in agreement, Jayson stepped closer to Jabari and studied his face.

LaToya could see the anxiety etched across her boyfriend's face, and she could tell that he wasn't sure if his oldest son would dismiss his youngest or if Jayson would accept Jabari into his life as his sibling. LaToya held her breath and prayed silently as Jayson continued to study Jabari's face.

After a moment of hesitation, Jayson took Jabari's hand, smiled, and said, "Bari come play?" Jayson sat on the floor and Jabari sat with him.

As LaToya released a sigh of relief, Jamal did the same

and handed Jayson his bag of toys. Jayson pulled out two trucks. As the boys began to play, LaToya felt her own worries going away. She thanked God that the boys hadn't started to cry or fight for Jamal's fatherly attention. She felt that everything might just work out. She and Jamal sat on the sofa and watched their children.

"Thank you," Jamal said, kissing LaToya's cheek.

LaToya smiled and rested her head on his shoulder.

Nicole sat in her room in the new house her mother had purchased a few months ago. She was still taking in the fact that this house was much larger than their old one. Her room in the old house could fit inside of her new room and her walk-in closet was twice as big as the one she'd had before.

Personally, she didn't think that her family needed a house this large, especially since Ronald wasn't living with them. They had two extra bedrooms that no one used, but apparently her mother had received a lump sum of money from Malcolm's parents for her "pain and suffering" and child support that Malcolm wouldn't be able to pay due to his incarceration. The money was to be used to take care of her and her children. So, Angelica had bought this house, and at Imani's suggestion, she'd hired Eddie's mother, an interior designer, to provide furnishings and other décor for their new home.

Despite all of that, Nicole still loved the house for two reasons: one, she needed to get out of the old house to get past the emotional turmoil she had been in, and two, she was within walking distance of her best friend's equally lavish home. She loved her room even more than the house. She had chosen everything from the queen-sized bed, to the daybed that sat by one of the three windows, to the small sofa that sat against the wall adjacent to one of her windows, to the beige paint and wallpaper that covered the walls. She had chosen it all, and it made her happy to be in different surroundings.

Nicole picked up her ringing phone and glanced at the name on the caller ID—it was her father using his one phone calls to contact her for the umpteenth time this week. She sighed before muting the ringer. It had been two weeks since her father's sentencing and she was just starting to get used to not having him around. And she liked it better that way. The house was friendlier and more loving. Angelica went to work, but always came home in time to fix the family dinner. Jeremy had stopped hanging around his thuggish friends and started doing his schoolwork. And Nicole had been doing better in school and her dancing was better than ever. She had even been chosen to be one of the lead dancers in one of the pieces in the regional competition. The only thing that was holding her down was the every-other-day, phone calls her father made to her private line. He never called the main line, but would always call Nicole's line, and it was starting to bother her. She hadn't known that when she'd given her father her new number, right before he was imprisoned, that she would have to endure the suddenly annoying sound of her ringing phone. She had answered the first time the call had been placed and accepted the charges, knowing it was her father and hoping he was calling to apologize.

"Hello?" she said when the phone was forwarded back to him.

"Heyyy, baby girl," her father slurred as if he was high or drunk.

"Hi, Daddy," Nicole said timidly.

"Whatchu been up to?"

"Nothin' much." Her voice still quiet. "What about you? How are you doing?" she asked him, but soon regretted it.

"How you think I'm doin'?" his voice suddenly became

sharp with animosity. "They got me up here, locked up wit' no place to go. All I do is eat, sleep, and try to keep all these prisoners away from me. Always tryin' to jack me for somethin' and I don't know why, 'cause I ain't got a doggone thing. How you think I'm doin,' baby girl?" he questioned again. "Just take a guess. If it wasn't for you, I wouldn't be here. If it wasn't for you, I could be at home with my family," he told her harshly as she began to cry.

Tears ran down Nicole's face like a river. She couldn't understand where all of his anger and hostility was coming from. "Daddy, why are you saying this? I didn't mean for you to go to jail. I'm sorry. I wasn't even going to tell, but they made me. I'm sorry, Daddy," she said, although she didn't understand why she was apologizing.

"Yeah, you sorry alright. You always gon' be sorry. You ain't gon' be nothin.' Ain't nobody gon' want you. Shoot, I don't even want you no more. You ain't nothin,' you hear me?" he yelled into the phone.

Nicole had hung up and cried into her pillow. She'd never heard her father speak in that tone before. He always spoke correct English and tried to be as professional at home as he was at work, but for some reason he sounded like one of the young boys she went to school with and she didn't like it at all. It was as if something evil had taken over his body and changed him from the honest, loving man he used to be a few years ago. She wished she could take back all that had occurred. She wished she hadn't gone to the house that night. But there was no point in wishing, she'd just have to endure the repercussions of her actions.

Since that phone call, Malcolm had called Nicole about five times. She didn't know why he was calling and she didn't want to find out. So anytime "new call" showed up in her caller ID, she completely ignored it. She hadn't told anybody that he called her continuously because she knew it would only cause more trouble.

Once again her phone rang, and she frowned when she noticed an unfamiliar number on her caller ID.

"Hello," she greeted cautiously, unsure of who would be on the other end.

"Wassup, Kiki?" Shawn greeted as if everything was cool between them.

Suddenly, Nicole wished it were the automated voice. She hadn't heard from Shawn in almost a month, and she wondered how he'd gotten her new number. She hadn't said a word to him since she saw him and Sheila in the hallway together. She had seen him around school, but he hadn't even approached her. He probably figured that he was no longer in a relationship with her, but Nicole had heard through the grapevine that he and Sheila had been hanging out together since school started. She couldn't believe he had been playing her from the beginning.

"How'd you get my number?" she asked, just as she had the first time he'd called her months ago.

Shawn laughed. "Not from Imani."

She wasn't in the mood for his games, so she left the situation alone. "What do you want?" Nicole asked, attitude sharp on her tongue.

"Dang, can't a man call his woman once in a while?" he said, making Nicole even angrier.

"Once in a while is right," she snapped. "And you must got me confused with Sheila, 'cause if I am your woman, I can't tell. Especially with Sheila all up in your face."

"What you talkin' 'bout? Sheila ain't been up in my face," he replied defensively.

"Oh you're right," she said sarcastically. "That must

have been you all up in hers. But it doesn't even matter, and just know that you have been cut," she said harshly.

"*What?*" Shawn questioned in surprise. "Girl, you must don't know who I am. I'm Shawn Maurice Underwood and I *never* get cut."

"Wow, you can say your whole name. Can you spell it too?" Nicole mocked. "You act like that makes you somebody, because you're letting me know you are who you are. You are nobody to me. And apparently you do get cut, since I just cut you. There's always a first time for everything," she said.

"So what if you cut me. People at school ain't gon' believe you."

Nicole laughed. "Shawn, you act like I really care if people believe that I broke up with you. I really don't care if you tell them that you broke up with me. I don't care if you tell them that I cried and begged for you to stay with me. I seriously couldn't care less if you tell them that I tried to commit suicide because I thought I couldn't live without you. You can tell them what ever you want. As long as I am finally rid of you, everything will be all good."

Shawn smacked his teeth. "Whatever. I was callin' here to give to you a second chance since you wanted to act like you ain't know me for the past month. But I've decided that we're better off separate. You think you somebody special, but you ain't. If I don't want you, who else will? You ain't ever gon' be nobody and nobody ain't gon' ever want you," he said, causing tears to form in the corner of her eyes as she suddenly heard her father's tone in Shawn's voice. "You ain't nothin,' " he spat.

Nicole hung up in his face and quickly dried her tears. Quite frankly, she was tired of people telling her that she was nothing and nobody wanted her. She'd been battling a sense of worthlessness for so long that having others reinforce it made the feeling more real. She got up from her bed and walked swiftly into the bathroom. Leaving the lights off, she turned on the faucet and splashed water onto her face. Looking into the mirror, she saw a glimmer of metal. She reached for the razor she had shaved her legs with earlier that morning. Holding it in her hands, it sparkled in the dark room. With tears still running from her eyes, she placed the cold metal against her wrist. Suddenly, her tears froze and her eyes opened wide at the sight before her. *Put the razor down*, her head said. *This is not worth it. You are somebody and someone does want you.*

Please, My child, don't do this. Come to Me. I want you.

She heard her thoughts and the words of God, but her brain shut down and she blocked them out. She held her breath as she slid the razor across her arm. She watched as the blood was released from her vessels. She exhaled as a sudden peace swept through her body. She relished in the feeling. She had wanted to feel peace for a long time, and she finally got what she had been longing for. After making two more cuts, she wrapped a bandana around her wrist, placed her razor on the countertop, and walked out of the dark bathroom.

Chapter 21

November 4

It had been six months since Eddie had asked Imani to be his girlfriend. Six wonderful months. And this night was a much-anticipated one. This night would be a celebration in more ways than one. It would be a celebration of the continuous emotional connection that they had shared throughout their relationship and it would also be a celebration of the beginning of their sexual bond. Imani had been preparing for this night for a long time and she was sure that tonight was *the* night.

She and Eddie were planning to have a romantic dinner at the off-campus apartment he'd decided to stay in after waiting too late to turn in his dormitory deposit. Though he paid most of the rent, his parents helped out with the utilities.

Eddie had said that if something was going to happen between him and Imani, it would happen. Imani was determined to make something happen *tonight*. Even if it wasn't the course that nature wanted to take, she had it all planned out.

Since Nicole had actually invited Imani to spend the night over her house tonight, Imani would ask her mother if she could stay with Nicole, although she had declined her best friend's offer without giving an explanation. After receiving her mother's permission, she'd have Eddie pick her up. In order to avoid questioning from her parents, she'd have to rush out of the house to keep him from coming to the door and ringing the doorbell. After that, her plan would run smoothly. *God, please don't let Nikki call over here tonight.* She wouldn't call it a prayer, but a wish that she so desperately needed to be granted.

With her mother already aware of where she would, or *wouldn't*, be this evening, but knowing that she would return tomorrow morning, Imani proceeded to get dressed. Since they weren't going to a fancy restaurant, she decided that casual dress was appropriate. She pulled on a long black jean skirt and a dark purple, button-down blouse. Knowing tonight's temperature wasn't warm enough for the thin cotton material her shirt was made of, Imani pulled out her black leather jacket. She twisted her hair up into a chic style and held it in place with a purple clip, then she slipped on a pair of three-inch, ankle-high boots and prepared herself for Eddie's arrival.

Minutes later, Imani heard a car pulling into her driveway. She peeked out of her window to ensure that it was Eddie before grabbing her coat and heading toward the door before he could ring the doorbell.

"Ma, I'm leaving," she yelled as she passed her parent's bedroom.

"Okay, sweetie, have fun," Michelle yelled back.

Suddenly, a churning feeling began to develop in the

pit of Imani's stomach. She knew it wasn't time for her cycle; she had made sure that she planned tonight around her period. She clutched her stomach as the pain grew. She wanted to get to the door before Eddie could, but was unable to move because of the aching. As suddenly as it had come, the pain left. She pushed the thought out of her mind as she quickly opened the door.

"Whoa," Eddie said as Imani rushed out of the house, almost knocking him down. "What's the rush?" he asked.

Imani stopped and breathed deeply. Smiling up at him she said, "Nothing, the . . . the door was stuck and I had to pull it open," she lied. Once again the sharp pain returned in her stomach. She moaned as she grabbed her abdomen.

"What's wrong?" Eddie asked in concern. "Are you okay?"

"Ye– . . . yeah, I'm fi– . . . fine," Imani said, holding her stomach tighter as the pain grew once again.

"Maybe we should take you inside and let your parents check it out?"

"No!" she said, quickly. Suddenly the pain disappeared as it had done before. "I'm fine. I promise." She smiled as Eddie continued to look concerned. "I'm *fine*," she stressed again. "Come on." She pulled him toward his car.

Eddie opened the door for her to get in. After shutting her door, he ran to the driver's side and climbed in. Turning on the car, he turned up the J Holiday album he had been listening to for the past week. He sang along as he pulled out of Imani's driveway and headed toward his apartment.

Imani sat quietly in the passenger's seat, which was very unusual because the song playing was one of her favorites on the album. But hearing Eddie's sweet voice sing "Suffocate" didn't help ease the queasiness in her stomach. The pain in her abdomen began to worry her. Although it was gone, she could still feel the churning of her stomach. She didn't know if it was a sign that tonight was a mistake, but she was starting to regret her plans. She was feeling a sense of guilt and deception, and she didn't like the feeling at all. Imani felt like she was going against everything she believed in and all of her convictions had become nothing more than meager promises she'd made to herself and others that she was ready to break all in the name of love. She had waited forever to be able to give herself to someone she loved and who loved her in return. Looking down at her hand, she was glad that she had removed the silver band that normally graced her ring finger, which would've been a constant reminder of her commitment to remain pure until her wedding night. She understood the importance of keeping a promise, but why should she wait if she'd already found what she'd been looking for?

Eddie looked over at Imani and smiled his wondrous smile—a smile she'd grown to love over the past six months. She pushed the feelings of guilt and deception aside. She wanted to be with Eddie and knew God would understand. She almost laughed aloud at the thought. *God will understand.* But whether He understood or not, she knew it was too late to turn back now. Eddie was pulling into his apartment complex.

He helped her out of the car. As they walked up a flight of stairs, the sickening feeling came back and Imani felt like running to a place where she knew she couldn't do any wrong. They came to a stop in front of a second floor apartment and Eddie pulled out a key to open the door. Stepping aside to let Imani enter first, he closed the door behind him. He watched as Imani admired the décor of his apartment.

His mother had personally designed his new home and Imani was impressed with the finished result. The plush cream carpet that covered the floor of every room in the apartment, with the exception of the kitchen/dining area, went perfectly with the tan leather sofa and two chairs that sat in the center of the room. The coffee table that sat in front of the sofa and the entertainment system that held a stereo system, a television, and a DVD player were all provided by his mother and her interior designing company.

"So what do you think?" he asked, walking up behind Imani.

"I . . . it's really nice." She smiled as she turned around to face him. "Your mom did a fantastic job. She really must know what you like because this room screams your personality."

"And what is that?" he asked, looking into her deep brown eyes.

Imani felt her heartbeat speed up slightly at his closeness. She cleared her throat. "Umm . . . ca– . . . calming and . . . at ease. Al– . . . always welcoming," she stammered.

He smiled as he noticed that she seemed very nervous. Changing the subject, he asked, "Would you like to take off your coat?"

Imani nodded silently as Eddie helped her out of her jacket.

"You look great," he added as he put her jacket on the coat rack that stood next to the door.

Imani smiled her thanks, afraid to open her mouth. If she did, she knew she would say something stupid. She walked over to the sofa and sat down. The cushions felt great, allowing her body to relax. She watched Eddie move into the kitchen to prepare their meal. Her edginess dispersed as she laughed when he pulled cartons of

Chinese food from his refrigerator and popped them into the microwave.

"Oh . . . you made my favorite," she joked as she walked into the kitchen.

Eddie smiled. "Girl, you know I don't cook."

She leaned against the counter. "Well, it's the thought that counts, right?"

"Exactly," he said, walking toward her. His stare was so intense it was starting to scare her, but at the same time, she was intrigued. "Faith . . . my precious Faith," he said, causing her brown face to turn deep red. "Have I ever told you how beautiful you are?"

Imani silently nodded as he came closer to her.

He caressed her face with the back of his hand. "Well, it bears repeating," he whispered as he leaned forward to kiss her.

Imani knew exactly where this was headed, and she certainly wasn't going to stop before it got there. The only feeling she felt in her stomach now was a bundle of butterflies. Eddie held her waist tightly and she clung to his neck for support as her knees weakened. The microwave beeped, signaling that the food was done warming, but neither of them wanted to interrupt the mounting passion between them.

Eddie picked Imani up in a swooping motion and carried her into his bedroom like a groom carrying his bride over the threshold. He placed her gently on his bed and she released her hair from the restraining clip, allowing her tresses to become mangled along with the sheets. She helped him out of his shirt and used her hands to explore his muscled torso. Eddie's kisses moved from her lips to her neck and toward the dip in her blouse. Imani tried to calm her senses as Eddie unbuttoned her top. He took a moment to gaze down into her eyes, as if asking if she was sure about doing this. She smiled, letting him know that she wanted this as badly as he did. They loved each other and wanted to show just how much. It seemed like this was the only way to do it. He returned her smile and protected himself as he prepared to make love to his love.

Imani lay next to Eddie who had his arms wrapped around her, something she wished he wouldn't do because she felt too impure to even be in the same room with him. Both of them were stunned into silence, not even close to believing what had just happened between them. At the time, it had felt right. Now, it seemed very wrong.

Making love to Eddie had seemed so satisfying at the time. But if Imani could take it all back, she would. As she lay in bed next to her first love, she realized that she'd made a mistake that couldn't be reversed. Silent tears ran down her face and she quickly dried them with her hands as she moved out of Eddie's strong hold.

Eddie sat up. "Faith, are you okay?" he asked, pulling strands of hair away from her face. When she flinched at his touch, he quickly moved away.

Imani continued to cry silently as she shook her head. She always thought that she'd cry after her first time, but she had imagined tears of joy.

"What's wrong?" he asked. "Did I do something wrong?"

She turned to face him. "No . . . no, it's not you. Really, it's not," she said when he gave her a skeptical look. "I . . . I just don't feel right anymore. I feel really dirty and unworthy of you right now."

Eddie was confused. "What are you talking about?"

"Eddie, I had this all planned. I had it in my head that I was going to do this once I got here, but you said you didn't want us to force each other and I did exactly what you didn't want."

He reached forward and wiped her tears, but hesitated when she flinched again. As he stared into her eyes, he tried once more to comfort her. "Faith, I knew what was going to happen tonight. I didn't plan it, but I just felt like the time was right. That's why I invited you here." He sighed. "But I do understand where you're coming from. I don't know if I really regret what happened, but I do feel like God's turned His back on me . . . on us. It's like, I'm afraid to even get on my knees and pray right now because of what just happened. Don't get me wrong, I enjoyed every minute of it." He smiled slightly. "But now that it's over, I feel unworthy of you, too, but mostly of God."

Imani wiped her tears as she sat up, making sure that the sheets were covering her naked body. "I'm sorry," she said, unable to think of anything else to say.

"Don't apologize; we're both wrong," he said. "I better take you home," he suggested, pulling on a pair of underwear before getting out of the bed.

"No!" she said. He gave her a questioning look and she lowered her eyes. "I kinda told my parents that I was staying at Nikki's and they aren't expecting me back until tomorrow morning."

His eyes budged. "What? You mean, they don't know you're over here?" Imani shook her head. "Why would you do something like that?" His tone was soft, but she could tell he was upset.

She shrugged. "I don't know. I didn't want them to start trippin' about me being at your apartment . . . alone . . . with you."

Eddie shook his head. "Well, can't I at least take you to Nicole's house?"

"Well . . . Nicole doesn't know that I'm supposed to be at her house. She asked me to come over," she explained quickly when Eddie gave her a disbelieving look, "but I told her that I couldn't without telling her that I planned on spending the evening here. So if you were to take me over there, she'd get upset because she already thinks that I neglect her to spend time with you."

He sighed. "Well, what am I supposed to do?" Imani shrugged as Eddie thought for a moment. "I guess . . . I guess it would be alright if . . . if you stayed here . . . tonight." He sounded unsure.

Imani studied his face. "Are you sure?"

"Yeah, it'll be fine," he said, more confidently. "I'll sleep on the sofa and you can stay in here." He handed her an extra large T-shirt out of his dresser.

"Are you *really* sure?" Imani asked him again.

"It will be fine," he assured as he leaned over and kissed her forehead. "I promise."

She smiled, but as he stood to gather his clothes and leave, she realized she didn't want to be alone. "Eddie?" she called him, and he turned to face her. "Would you stay?"

He hesitated before saying, "Sure." His smile was awkward, but reassuring.

"But I need a minute alone first," she requested.

"That's cool." He nodded in understanding, and she was certain he felt as if he needed to be alone for a while also.

As he proceeded down the hall to the bathroom, Imani looked down at the floor to find every piece of her clothing strewn across the room. Her top was by the mahogany dresser, her boots were on the floor near the door, and her skirt and underwear were by the chaise that sat near the window. She couldn't believe what had happened. Now that she was fully alert, she realized that she never really wanted this and she regretted every-thing. She wished she had listened to the whispers down in her soul asking her to stop before it was too late, but instead, she permitted the screams of her body to over-power her judgment.

She slipped into the shirt, Eddie had given her, before kneeling to pray. "God, I just ask that you please forgive me," she began as tears rolled down her cheeks. "I know it's kinda late to be coming to you now, but I'm so, so, so sorry. I ask that you forgive Eddie also, although I know he's probably asked you to do so a billion times already. I promise I will never do anything even remotely close to this ever again, until you send me a soul mate that I will make my husband. I pray that you will wash us clean. I love you, Lord. Amen." She stood and climbed back into the bed, pulling the sheets over her body.

Almost a half an hour later, Eddie came back into the room and accompanied her. Imani took his arm and wrapped it around her waist, wanting to feel protected.

"I love you, Imani," he whispered.

She smiled slightly. She loved when he called her "Faith," but the times he used her real name made her feel even more special.

"I love you, Eddie."

She closed her eyes and hoped that they could con-tinue to have a good relationship without falling into temptation again.

Chapter 22

Sierra rummaged through her closet, trying to find her orange stilettos. She threw boxes of shoes out into her bedroom and opened one after the other with no luck in finding the right pair. *This is why I hate having so many shoes.* Every time she went to a store, she'd have to buy a new pair, for no particular reason. So over the years, she had accumulated too many to count. Some she hadn't even worn yet, and that was because she had not found the right outfit to complement them.

"Thank you, Jesus," she said as she pulled out the box she had been looking for. She opened the box, looked down at her outfit, and then let out an aggravated scream.

LaToya ran into her best friend's room, leaving her son in the living room with his toys. "What's wrong?" she asked Sierra.

Sierra looked as if she wanted to kill someone. "I have just spent the last half hour looking through all of these stinkin' shoes trying to find these." She held up the orange heels. "And when I finally find them, I notice that they don't even match my stinkin' outfit!" She pointed to the reddish-orange evening gown she wore.

LaToya stood in the doorway and laughed. "Why is your outfit such a big deal? You haven't figured out that after four years of dating my brother, he doesn't care what you're wearing. It's always the same reaction: 'You look great,'" LaToya exaggerated with excessive hand motions. "You could show up in a pair of ripped jeans and an old college sweatshirt and you'd still look *great* to him."

"But tonight may be *the night*, Toya." Sierra sighed. "I just want it to be perfect, you know. If he is planning to propose to me tonight, I want to look so good that when he sees me, he forgets what he was planning to ask." She paused and thought about what she'd just said. "Well, not so much that he forgets totally, but I want him to be speechless."

"I understand where you're coming from," LaToya said, "but trust me, he's not going to care what you have on." She saw the pitiful look on her friend's face. "Why don't you wear that long blue gown with the silver sparkles . . . you know, that sleeveless one?"

"Toya, it is the middle of November," Sierra stated with her hands on her hips. "Do you honestly believe that I'm going to go outside with nothing on my arms?"

LaToya returned the stance and added a roll to her neck and a smack in her tone. "That's why you wear the shawl that goes with it," she said, causing Sierra to burst into laughter.

"Girl, you are crazy. But I know what you're talking about." Sierra went to her closet and pulled the dress from the back corner. "I haven't worn this since our first Valentine's Day." She held up the dress and pretended to brush dust from its shoulders.

"That'll make it even more special," LaToya said. "Now just put that one on, find some blue or silver shoes to match, and do your hair in that little fancy wrap-around thing, and you're good to go."

Sierra smiled. "Thanks."

"No problem. So you really think tonight is the night, huh?" LaToya looked skeptical. "You think he's going to be as predictable as to propose on your birthday?

Sierra shrugged. "All I know is that he's taking me somewhere special for dinner for my birthday, but I'm hoping . . . no, I'm *praying* that he asks me tonight. Shoot, I've been praying for the past year now and I know God is hearing me up there," Sierra said, looking upwards. "And it's not so much that it's my birthday, I just feel it."

"Well, good luck," LaToya said, hoping that her friend was right.

"What about you?" Sierra asked LaToya. "What do you and Jamal have planned tonight?"

"Girl, I don't even know, but I *do* know that it's going to be all of us tonight. The four musketeers."

"So little Jay is starting to grow on you?" Sierra asked as she slipped out of her dress and threw it across her bed.

"I guess he is, but it's Jabari who can't stop talking about him. All it's been is, 'Day comin'?' and 'Day play?'" she said in her best childlike voice. "And he can't even say Jay. He says 'Day,' so sometimes I don't even know what he's talking about."

Sierra laughed as she stepped into the blue gown. "Well, I'm glad you are starting to like the arrangement. I'm sure Jamal is glad too. But what about Miss Thang?" she asked, referring to Kim.

"Oh, as far as I know, she's fine with it. She hasn't con-fronted me *yet*, so I guess she's happy that we're happy. I figure she's okay as long as I don't try to steal her baby boy, and trust me, she ain't even got to worry about that 'cause I got my hands full with mine and I definitely don't have the time or the patience for another."

"O-kay," Sierra said, giving LaToya a high five. She walked into the bathroom. "Well, can you call me when my baby gets here, please?"

LaToya laughed. "Sure." She walked out of her friend's room.

Sierra put on a robe over her clothes and began to fix her hair. She gathered it piece by piece and rolled it up into a bun in the center of her head. Sticking bobby pins in her hair to hold it in place, she smiled as she admired the delicateness of her face. She said a silent prayer that if it was God's will for them to be together, Corey would propose tonight. She heard a knock at the door and waited for LaToya to call her out front before going, so she wouldn't seem too anxious.

"Sierra, get out here, girl," LaToya yelled after letting Corey in the apartment. "I know you heard this boy out here knocking for you," she said.

Leave it up to LaToya to ruin her grand entrance. Sierra applied makeup to her face, slipped out of her robe and into her silver stilettos, and grabbed her small silver purse that held nothing but a tube of lipstick, a compact, eyeliner, a small bottle of lotion, and a few mints. She walked out front to find Corey sitting on the couch playing with his nephew. Sierra held her finger to her lips to silence LaToya. She snuck up behind Corey and placed her soft, manicured hands over his eyes.

Caught off guard, Corey placed his hands atop Sierra's and inhaled her perfume. "Smells like . . . Chanel," he said, removing her hands from his eyes. He stood up and turned around to face her. "Very sexy." His eyes scanned her attire; it seemed he had to catch his breath before saying his next words. "You look . . . great," he said to LaToya's amusement.

Sierra eyed her best friend.

"I told you," LaToya mouthed.

Sierra looked back at Corey and smiled. "Thank you," she said.

"Are you ready to go?" he asked, holding out his arm.

She looped her arm with his and looked into his light brown eyes. "God, am I ever ready," she whispered.

The band played in the background as she and Corey danced in the empty ballroom at the Renaissance Grand Hotel St. Louis. The atmosphere couldn't be more perfect. Dimmed lights, soft music, and her man. As the song came to an end, Corey stopped dancing and slid down on one knee. Sierra couldn't control the tears that immediately sprang into her eyes. He pulled a small blue velvet box from his pocket and gripped her left hand softly.

"Sierra," he began. "I love you with all of my heart. I can't imagine living my life without you by my side." He opened the box and revealed the diamond ring. "Will you marry me?"

Sierra couldn't form the words. She opened her mouth, but nothing came out. Corey waited on one knee with the beautiful ring glistening in the dimly lit room. Since she was literally speechless, she just nodded her head, silently. Corey took the ring out of the box and slipped it onto her finger. He stood up, kissed her, and they resumed dancing the night away.

The buzzing of her alarm clock startled Sierra out of her sleep. She woke up with beads of sweat dripping from her forehead and hit the "off" button on the radio. *Stupid, stupid dream* as she looked down at her finger and noticed that nothing was there. To some girls that would have been one of the most wonderful dreams to have, but to Sierra, it was a horrific nightmare. Last night had turned out to be a major disappointment.

After she and Corey left the apartment, he drove out to the Renaissance Grand Hotel. Sierra was so excited that she couldn't seem to stop moving around in the car as he drove. When they arrived at the hotel, Corey walked up to the front desk, whispered something to the man sitting behind it, and seconds later, they were being led to the large ballroom that usually was filled with people celebrating birthdays, weddings, or attending a ball of some sort. But tonight it was empty, with exception of the live jazz band that had been playing soft music in anticipation of their arrival.

Immediately, they began to dance. Sierra fell into the feel of Corey's muscular arms embracing her. She gazed into his eyes and hoped that she had transmitted the message to him: She was ready to get married. Corey seemed nervous and that made Sierra's anticipation level escalate. His anxiety had to be a good sign. What man wouldn't be nervous about asking the love of his life to marry him?

But as the night progressed, Corey showed no signs of asking any questions anytime soon. He held general conversation all night. He hadn't even brought up the subject of marriage as he usually did when they were together. Maybe Sierra had been wrong. Maybe he wasn't going to propose tonight. Or maybe he wasn't going to ask her to marry him at all. Maybe he didn't want to be with a woman who'd probably die after a few years of marriage because she'd failed to control her hormones when she was in high school. Maybe she should just forget he had ever brought the subject up.

But when Corey had pulled a jewelry box out of his

pocket while they were eating, Sierra's excitement heightened to its peek level. He didn't kneel on one knee, but who cared how he was positioned when he asked? She just wanted him to ask. The box seemed a little big, but Sierra didn't concern herself with that either. With any luck, it would be a big ring. When he opened the box and revealed the diamond-encrusted bracelet, she tried not to let her disappointment show on the outside, but on the inside, her heart broke in two and fell.

Having that dream made Sierra even more upset. She looked at her nightstand and saw the box that held the bracelet. She wanted to take it and throw it across the room, or better yet, right upside Corey's big head. She was getting tired of waiting. She was twenty-two years old, nearly finished with college, and ready to settle down. She thought Corey had been ready too. He'd said that he was, but his actions were definitely saying otherwise.

Climbing out of her bed, the smell of bacon, eggs, grits, and homemade biscuits greeted her nostrils. She wrapped her silk robe around her body and walked out into the den. *Jabari needs to learn how to put his toys away*, Sierra thought as she stepped over blocks and toy trucks. She walked into the kitchen and found Corey standing over the stove preparing Sunday morning breakfast. She pulled the robe closer to her body and cleared her throat.

Corey turned around and smiled. "Morning, sweetheart," he said like his being there was normal.

Sierra reached up and made sure her silk head wrap was still in place. "What are you doing here?" she asked with a bit of an attitude

"Cooking," Corey said, obviously unaware of her demeanor. "What does it look like?" he asked as if he thought her question was extremely foolish.

Sierra looked around the house like she had no earthly idea where she was. She turned and walked out of the kitchen toward her best friend's room like she needed to be reassured that she wasn't in the wrong apartment or just having another silly dream.

"Toya's not here," Corey's voice stopped her. "Jamal came by and took her, Jabari, and Jayson out for an early breakfast. They are planning to come to church with us this morning."

Sierra walked back into the kitchen as Corey began to prepare two plates of food for them. She stood, staring at him. He was dressed in a pair of khaki slacks and a blue polo shirt. He looked gorgeous in his casual wear and she wished, now more than ever, that he had popped the question last night.

He turned and smiled at her. His smile looked a little mischievous and she couldn't figure out why, but she knew today was not going to be a normal day. "Come eat with me," he said, holding out her chair.

Sierra shook her head. "I need to go get dressed . . . and I need to wash my face and brush my teeth."

"Girl," he said when he noticed that she looked uncomfortable with her appearance, "you act like I've never seen you look like 'the morning after.' " He laughed. "You look fine. Now come sit down and eat."

Sierra walked over to the chair he was holding for her and sat down to the breakfast that he had prepared. After saying grace, they began to eat in silence. As he ate, Corey would look up at Sierra and smile, only when she took a sip of her grape juice, which he had poured in wine glasses. She would return the gesture and then give him a strange look. As she continued to eat, she wondered if he was up to something. A passing thought teased her mind, and she looked into the glass of grape juice and tried to figure out if he just might have placed a piece of jewelry in it, amongst the small cubes of ice. Not seeing any glimmer of a sparkling rock, she placed her glass down and didn't bother to touch any more of her food. She pushed away from the table and walked out of the kitchen.

"Baby, where are you going?" Corey asked as she walked into her bedroom.

"I'm no longer hungry. I'm getting dressed." She slammed the room door and fought oncoming tears.

By the time she'd finished getting ready for church, LaToya and Jamal had returned with the boys, who were dressed in Girbaud outfits identical to their father's. As they prepared to leave, Corey's ignorance to the fact that Sierra was upset only made her angrier. She continued giving him the silent treatment as they piled into his Navigator and headed to church.

Throughout the worship service, Sierra resisted the urge to burst into tears. She couldn't believe that after four years of a blissful, though sometimes trying relationship, it was all about to end just because, after all, Corey didn't want to commit himself. She should have known better. What man would want to spend the rest of his life with her? She was carrying the virus of a deadly disease. That was reason enough for any man to pass her by. Part of her actually understood why Corey had decided not to make a full, lifetime commitment to her. She should just be happy that he was still dating her despite her health. Sierra knew that she should be content with what they shared now, but, honestly, she wanted more.

When worship service ended, Sierra hadn't noticed that Corey had slipped from his seat next to her until she saw him in the pulpit standing next to the presiding pastor. As the pastor handed Corey the microphone, Sierra cast a sidelong glance at LaToya, who only shrugged as she pulled Jabari back onto her lap to keep him from playing around with Jayson during the service. Sierra turned her attention back to Corey who now held everyone's interest.

Corey smiled as he began. "I know everybody's wondering what I'm doing in this pulpit because most of you who do know me, know that I am not even close to being a preacher. And let me tell you now, I am *not* about to preach. So fellas, y'all can get off the edges of your seats," he said to a few of the younger brothers that sat near the front row as laughter filled the room. He cleared his throat. "I am here to say a few words about someone special in my life, who has been through so much in her short lifetime." His eyes rested on Sierra. "I'm not gonna tell all her business because I know she's already upset with me." More laughter came from the congregation. "But I pray that I can make that frown on her beautiful face turn into a smile. So I'm going to ask that she join me up here. Miss Sierra Monroe," he called, grinning as applause erupted from the congregation.

"Go girl." LaToya nudged her friend who was just sitting like she hadn't heard Corey call out her name.

Sierra slowly got up and the applause became deafening as several males among the congregation began to bark, hoot, and holler. She smiled slightly at the "compliments" as she joined Corey in the pulpit.

"Alright now, we are still in church," Corey said into the microphone and joined in the laughter. He turned and looked at Sierra, love pouring from every part of his body into hers as he held her hand. "Sierra, I know you are not happy with me right now and I think I have a way to turn that all around, but first let me tell you how wonderful you are to me.

"Knowing you since you were seven years old, I've always thought you were beautiful. You always had a smile that could light up a room and a glow that made you seem so unreal." His comments made her smile. "But I never thought we'd end up together because you always seemed to think of me as your brother and you as my little sister." He turned and smiled to the audience. "Then she got grown." They laughed and he faced her again. "And you look even more beautiful now than you did then, and I am thankful for *every* day I have to spend with you." He looked deeper into her eyes and she realized there was a double meaning to his statement. "I love you so much. You make me smile. You make me laugh. You make me feel complete and I can't imagine my life without you. I want to spend the rest of my life making you happy."

The tears of anger she'd been trying to hold back earlier now began to flow as happy ones as Sierra watched Corey kneel before her and take a small jewelry box out of his pocket. Whispers filled the sanctuary as Corey revealed the one-half karat three-stone diamond ring. Sierra covered her mouth and whispered "Oh my God," breathlessly over and over again as Corey continued his proposal.

"I know you were expecting me to ask you this last night, on your birthday, but that was way too predictable for me." He looked deeper into her eyes, which were overflowing with happy tears, and smiled. "Sierra Celeste Monroe, would you do me the honor of becoming my wife?"

It was just like her dream, only better. "Yes," she whispered. "Oh God, yes."

He slipped the ring on her finger before rising. The couple shared a lingering kiss as a roaring applause erupted in the sanctuary, filled with more than a hundred worshipers relishing in their happiness.

Chapter 23

Shimone and Ebony walked up the cobblestone walk-way and the stairs to the front door. Shimone rang the doorbell, and, seconds later, Timothy welcomed them in. Shimone had called Tyler last night and asked him if it was okay for her to stop by after her last class, which ended at two o'clock. After hearing Pastor McKinley's message series on living life as a Christian and forgiving those who have done you wrong, she felt it was time to let go of the past and grab a stronghold onto the future.

"Wassup, Shimone?" Timothy greeted her with a hug. "Where's my favorite niece?" he said

"I right here," Ebony answered, stepping from behind her mother and walking into her uncle's opened arms.

"Is that my CD blastin' up in here?" Shimone asked as she stepped into the house.

"Yep," Timothy said as he bobbed his head to the rap portion of the song. "Who you record this with?"

Shimone smiled. "That's Nova 4 Jehovah."

Timothy's eyes opened wide. "For real?" he asked as Shimone nodded.

"He was real cool about working with me, especially after he heard me sing."

"So, tell me again, why didn't you want to do this full-time?" Timothy asked with a crooked smile.

"I'm not trying to go there." Shimone chuckled while shaking her head. "Where's Tyler?"

"Oh, he went to the store like thirty minutes ago. He should be back soon," he said as he walked over to the stereo and turned up the volume and bass.

Timothy and Ebony started dancing around the house as Shimone watched them and shook her head. Timothy was singing every song on the CD, and it was apparent that the singing gene had passed him by. He strained to hit the high notes and ended up off key when he tried to carry the low tunes. But he did extremely well with keeping up with Nova 4 Jehovah's rap. Shimone walked over to the stereo and turned down the volume as one of the slow ballads began to play.

"Hey, whatchu doin'?" Timothy asked when he noticed that his off-key voice was louder than the actual CD.

"I need to ask you something." Shimone took a seat on one of the couches, pulling Ebony with her.

Timothy followed her lead. "Okay. What's up?"

She inhaled. "How do *you* feel about your dad marrying my mom?"

He gave her a strange look. "*My* dad? I could have sworn that he was your dad too," he said.

Shimone gazed nervously out of the window. "Yeah, but you've known him longer and you know him better."

"Yeah . . . so?" Timothy shrugged indifferently. "He's still your dad. I mean, even though he wasn't there for you, biologically, he's your father just as much as he is mine."

"I know," she said. "So, how do you feel about *our* dad marrying my mom?"

Timothy shrugged and leaned back into the sofa. It reminded Shimone of the way a lot of the younger boys sat, slouched back and legs wide open. "It really doesn't matter to me. I'd love for our parents to get together, but ultimately, if you don't want this, neither will they. Well, they might still want it, but they aren't going to do anything unless it makes you happy. I know Dad won't."

"Well, I've already made my decision," Shimone revealed. "I just wanted to see how you felt about it."

"Well, I'd love for you to tell Dad he could marry Ms. Misty."

"So, you wouldn't feel like she's trying to take your mother's place?"

Timothy looked at her incredulously. "Naw! I was like nine or ten months old when my mom died and I was too little to know what was going on with her cancer. Dad tells me about her sometimes, and of course I love her 'cause she's my mom and she literally gave up her life so that I could live. Dad told me that when she was pregnant with me, she refused any treatment so that I wouldn't be affected, so that's why she passed so soon after my birth. It means a lot to me that she did that, but what matters most is what she wanted and that was for Dad to move on."

Shimone looked at him. "How do you know that?"

"I was going through some old stuff like two years ago. Dad was making me clean out the garage and it was this one box with old love letters that he and my mom had written to each other. I went through all of them." He tossed Shimone a mischievous grin. "The letters were dated, and as I got closer to ones that were dated near the day my mom died, I noticed that they started to get more and more sentimental. She would write about their old times in college and how much she would miss him once she was gone. And in one letter, several weeks before she died, she was telling him that it was almost her time and that when she left, he didn't need to grieve. She wanted him to move on with his life and, when he felt the time was right, he should remarry so he'd have someone to spend his time with so he wouldn't feel so sad, I guess."

"And I'm assuming that time is now," Shimone said as she sat back.

"Exactly." Timothy nodded. "So I hope your answer is yes, because personally, I think our parents are great for each other. I've gotten to know Ms. Misty during the Sundays she goes to church with us and has dinner with us afterward. She's funny and treats me like her son already . . . threatenin' to whip me and stuff when I get out of line." He laughed. "She definitely makes Dad happy, and for that, I love her. Why not let them make it official." He got up and turned the stereo's volume back up.

This time they all started dancing and singing along. Minutes later, Tyler walked through the front door and was shocked to see his children dancing in the middle of his den. He walked past them and placed the grocery bags in the kitchen. When he returned, Ebony began dancing around him.

"C'mon, Papa," Ebony said as she moved from side to side. "Come dance," she demanded as she continued to move to the beat of the song.

"Yeah, Dad," Timothy said as he and Shimone did their rendition of the two-step.

"I don't think so," Tyler chuckled as he walked over to the stereo and lowered the volume of the music.

Timothy and Ebony continued dancing, but Shimone followed Tyler into the kitchen. "Need help?" she asked as he began to unpack the groceries.

Tyler looked up and smiled. "Sure."

Shimone picked up a bag with milk in it and another one with apples. She placed the milk in the refrigerator and handed Tyler the apples to put in the fruit bowl. She placed two jugs of orange juice in the refrigerator, and then turned toward Tyler who was placing bread in the cabinets.

"Tyler," she called his name. He faced her. "Can I talk to you for a minute?"

"Sure, sweetie," he said as he motioned for her to sit at the table. He shut the sliding doors that separated the kitchen area from the den before sitting next to her. "What's on your mind?"

"Okay," Shimone started. "I know that you have been waiting for me to give you an answer about you and my mom." Tyler nodded and she continued. "But before I tell you my decision, I need to ask you a couple of questions."

"Sure, go ahead," he said without hesitation as if he was expecting her to have questions for him.

Shimone tucked her hair behind her right ear and pulled at her lobe, bringing a smile to Tyler's face, before she began. "Okay, I want . . . I need to know . . . if you want to marry my mother because you love her, or because you want to have a better relationship with me." She paused for him to answer.

Tyler didn't miss a beat. "Shimone, I love your mother with all of my heart. When I first started thinking about asking her to marry me, I thought about the advantages and disadvantages. I knew that I would have to ask you to grant me your blessing first, and I considered that a disadvantage because I knew that you weren't too fond of me in the beginning. I knew that if you were to say no, I might as well give it up. I also knew that if you were to say yes, that it would help better my relationship with you, an advantage. So to answer your question, no, I don't want to marry your mother just to establish a better relationship with you, because my main motive is the love that I've always had for her. I consider it a benefit in asking your mother to marry me because you and I would have a better chance at becoming closer."

Shimone was satisfied with the answer he gave. She moved on to her next question. "Umm . . . what about your first wife? How do you think she would feel about you being in love with another woman and wanting to remarry?" she asked, although Timothy had just explained all of that to her.

Tyler smiled. "Nadia knew about Misty from the beginning of our relationship. She knew that I still had feelings for Misty, and she knew as much about you as I did at that time in our life. Truthfully, I didn't expect Misty to have an abortion, especially after she left our school, but I didn't think that she would actually raise you. So all I knew was that I lost my first love because I didn't want to take care of you, and that's what Nadia knew. She understood that I would probably never get over your mother, but she wanted to have a place in my life, and I allowed her to. I loved Nadia, I still do, and after she became really sick, she told me that once she was gone, she wanted me to try and find Misty. She said that God had revealed to her in a dream that Misty would be the only person that could make me truly happy after she was gone. So once she started to get really sick, she would constantly tell me not to grieve for her, but once I felt it was time, I should find someone, namely Misty, to spend the remainder of my life with."

"Wow." Shimone sat back in her chair, amazed that God had this ordained from the very beginning. Her blessing was just another part of the plan God had for their lives and she was ready to give it. "Well, I've thought about this really, really hard. I've received spiritual counseling from my pastor and others from my church. I talked to Tim about it today, and he's fine with you marrying Mama. I even talked to Mama about it without really telling her why I was asking, and she's ready to spend her life with you," she informed, looking into her father's eyes. "And I know in my heart . . . that if somebody was to come and sweep my mama off her feet"—Shimone broke into a wide grin—"you . . . would be the best man . . . for the job."

Tyler's smile matched hers. "Really?"

Shimone nodded. Tyler got up from his seat, picked Shimone up, and spun her around.

"Daddy, put me down." She giggled like a five-year-old as Tyler released her.

He stared at her with love in his eyes. *"Daddy?"* he asked.

Shimone hadn't realized that she had called him "Daddy," but for some reason, it felt natural. She smiled. "Daddy," she said as Tyler hugged her.

"I love you so much, Shimone," he said as he continued to hold her like he never wanted to let go.

She released her tears on his chest. "I love you too, Daddy," she whispered.

Chapter 24

Nicole and Imani sat in the middle of Imani's bedroom. The curtains were closed, preventing any moonlight from entering their space. Only the lamp on Imani's dresser was on, providing them with dim lighting. Nicole was staring at Imani with so much anger in her eyes that it was scaring them both. After not having talked in almost a week, Imani wanted to say something to her friend in her own defense, but she didn't have the words that would justify her actions. She had never seen Nicole like this before. She looked angrier now than she had when she caught Shawn hugged up with his ex-girlfriend. Nicole was aware of the night Imani had spent with Eddie because Imani had told her about it the next morning, but Imani's honesty hadn't changed Nicole's reaction.

Imani had called Nicole right after Nevaeh questioned her about where she had been the night before. Her wish had been granted. Nicole had not called her house that night, but Nevaeh had called Nicole. She wanted to know if the girls would want to go shopping the next day and Nicole, unknowingly, asked to speak to Imani after briefly conversing with Nevaeh. Nevaeh, confused at first, told Nicole that Imani was supposed to be at her house. When Nicole had divulged that Imani was not at her house, Nevaeh drew the only obvious conclusion. She couldn't believe that her sister had given up her virginity. After Nevaeh yelled at her, they cried and prayed together.

So now, as Nicole sat in front of her best friend with her nostrils flaring in anger, Imani wanted to apologize as she had done before, but she couldn't say a word. Finally, Nicole let her first tear escape. Imani immediately grabbed hold of her and held her close.

"I'm sorry," Imani whispered. "I'm so sorry."

"Get off of me," Nicole said through tears. "Get . . . off . . . of me!" She jerked away.

Imani watched Nicole run into the bathroom. She listened, but only heard silence before the faucet began to run. She guessed that Nicole was crying and didn't want anyone to hear her.

Imani tried hard to think of how she could make their relationship better. It was like things were reverting to the way they had been before they became close. In eighth grade, Imani had been jealous of Nicole's gift of dance. Though she herself possessed the same talent, the skill had never come as easy to Imani as it had to Nicole. Now, it seemed Nicole was jealous of Imani and her relationship with Eddie, or maybe it was just the time Imani spent with Eddie. Either way, Imani felt she could only wait for Nicole to get over it just as she'd had to do.

Imani sat in her room for about fifteen minutes before she realized that the only sound coming from the bathroom was the running faucet. She walked toward the bathroom and knocked on the door softly.

"Nikki?" Imani called. When she didn't receive an answer, she knocked again. "Nikki, open the door," she said.

Still no answer.

She knocked harder. "Nicole, open this door now!" she said more firmly.

Imani looked down at her feet as she noticed the dampened carpet. Water was seeping under the door and she guessed Nicole had turned on the faucet with the clogged drain. She began to bang on the door. "Nicole . . . Nikki . . . please open the door." When there was still no response, Imani began to panic. "Daddy! Mama! Nevaeh! Somebody please come help me!"

It sounded like a stampede of horses was coming her way as all members of her family rushed to her aid.

"What is it?" her mother asked frantically as she searched Imani's tear-soaked face.

Her father turned on the hall light. "Why is all this water on the floor?" he demanded in his man-of-the-house tone.

"Nikki . . . locked . . . bathroom," Imani said through her tears.

Nevaeh began to bang on the bathroom door. "Nicole, if you can hear me, please come open the door."

When all they heard was the sound of running water, James immediately began to thrust his large body against the door. As he did so, Michelle questioned Imani.

"What is going on?" she asked.

"She's so mad . . . at everybody. . . . She won't talk . . . to me . . . I'm sorry . . . all my . . . fault," Imani said as she soaked her mother's robe with her tears.

Finally, James burst through the bathroom door. "Oh my goodness!" he bellowed at the sight of the limp body before him.

"God no!" Imani yelled as she pushed her way past her father and into the bathroom. "God, please no!" she

cried as she kneeled next to Nicole who had blood pouring from both of her wrists onto the carpeted floor. "God
no!" she continuously repeated, noticing the razor that
sat on the floor next to Nicole.

Nevaeh pulled her sister out of the bathroom as James
lifted Nicole into his arms and carried her out of the
bathroom. "Michelle, call Angel," he said in a calm, but
emotional tone. "Call Ronald, and anybody else you can
think of. We need all the prayers we can get or this child
is not going to make it," he said as he tied two cloths
tightly around her wrists and carried her to the garage.
He placed her in the backseat of his SUV and drove out
toward the hospital, knowing that he could get Nicole
there before the ambulance could reach them.

"And Lord, we just ask that you watch over her. God,
please don't take her from us just yet. She has a mighty
work to do for your Kingdom. Just give her a second
chance, Lord. Let her come back home to you, Jesus,"
James led the prayer as Nicole's family and friends stood
in the waiting room of the hospital. "Lord, only you
know her heart and you know the reason behind this
tragedy. Lord, just please, please give her a mind to want
to be alive and to want to live for you. Father, we asked
that you bless her and keep her. Surround her with your
grace and mercy. Show her your loving kindness. In your
name we pray. Amen."

"Amen," they all said.

Michelle sat in a seat next to Angelica and consoled
her emotional friend. Shimone and Marques kept Jeremy
in the corner playing with Ebony, so he wouldn't ask too
many questions. James tried to keep Imani from breaking
down again by talking to her softly, and Nevaeh sat in
the far corner next to Ronald as she rubbed his back for
comfort. Ronald sat with his head in his hands as his right

leg continued to shake, signaling that he was extremely worried about his baby sister.

"Baby, everything is going to be okay," Nevaeh spoke softly in his ear. "God's got this all in control."

"But why would she do something like this?" he asked with his head still down. "Why would she feel the need to cut herself? I thought everything was all right."

"Ronald, I don't know why she would do this to herself," Nevaeh said, tears streaming from her own eyes for the girl she had considered a little sister for the past four years. "All I can tell you is that everything is going to be okay."

"How can you be so sure?" he asked.

Nevaeh cupped her hand around his face and raised his head so she would be looking into his tear-soaked eyes. "Because . . . I have faith," she whispered before pulling him into a loving embrace.

"Angelica McAfee?" a female doctor called out as she walked into the waiting room.

Angelica looked up and stood as the doctor greeted her with a friendly handshake.

"Hi, I'm Dr. Gleemen," she greeted.

"How's my baby?" Angelica asked as everyone crowded around, hoping for good news.

"She's doing well," Dr. Gleeman informed to their relief. "But she's not out of the woods yet. She has lost a lot of blood and she fractured her left arm in the way that she fell, I presume, so we had to take care of that also. She has a small concussion from when she passed out, so we have to run more test to make sure that the fall didn't cause any brain damage or a hemorrhage in the brain area. But other than that, she is going to be fine."

"Thank you, Jesus," Angelica said.

The doctor looked at Angelica and smiled. "Let me tell you," she said, "He is the only reason your daughter is alive. So if you started to shout right now, I wouldn't blame you," she said as they shared a light laugh.

"Doc," Ronald said, "when can we see her?"

"Well, we're already done stitching her wrists and we've placed a cast on her arm. Now we're about to run a few more tests and monitor her brain activity, and then you may be able to see her."

"Thank you," Michelle said as the doctor walked off.

They all returned to their seats and let their thoughts consume them once more. Ronald looked at Imani, who had remained seated in the corner the entire time the doctor was updating them on Nicole's condition. He walked over to her, drying his own tears, and took a seat next to her.

"Hey," he spoke softly. "You all right?"

Imani continued to cry as she had been doing for the last couple of hours. "No, it's all my fault."

"Why would you think that?" he asked as she wiped a few of her tears. "Did someone tell you it was your fault?"

She shook her head. "I just . . . know. If I would have gone to her house last weekend this would have never happened."

Ronald didn't understand. "Imani, what are you talking about?"

Imani looked up at him. "Last Friday, she invited me to spend the night. I told her I couldn't, but I didn't tell her why. It was because that night was me and Eddie's six-month anniversary and I wanted to spend that time with him. So I went to his apartment instead of going to her house. I didn't want to tell her because Nikki thinks that I spend too much time with him anyway. I did end up telling her the next morning, though, but I couldn't even finish before she got upset with me."

"What were you doing at Eddie's apartment?" he asked as if he hadn't heard anything else she'd said.

"I was planning to . . . I did . . . spend the night," she said as he gave her an admonishing look. "I know . . . please don't yell at me. Nevaeh already handled that part," she said as if Ronald was threatening to punish her.

Ronald's face held a look of disappointment. "You actually . . . ?" She nodded. "Why would you feel that you have to sleep with this guy anyway?" he asked.

Imani wiped more tears. "Because I love him . . . and because . . ." She turned to face him. "It's so hard, you know. Hearing these girls talking about how they love being with their boyfriends. I really wanted to experience that. But now I regret it so much."

Ronald studied her face. She had grown so much over the years and had developed into a beautiful, mature, young lady who had a bright future ahead of her. It disturbed him to see that she was allowing others to influence her actions. "Imani, you can't let what other people say pressure you into doing something that you know you don't want or shouldn't do. You have to listen to your own heart and do what you know is right. And all these lil' girls runnin' around out here thinking that they got something special just 'cause they having sex with their boyfriends, don't know what they are getting themselves into. Most of them will end up with consequences for their actions before graduation.

"You say you wanted to do this because you love Eddie, but if you love someone you don't try to make them do something they don't want to do," he said, placing his arm around her. "Trust me, I know. I almost lost your sister that way."

Imani smiled faintly. "Oh . . . I remember that," she said, recalling how distraught Ronald and Nevaeh were when their differences on the subject of abstinence caused them to break up.

"See," Ronald said, returning her smile. "And though we still struggle, we know what can happen if we were to pressure each other into doing something that wasn't on our list of things to do. Plus, Eddie is cool, so you definitely don't need to lose him over something as meager as sex."

"I know," she said, "and I won't. We've already talked about it and we've decided not to put ourselves into anymore compromising positions, so we won't be tempted. But it's because of my relationship with him that Nikki is in this place now."

"Stop saying that," Ronald said firmly. "Nikki . . . she is just having some issues right now that she needs to learn to handle in the right way."

"Yeah, she's dealing with a lot of issues," Imani mumbled. "She thinks no one loves her. She told me that no one cares about her and that we are all wrapped up in our own stuff that we don't realize that she needs attention."

"She said that?" he said as Imani nodded. "Why would she think something like that?"

"I don't know," Imani shrugged. "Probably because it's true," she said quietly.

They sat in silence until the doctor returned. When Dr. Gleeman came into the waiting room, Imani stood, and this time, walked over to the doctor as everyone gathered around her once more.

"Can we please see her now?" Angelica asked, hoping that their wait was over.

Dr. Gleeman smiled. "I just came to let you know that Nicole has done well with all the tests that we have given her, and you can see her now, but she has requested to see Imani Madison first," Dr. Gleeman said.

"Me?" Imani asked in surprise.

"I guess, if your name is Imani," the doctor laughed. "But she said to assure the rest of you that she feels fine, and she is thankful for your prayers."

Everyone returned to their seats as Imani followed the doctor to Nicole's room. Dr. Gleeman opened the door and Imani followed close behind her.

"Hi, I have a visitor for you," the doctor said to Nicole. She stepped aside so that Nicole would have full view of her best friend. She turned to Imani. "You can only stay a few minutes." She walked out of the room to give them some privacy.

"Hey," Imani said quietly as she stood by the door.

"Hi," Nicole replied.

Imani walked slowly over to the bed and looked at her friend. Tubes ran into Nicole's arms, bandages covered her wrists, a cast swathed her left arm, and monitors tracked her heart and brain activity.

She touched Nicole's right hand. "I'm so sorry," she said, tears springing into her eyes.

"Why didn't you just tell me that you and Eddie had plans that night instead of lying *to* me, and then turning around and lying *on* me? Telling your mom that you were at my house when you were really at Eddie's apartment. Even if you would have told me that you had plans to go to Eddie's, but you wanted for me to cover for you if your mom happened to call, I would have done that."

"I'm sorry," Imani said again. "I didn't want you to think that I was blowing you off for Eddie, which I know I was, but I really wanted to spend that night with him. I'm so sorry."

Nicole softened her eyes and her voice. "No, I'm the one who should be sorry," she said as her eyes began to get watery also. "I should be able to understand that you aren't going to be able to spend all of your time with me. You have a man—someone who is going to want to spend time with you—and I should be able to handle that without having someone think I should be in a mental institute."

Imani's eyes opened wide. "They're going to put you in a mental institute?"

Nicole shook her head. "Worse. They are making me see a therapist. Somebody who is going to try to get all up in my business and try to tell me how I feel about myself when I already know that I'm worthless."

"Nikki, why do you continue to say that?" Imani asked, almost to the point of being aggravated with her friend's low self-esteem. "Who is telling you that you are not worth anything and that no one cares about you?"

Tears began to roll down Nicole's cheeks and onto her pillow. "My daddy," she cried. "He calls me every day now. I haven't even talked to him since the first time he called. He put me down so bad that I just had to hang up on him. He was talking about how it's my fault that he's in jail and how nobody will ever want me and how he didn't even want me anymore."

"How did he get your new number?" Imani asked.

"I stupidly gave it to him," Nicole sniffled.

"Have you told your mother about this? About his calls?" Imani asked, not believing that Malcolm would have the nerve to do something like that.

"No," Nicole said. "I just wanted to forget about it."

"Nikki, you need to tell somebody. He's harassing you and it needs to stop. He's only saying those things to make himself feel better about what he did. He is feeling down on himself, so he calls you and harasses you because he knows that it will affect you. And that's what you are doing . . . letting what other people say and do affect who you are." Imani realized that she was talking about herself, also. She'd been allowing the opinions and beliefs of others to influence her decisions, and it was time for that to end, too.

"I know, but it wasn't even him who had started to make me feel really bad about myself. It was Shawn. He called about a week after my dad first called. I still don't know who gave him my number, but I figured it was probably one of the dancers. I know all he has to do is sweet-talk them and he gets whatever he desires." She rolled her eyes. "But anyway, he started talking a bunch of mess and then when I told him that we were through, he started saying the same stuff my dad had said to me." She closed her eyes. "That's when I first cut myself," she said softly.

"Girl, Shawn ain't worth a rusty penny and I should've never tried to hook y'all up." She shook her head. "But why are you letting what he says get to you. He's just mad because *you* broke up with him instead of it being the other way around. Nicole you are the most wanted . . . the most *needed* person I know. If you weren't, do you think that all of your family and friends would be out in that waiting room, praying for your life right now? We all need you, Nikki, especially me." Imani looked down at Nicole's wrists. "What made you think this was going to make it all better?"

Nicole shrugged. "I didn't think that. I wasn't even planning to do it the first time, after Shawn called me. I just saw the razor and it seemed like my only option. And when I did it, it made the emotional pain I was feeling go away." She sighed. "Tonight, I just went too far to get rid of the pain. I kept cutting myself until the sight of the blood on my wrists made me pass out."

Imani shook her head, slowly from side to side. "I just never thought . . ." Her voice drifted. "Are you going to keep doing this to yourself?"

"I don't think so," Nicole replied. "I can't stand being in hospitals. If cutting is going to land me in another one, it's not even worth it."

"Thank goodness." Imani smiled.

They were silent for a moment, and then Nicole said, "You know I never did let you finish telling me about your special night. So did you and Eddie really . . . ?"

Imani smiled from the memory. "Yes." Nicole gasped. "But we're not going to anymore."

"Oh . . . was it bad or something?"

Imani laughed. "No, it wasn't bad . . . it wasn't bad at all. But afterward, we just felt kinda dirty—like how Adam and Eve felt when they ate that fruit. It felt like we realized that we had no clothes on, and we were out in the open for God to see. It felt horrible."

"Well, I'm glad you've decided not to do that anymore."

"Me too." She sighed. "Well, I'm going to go. I'm sure your mother is dying to see you." She leaned down and kissed Nicole's forehead. "When you get out of here, and I hope that is very, very soon, we'll go to the mall and spend all of my dad's and your brother's money."

"Promise?" Nicole said, holding out her pinky finger.

Imani entwined her pinky finger with Nicole's. "Promise," she said.

Chapter 25

Jayson and Jabari played on the floor in the living room while LaToya made dinner. She couldn't believe that Jamal had dropped Jayson off and left her alone with the boys, again. For what reason, she didn't know, but one thing she knew was that this was definitely not going to become an everyday thing. *Although it practically already has*, she thought. She wished Corey hadn't come to take Sierra out, but the newly engaged couple couldn't go one day without seeing each other. She stirred the pot of creamed corn and placed a lid over it. She opened the oven to check on the chicken breasts she was preparing and placed ten minutes on the timer so she wouldn't overcook them.

"Ms. Toya," Jayson called her name as he walked into the kitchen.

LaToya jumped; she didn't know why she was so nervous around Jayson. He was only four. What could he do to her? She turned to face him. "Yes?"

"Mama said call her," he stated simply before walking out of the kitchen.

She followed him. "Jayson, what do you mean?"

Jayson turned around. "My mama said call her," he said, much louder and much slower, as if he thought she was deaf and needed to read his lips.

"Oh . . . okay," she said as he walked back into the living room to continue playing with his little brother.

LaToya walked into the kitchen to check on the rice before taking the cordless phone and walking into her bedroom, leaving the door open, to do as the child had said. She retrieved her phone book to look up Kim's number, which she had to force Jamal to give to her in case of emergencies. She dialed the number and waited for an answer.

"Hello?" Kim's voice came in loud and clear.

"Hi, Kim. It's LaToya. Jayson said you wanted me to call you?" LaToya replied.

"Oh yeah. Hey, girl," Kim said surprisingly cheerful. "I was just wondering if we could get together for lunch tomorrow. I know the boys are staying over at your place tonight and—"

"The boys are *what*?" LaToya asked, knowing that she couldn't have heard Kim correctly.

"Yeah, when Jamal came to pick up Jay earlier, he asked if it was okay that he stay with you tonight . . . you know, so him and Jabari can have some more bonding time?"

"Oh, well, I guess I'll have a full house tonight," LaToya said. *I'll have to deal with Mr. Jamal later.* She couldn't believe he'd propose something like that and not even ask her about it first. "Well, why do you want to meet me for lunch?" she asked cautiously. "Last time I saw you, you were trying to have me lose my rights as a citizen."

Kim chuckled nervously. "Girl, that's all water under the bridge. I just wanna talk to you about some things."

"And you can't talk to me about them over the phone?"

"Please, LaToya, I'm trying to make things right." Kim's voice had suddenly become soft and wavering, almost as if she were crying.

Feeling that they needed to make amends now that their sons were spending so much time together, LaToya agreed. "My last class is over by 3:30, and then I'll have to go by Jamal's and pick up the boys, so I think I can squeeze in a late lunch. Where do you want to meet?"

"What about the Subway right down the street from your apartment building?" Kim suggested. "It's not too far from my job, so neither one of us has to drive too far."

"Sounds good. So we can meet around four, then?"

"Sure," Kim said. "Thanks, LaToya."

"You're welcome." A loud thud drew LaToya's gaze toward the living room and her eyes opened wide in disbelief. "Kim, I have to go 'cause Jayson and Jabari are literally fighting over some toy."

"Tell Jay I said he better behave himself or he'll be looking at a leather strap when he gets home," Kim threatened.

"I will," LaToya assured, placing the phone in its cradle.

She ran into the living room to find the boys tussling over a toy car. She pulled her son off of his older brother and held him in the air as he continued to kick.

"Jabari, what is wrong with you?"

"Gimme," he said, struggling to get out of his mother's grasp.

"No, it's mine," Jayson said, holding up the toy. "He tryin' to take it."

The timer went off on the oven, causing LaToya to shorten her lecture on sharing and being cordial to one another when playing. She walked into the kitchen, still holding Jabari so they wouldn't start going at it again.

She turned off the oven, the corn, and the rice and walked back into the living room, where Jayson was playing with his toy car. LaToya put Jabari on the floor and sat next to him.

She stared into the eyes of both boys. "We *do not* fight in this house. We don't fight each other because we are a family and families love and protect each other. And we are going to share toys because families do that also." She looked back and forth between the two boys. "Do we understand?"

"Yes," Jayson said as Jabari nodded.

LaToya smiled. "Good. Now, who's ready to eat?" she asked as she got up off of the floor.

Both boys raised their hands. LaToya sat them at the table and proceeded to fix their dinner. As she did, Jamal knocked at the apartment door. She hesitated before opening the door. After she did, she returned to the kitchen without greeting him. LaToya tossed an annoyed glare his way before she continued cutting the boys' chicken into smaller pieces.

"Daddy," Jabari and Jayson said at the same time.

"What's up, little men," he said as he kissed both of their heads. He walked over to LaToya and tried to kiss her, but she quickly moved out of his reach.

"Why didn't you tell me that I was supposed to be keeping Jayson tonight?" she asked quietly, but with plenty of attitude.

Jamal snapped his fingers. "Dang, that's what I forgot." He smiled apologetically. "Do you mind?"

His gorgeous smile softened her tone. "No, I don't, but I'd like to be informed when I'm supposed to be hosting guests. Where is he supposed to sleep?"

Jamal looked around the apartment. "Umm . . . can he sleep with Jabari?"

LaToya shrugged nonchalantly. "It doesn't matter. Guess that means the floor is my friend tonight, but it seems, all of a sudden, that our boys have a problem sharing, so hopefully it'll work out without another fight."

He chuckled. "Boys will be boys."

She shook her head. "Do you want something to eat?" she asked him.

"Sure," he said, sitting at the table in between Jayson and Jabari.

LaToya placed the boys' plates in front of them and then fixed plates for her and Jamal. They sat down, blessed the food, and began to eat.

"So what you got planned tomorrow?" Jamal asked. "Maybe we can take the boys to the park after your classes or something."

LaToya looked up and wondered if she should tell Jamal that she had plans with Kim. She didn't know if he'd be okay with her meeting with his ex, so she decided against telling him where she'd be tomorrow.

"I don't think that's a good idea. I have a lot of studying to do tomorrow afternoon, but maybe we could go out tomorrow night."

Jamal nodded that the plan was okay with him, but she knew he was wondering why she preferred studying to going out with him.

"Mama," Jayson shouted as soon as they walked into the Subway restaurant.

A couple sitting at a nearby table smiled as Jayson ran toward his mother, who was sitting at a table for four, with LaToya and Jabari close behind.

"Hey," Kim said as she scooped him up into her lap and placed kisses all over his face. "Did you have fun at Ms. LaToya's house last night?"

Jayson nodded as LaToya and Jabari came to the table.

"Hey." LaToya smiled as she sat in the chair across from Kim and put Jabari in the chair next to her. "What's up?"

"Nothing much," Kim replied. "Did you want something to eat?"

LaToya's stomach growled. "I guess I could get something," she said as she approached the counter and ordered a six-inch cold cut sub and two bags of chips.

When LaToya came back to the table with her food, she handed Jayson a bag of chips and opened the other bag, handing Jabari a few chips out of it before saying grace and biting into her sandwich. As she ate, LaToya noticed that Kim looked very uncomfortable, and she kept moving Jayson from one leg to the other until she finally sat him in the chair next to her. "Is something wrong, Kim?" she asked.

"Not really. I just wanted to set some things straight," Kim said as she looked down and picked imaginary lint off of her shirt. She looked up at LaToya. "I know you probably think that I don't like you very much, but that's not true. I mean, I think you're a really sweet person and everything." LaToya smiled and took another bite of her sandwich as Kim continued, "And I don't have any reason not to like you, and I just wanted you to know that."

LaToya gave her a confused look. "O-kay. I think you have the *potential* to be a cool person too, but I have a feeling that's not why you asked me here today."

Kim nodded. "I know we got off to a rocky start 'cause of Jay, and Jamal not telling you about him, but Jay and Jabari love each other and I don't want to take away what they have."

"Kim, what are you trying to say?" LaToya asked, tired of the girl's stalling.

"I know how much you love Jamal," Kim continued,

"and I know how much he loves you . . . but I have to tell you something."

LaToya sat on the edge of her seat and prepared herself for the worst. "What is it?"

Kim swallowed in an effort to moisten her suddenly parched throat. "I . . . me . . . Jamal and I are . . . we still see each other," she said quietly, her head lowered.

LaToya stared emotionlessly at the woman who had mothered her boyfriend's firstborn. "What do you mean you still see each other? What? When he comes by to play with Jay?" she asked, hoping that was the case, but knowing it wasn't.

Kim slowly shook her head. "No, we still have a sexual relationship. I'm so sorry, LaToya," she said when she saw the look of anger and hurt in LaToya's eyes. "I'm really sorry, but—"

LaToya's hand in the air stopped her next words. "Why . . . why are you telling me this? Are you *trying* to hurt me? I mean, why would you do something like that when *you* said that I was the best thing to ever happen to him? Why?"

"Because I love him, LaToya," Kim defended, looking LaToya straight in her eyes. "I love Jamal. I've always loved Jamal."

LaToya looked angrily at Kim. "Why would you leave someone you love?"

Kim looked down at Jayson, who was making faces at his younger brother, oblivious to what was going on with their mothers. "When I found out I was pregnant, I got scared. I didn't know how Jamal was going to react, and I didn't want to lose my baby, so I left without saying good-bye. I think it was the hardest thing I've ever had to do because I loved Jamal so much, but I just didn't want to mess up his life.

"After Jayson turned two, I left him with my mom and came back to school thinking I was just going to waltz in there and get my man back. But I guess he had gotten tired of waiting for me to return his calls, because when I saw him, you were on his arm, and you were pregnant. I remembered hating you because I thought you were so beautiful. And I hated myself even more because all I could think about was what if I had stayed. So, when you had your baby, I brought in mine because I didn't think it was fair to Jayson. And Jamal was a good father from jump, he never denied my baby. Even before he got the paternity test, he never said a word about Jayson not being his, and that's why I love him so much." She closed her eyes briefly and then continued. "I don't want to be the one to break up what you guys have, but I want to be happy. I want to be loved. And I want Jamal."

LaToya felt the hot, angry tears that ran down her cheeks and tried to wipe them away before Jabari saw. She realized that while Kim may actually love Jamal, he might only be using her for his own sexual pleasures. Since having Jabari, he and LaToya were not having sex at all, and she thought Jamal had been fine with that arrangement, but apparently she was wrong. "So . . . how long has this been going on?" she asked as she stared at Kim, who seemed to be afraid of answering the question.

"The past seven months," she said as LaToya's face dropped.

"Oh my God." LaToya's whisper sounded like a scream. "You can't be serious," she said as she shook her head. "You're lying . . . you have to be."

"LaToya, I'm sorry because I know this is hurting you, but I promise I wouldn't lie about something like this."

LaToya looked up with fire burning in her eyes. "Give me one good reason why I should believe you."

Kim looked down at Jayson. "Jay, baby," she called for his attention, "when Daddy comes to Mommy's house, where does he sleep?"

LaToya's heart stopped as she watched a wide smile spread across Jayson's face.

"In bed with Mommy," the four-year-old spoke, causing LaToya's mouth to drop open in shock.

Kim looked back at LaToya. "I'm sorry."

LaToya tried to fight the tears that poured from her eyes by shutting them tight and trying to avoid the image of Jamal holding, kissing, caressing Kim like he did her, but it was no use. LaToya opened her eyes and wiped her tears away. She couldn't believe this was happening to her. She had done nothing to deserve this heartache. Jamal had lied and cheated, and at this point, LaToya felt as if she didn't know him at all. She turned her attention to Kim. "Does Jamal know you're telling me this?"

Kim shook her head slowly. "I've been trying to get him to tell you about us since you found out about Jay, but he said he'd do it when he felt it was the right time. I know he was just scared of losing you over it and that's understandable." She paused for a brief moment. "But this is why the boys have been spending so much time with you." She looked apologetically at LaToya.

LaToya realized that this relationship had practically been going on in her face the whole time. It was why she had been keeping the boys. Jamal would dump them on her, and then go kick it with his ex-girlfriend. Suddenly something hit her. "When was the last time you were with him?" she asked, though she didn't want to hear the answer.

"L–... last night," Kim muttered, but LaToya heard her very clearly. "I'm sorry," she said with tears coming from her own eyes.

LaToya wanted to accept the girl's apology, but something in her wouldn't allow it. The only thing she could muster was a firm "Me, too," before picking up her purse and her child and exiting the restaurant.

Chapter 26

Thanksgiving

The Calhouns, the Johnsons, the Madisons, and the Andersons had gathered at the McAfees' home to celebrate another Thanksgiving that God had so graciously bestowed upon them. The women were seated at the table while the men stood as Tyler continued leading them in prayer over the food.

"And Heavenly Father, we thank you for all that you have done in our lives and we thank you for what you will do. Lord, we ask that you bless this delicious food so that it may be good to our bodies. In your name we pray . . . "

". . . Amen," they said collectively.

Immediately Marques, Ronald, and Timothy ran to the turkey. Tyler pulled Timothy's collar, and Angelica and Shundra popped their sons on the back of their heads. Everyone laughed as the boys pouted when the women and children were allowed to fix their food first.

"Mama, get that," Ebony said, pointing to the collard

greens. "And that," she said, pointing to the yams. "All those," she said, pointing to the roast beef, turkey, ham, and chicken.

"Girl, why don't you go sit with your daddy or Uncle Tim while I do this?" Shimone said, pushing her daughter toward the den, where the men had retired until it was their turn to prepare their plates.

"Ms. Angel, this food looks appetizing," Imani said as she heaped a spoonful of macaroni and cheese onto her plate.

"Girl, don't give me all the credit," Angelica smiled. "Your mom, Shundra, and Misty were over here helping me late last night and early this morning."

"Well, I can't wait to dig into it," Nevaeh said, grabbing a piece of cornbread.

"Yeah, and neither can we, so hurry it up," Ronald yelled from the den followed by loud agreements from the men who were watching the Falcons take on the Bucks.

"Nikki, tell your brother to hush and wait his turn," Nevaeh said, just loud enough for Ronald to hear.

Nicole shook her head. "That's *your* boyfriend." She laughed along with the other women.

Once the women finished preparing their plates, the men ran into the kitchen to devour whatever was left. They all found a spot to eat, whether it was at the kitchen table, the dining room table, or on the sofa in front of the television. The house was so loud that everyone had to just about scream in order to hear the person next to them.

"So how are you feeling, sweetheart," Misty asked Nicole.

"I'm fine. Thank God for the second chance," she replied.

Nicole had just gotten out of the hospital the week be-

fore. She returned to school to rumors that she had tried
to commit suicide. She didn't listen to any of them, especially the one Shawn had started. He had told everyone
that she couldn't go on living without him, so she tried to
kill herself. It was the exact same thing she had told him
he could say after they broke up, so she wasn't fazed by
any of the drama he was trying to push her way. She was
just glad that the doctors allowed her to see Patricia for
her therapy sessions. She felt most comfortable talking
with the woman who she'd been sharing her problems
with since her freshman year of high school.

Nicole tried her hardest not to think about what she
had done to herself. When people asked her about it,
she'd say she was fine and give God the thanks He deserved. The only reminders she had of the incident were
the stitches that were still in her wrists and the cast she
was still wearing on her left arm.

She had told her mother about her father's daily calls.
When Angelica had said that they would come to an end,
Nicole knew her mother was serious. Angelica informed
the prison supervisor of the problem and Malcolm was
temporarily stripped of his phone privileges. Nicole was
thankful to be alive. She knew that if it weren't for God,
she wouldn't be here. She smiled as she looked across the
table at Ebony, who was fussing at Timothy for trying to
take something off of her plate.

"That's yours," Ebony was saying. "This is mine." She
pointed to the food on her plate.

"Okay, okay." Timothy put up his hands in surrender.
"I'm sorry." He went back to eating his food.

"Marques, will you let that girl eat her food?" Shundra
said as she watched her son whisper something in Shimone's ear.

They wouldn't admit it to anybody, but everyone
knew that Shimone and Marques were back together, or

at least that they were in the process of reconciliation. Shimone had told Marques that they would start from the beginning with a clean slate, as friends first and they would let things progress in their own time, and Marques had been all too eager to prove that he could do right. So far he was doing well, but it would still be a while before Shimone could officially call him her boyfriend once again.

Shimone had something more to be thankful for. Her family had convinced her to renew her contract with Power Records. After praying and fasting, she knew that God would have it no other way, so she sat down with Marques's father and mapped out a plan. They called up Vincent Gardiner and asked them if the company's offer was still open. He graciously accepted Shimone back and promised that he'd take care of everything from the remainder of her schooling to the recording time and they'd get started on a new album as soon as possible.

In the den, Nevaeh sat next to Ronald as they watched the Falcons score another field goal, putting them ahead of Tampa Bay by seven points.

"Yeah!" Ronald exclaimed as he turned and kissed Nevaeh. "That's what I'm talkin' 'bout," he said as he returned his attention to the game.

Nevaeh continued eating as if his kiss had no effect on her, but inside her stomach was doing flip-flops. She knew some people would look at her and say she had the perfect life, the perfect boyfriend, and the perfect relationship. Even though everything was far from perfect, her life was still good. She couldn't ask for anything better, even with all the drama and problems her family and friends had been through in just the last few months, she still believed that God had blessed her.

No one in their families knew that she and Ronald had been talking about marriage, but once she finished medical school and found a steady job, they'd make the big announcement and begin making arrangements. She believed God had blessed her in that area. Some guys wouldn't be okay with waiting for their girlfriends to finish school, especially if they would have to go longer than the expected four years, but Ronald was willing to wait, and she loved him for it. *Two more years,* she thought as she gazed at Ronald's handsome profile.

Ronald felt her staring and turned toward her, locking their eyes in a lingering gaze. "I love you," he said.

Nevaeh smiled. "I love you."

He kissed her once more and turned back to the television. She felt so special and so blessed, She didn't know what else God could have in store for her.

Imani sat at the dining room table next to her parents thanking God for the gift of forgiveness. The same night Nicole went into the hospital, Imani decided that it was best to tell her parents what had happened between her and Eddie. Their reaction was worse than what she had expected: disappointment. She hated when they were disappointed in her; she could handle anger or even rage, but the disappointment on their faces made her want to tell them that she has just been kidding around. Her mother cried on her father's shoulder and her father continued to shake his head in displeasure while trying to fight off tears of his own. Her punishment was not a major surprise to her, but at the same time, it made Imani feel even more remorseful about the night she'd spent with Eddie. For the next several weeks, she would not be able to talk to or see Eddie. Her parents had also taken every enjoyable leisure activity away from her. No phone, television, computer—other than for homework assignments—shopping, or hanging out with friends. Imani knew the next few weeks would be hard on her, but when she thought about how much she'd allowed her relationship with

Eddie to pull her away from God, she knew that the time apart would be good for them both.

When everyone was finished eating, they gathered in the den, switched off the game, to many of the men's dismay, and turned on the stereo. Marques put in Shimone's album and they formed a soul train line and began to dance. When Tyler's favorite slow ballad came on, he took Misty's hand and began to slow dance with her. The other men followed his lead and began to dance with the ladies, some alternating between partners.

Misty looked into Tyler's light brown eyes and noticed something different about him. He looked happy . . . excited even. She wondered what was going on in his head, but didn't even have a chance to guess because during the second verse of the song, which spoke of loving to love the one you love, Tyler began to softly sing the words. Misty didn't bother to wipe the joyful tears that fell from her eyes. She couldn't ask for a better person to love, and she loved to love Tyler.

As he continued to sing, he slipped down on one knee and pulled the small red box from his pocket. Noticing that Tyler was in proposal position, Timothy turned down the music. Everyone stopped dancing and gave Tyler their shocked, but undivided, attention.

Tyler gazed into Misty's eyes. "I love you so much," he began. "I've loved you since we were in high school. I love Shimone, and I love Ebony. I want us to be a family. I can't see it any other way. God has ordained this. So . . . Misty Johnson"—he opened the box revealing the two-karat diamond ring—"will you marry me?"

Tears clouded Misty's vision as she readily shook her head "yes". Tyler slipped the ring on her finger, stood, and kissed her passionately. He pulled back and wiped her tears as everyone clapped.

"I have another surprise for you," he revealed as Shimone went into the dining room to retrieve her purse.

When she came back she had her birth certificate with her. She handed it to her mother. Tears continued to run down Misty's face as she looked in confusion at her daughter and Tyler.

Shimone smiled. "I'd like to have that blank above the word 'father' filled in, if it's okay with you."

Misty tearfully gazed at Tyler. "You want to sign her birth certificate?"

"Why not make it official?" Tyler shrugged. "All we have to do is go to the Vital Records Office in North Carolina, where she was born, and fill out a Paternity Acknowledgement Form."

Before Misty could respond, Shimone handed her more papers.

"Petition for Change of Name?" Misty questioned.

"Like Daddy said, we'd like to make it official," Shimone began to explain. "Once you guys get married, I'll be the only one in the family without Calhoun as my last name." She broke into a huge grin as tears filled her eyes. "I don't like feeling left out."

"Oh," Misty breathed deeply. "This is just so much."

"Too much?" Tyler questioned worriedly.

Misty looked into his eyes. "No, not at all. Let's make it official," she agreed.

Tyler looked at Misty and smiled. "So when do you want to become Mrs. Tyler Calhoun?" he asked as he pulled her closer to him.

"As soon as possible," she whispered, kissing him.

Chapter 27

Sierra looked at her friend, who had a rather hostile expression on her face. "Toya, put a smile on. It's Thanksgiving."

"Sierra please," LaToya grumbled as she stirred the pot of greens. "There's nothing to be thankful for."

Sierra stopped watching over the frying catfish and stared at her friend. "Girl, if I, a woman who is living with Human Immunodeficiency Virus, can be happy and thankful about something, then certainly you can."

"Well, that's easy for you to say," LaToya snapped. "You may be sick, but you look healthier than I do. You have a man who loves you, and . . ." She looked down at Sierra's left ring finger. "And you are getting married next summer. So you have a lot to be thankful for.

"But what about me? Umm, let's see," she said, placing her finger on her chin as if in deep thought. "First, my boyfriend doesn't tell me he has a son, then, he cheats on me with his son's mother." Tears began to roll down her cheeks. "So I'm sorry if I can't find anything to be thankful for," she said as she continued to stir the greens.

Sierra dropped the last of the catfish into the frying pan and walked over to LaToya and pulled her into a tender embrace. "It's going to be okay," she whispered as LaToya let all of her emotions out on Sierra's sweater. "God's got this under control. You just have to let it go or else you are going to let it ruin your life. Jamal was wrong, but he's apologized and he's giving you your space." Sierra pulled back. "All you have to do is forgive him."

LaToya looked at Sierra through her tears. "But it's so much more than that." She wiped her cheeks. "I loved him so much and I didn't want to lose him, but after this I know I don't want him back. And the hard thing is I don't want anyone else to have him either, but Kim *already* got him. I don't have anything against her; I just don't want her to have Jamal," she rambled.

"I can understand that," Sierra said. "But you can do so much better than Jamal. I know you love him, but the only thing holding you to him is Jabari. I'm not saying don't let Jabari see his father, but don't let that be the reason you're trying to hold on to something that's no longer there." She went back to monitoring the fish. "Honestly, I think that Jabari is the only reason you guys were still together. I know Jamal loves you, but it seems like there's still something with Kim that he hasn't gotten over yet and you need to let him handle it without having any extra burdens on his back."

LaToya wiped her eyes and began to monitor the chitterlings. She didn't know if she would be able to let go of Jamal. She did love him, but was he really worth the fight? She recalled that day at the park when she asked him if he really had feelings for her. When he said that he loved her, it made her feel so special. But he had still been with Kim then. LaToya was ready for a commitment, but could Jamal fully give himself to her if he was still attached to someone else? She didn't think so.

She'd questioned Jamal about his relationship with Kim after she'd come home from lunch that same day. He had been surprised that she had actually lied to him and gone out to lunch with his ex-girlfriend, but when she told him what was revealed during the lunch, he hadn't denied anything. He told her that, although he loved her, he did have mixed feelings for Kim. He said he didn't understand the feelings he had for her, but they were in existence. LaToya told him that until he resolved those feelings, they couldn't see each other. He didn't pressure her into changing her mind, and she didn't cry until after he walked out of the door. Her father always told her that a person's heart was capable of loving more than one person. She never understood that until now.

"I guess you're right," LaToya told Sierra as she placed a top over the chitterlings. She opened the oven and checked on the peach cobbler. "Maybe it's just not meant to be. But I sure wish she wasn't pregnant, then maybe I could just forgive him and we can go on with our lives. I don't hold anything against her though." She looked at Sierra. "You know I can't stand it when women get mad at the other woman, but not at their man."

"I know that's right," Sierra said, taking the fish out of the pan and placing it on a draining pan. "But you do need to forgive him because it's not going to help the situation if y'all are mad and you show that anger around Jabari."

"Yeah, I know. I definitely don't want Jabari to see the tension between us right now." LaToya sighed. "What time are they supposed to be here?" she asked as a knock came at the door.

Sierra smiled. "Right now," she said as LaToya took a

deep breath. "I promise you're not going to regret this," Sierra said as she walked over to answer the door. "Hi," she greeted the guests.

"Hey, baby," Corey said, before kissing her lightly on the lips. He walked into the apartment carrying Jabari. "Mmm, it smells good up in here." He went into the kitchen and began lifting pots. He looked up in surprise. "Am I in the right house?" He looked around as if he was trying to make sure he was where he thought he was. "Are these chitterlings and pig's feet on this stove?"

Sierra laughed. "I only let LaToya make them because I know you love them," she said. "But hurry and eat them because they are stankin' up my house."

"You don't have to tell me twice," he said, looking though cabinets for the hot sauce.

"Mama," Jabari said, reaching for his mother.

LaToya grabbed him, kissed his forehead, and looked at her brother. "Corey, where are Jamal and Kim?" she asked, hoping she wouldn't regret inviting them. With encouragement from Sierra, she'd called Jamal last night and invited him over. She surprised not only him, but herself, when she unconsciously asked him to bring Kim.

"They were pulling up right after me," he said, using a fork to help himself to a pig's foot.

"Here we are," Jamal said as he walked through the open door with Jayson holding onto his leg and Kim following behind them.

It took everything in LaToya to hold back tears. They looked like such a happy family: a father, a mother, and a son. LaToya plastered a smile across her face and greeted them. "Hi," she said, but smiled a genuine smile as Jayson ran toward her.

"Hey, Ms. Toya," Jayson said as she stooped down to give him a big hug.

"Dayson" Jabari said, calling for his brother's attention.

LaToya placed Jabari on the floor and immediately the boys began to play with the toys that were in the den.

"Hi," Jamal said as he walked into the apartment.

"Hi." LaToya's voice was firm, but her eyes showed that she had forgiven him. She looked into his eyes and saw regret, but she refused to let her guard down for fear of being hurt even further. She looked beyond him and smiled at Kim. "Hi Kim."

"Hey," Kim said as she surprisingly pulled LaToya into a hug.

It wasn't a hug that promised friendship, but it was one that vowed to lay the past to rest. They both felt remorse for the way they'd acted toward each other over Jamal and knew it was time to let go of the jealousy and anger they'd been harboring. When they released each other, they both had unshed tears in their eyes. Silently, they made a truce.

Sierra cleared her throat and said, "Who's ready to eat?"

Corey smiled and yelled, "You don't have to ask me twice 'cause the answer will be the same: Let's do this," he said, rubbing his hands together as they all laughed.

After dinner, Jamal volunteered to help LaToya clean up. Everyone else went into the den to give them some privacy, though the small apartment didn't offer much. LaToya washed the dishes and handed them to Jamal to be dried. Neither of them said a word for several minutes, but LaToya could sense that Jamal wanted to say something by the way he kept glancing at her. She just hoped that it wasn't another apology because, truthfully, she was tired of hearing them.

"LaToya," he said quietly as she handed him another dish.

LaToya let out a deep sigh. "Jamal, if you are about to apologize to me, please don't waste your breath. I know you're sorry"—*In more ways than one*—"and I forgive you, so there's no need to continue to repeat yourself."

Jamal looked at her side profile. "LaToya," he said her name again.

She continued to wash the dishes. "Yes, Jamal," she said as she handed him another dish.

He refused to take the plate. "LaToya, would you look at me. How am I supposed to believe that you have forgiven me if you won't even look at me when I'm trying to tell you something?"

LaToya glared at him. "What is it, Jamal?" He looked like he didn't know what to say, so she rolled her eyes at him and continued to wash and dry the dishes herself.

"I . . . I just want you to speak to me. Say something other than the angry stuff you been throwin' at me since you found out about this," he finally said.

LaToya looked at him as if he had lost his mind. She placed the dishtowel by the sink. He stepped back just in case she was about to hit him. "What do you expect me to say, Jamal? In what tone of voice am I supposed to speak to you? Do you want my congratulations?" She plastered a smile on her face and livened up her voice. "Well, Jamal, you messed up the best thing that's ever happened to you, how does it feel to be labeled the biggest dog in the Midwest?" she asked as she took a spoon and placed it to his mouth, acting like a news reporter. "Is that how you want me to act . . . or . . . or do you want this?" She flipped her hair over her shoulder and began to speak like a "Valley girl". "Oh my gosh, Jamal, you really cheated on me. Like, I totally cannot believe you. How could you, like, do this to me?" She looked at him as if she wanted him to say something, but would slap him if he uttered one word. Then she glanced toward the den and noticed Kim looking in their direction, so she lowered her voice. "Well, I'm sorry. You might be able to pull something like that up here in the Midwest, but that's not how it works down South. You can't play a Southern girl and expect her to not get upset." She resumed washing dishes as tears began to well up in her eyes.

Jamal walked closer to her and pulled her into his arms.

"I'm not mad at her, Jamal. Me and Kim are cool," LaToya said quietly as she cried into his shirt. "I'm mad at you, and I don't even wanna be. I want to truly and completely forgive you . . . not just say it, but really feel that way in my heart. I wanna get past this and move on . . . without you tugging at the ends of my heart." She pulled away from him. "But I wanna be able to come to you as a friend, or as my son's father when I need to, without there being any hard feelings, especially when we have Jabari tying us together."

"I want that, too," Jamal said, still holding on to her arms. "But I want you to know that I *do* love you and that I am sorry. You deserve someone who is going to do better than me. Someone who is going to pay attention to you and someone who is going to love you completely like you should be loved."

"Don't I know it." LaToya laughed while Jamal, playfully, rolled his eyes.

He placed a soft kiss against her forehead as one last goodbye to their relationship. Surprisingly, all LaToya felt was love for Jamal. She thanked God that, after all they had been through, she was still able to love him because of God's love for her.

Epilogue

February 14
Greater Faith Tabernacle

It had taken all of two and a half months to plan the small, but eloquently arranged wedding. To Misty, the last couple of months seemed like a couple of years, but the day had finally come. She stood behind the closed doors of the church and awaited her grand entrance.

As the instrumentals to Musiq Soulchild's "Love" began to play, Shimone stepped out of the bridesmaid line and into the pulpit and took the microphone off of the stand. She began to sing as the doors of the church opened, revealing the blushing bride.

As her daughter continued to sing, Misty walked gracefully down the aisle, her eyes focused on her groom. Tyler looked so handsome in his black tux that it took everything in Misty to keep from running toward him. Camera lights flashed from the two hired photographers as they captured her walking down the aisle, on top of the red rose petals that Ebony had dropped right before her entrance. Her beautiful cream gown flowed as she took her last steps. Finally, she was standing next to her first and only love. He intertwined their arms together before whispering in her ear how beautiful she looked.

Assistant Pastor John Wallace was honored to preside over his pastor's nuptials. He opened with The Lord's Prayer and when he was done, he began the ceremony. Doing his best not to stumble over words or miss any parts, Pastor Wallace sounded like he had spent weeks practicing.

"May I have the rings please?" Pastor Wallace asked after the couple had exchanged traditional wedding vows.

Timothy proudly stepped forward and handed the pastor the wedding bands.

Tyler took one of the rings and repeated after Pastor Wallace as instructed. "With this ring . . . I thee wed," he said as he slipped the ring onto Misty's trembling finger.

Misty took the other ring and repeated after the pastor also. "With . . . this ring," she said as a tear ran down her face, but she dismissed it as she continued to look into the eyes of her beloved. "I thee . . . wed."

"What God has joined together let no man put asunder." Pastor Wallace smiled as he said his next words. "By the powers invested in me by the Almighty God and the state of Georgia," he stated proudly, "I now pronounce you, husband and wife." He looked at Tyler. "Pastor, you may kiss your bride."

Camera flashes captured the couple enjoying their first kiss as husband and wife.

"Ladies and gentlemen, I present to you Pastor and Mrs. Tyler Jacob Calhoun," Pastor Wallace said as the couple faced the audience.

The recessional music began to play as the wedding

party walked out of the church. After posing for pictures, they headed to the awaiting limousines that would take them to the banquet hall of a nearby hotel. When the limos pulled into the parking lot, cameras began to flash once again. The bridesmaids and groomsmen walked into the building first. They smiled as the guests used the disposable cameras that had been purchased to capture this moment.

"Two more years," Ronald whispered in Nevaeh's ear as they walked to their reserved table. Nevaeh continued to smile as he pulled out her chair. "Maybe Shimone could sing at ours," he said as Marques and Shimone joined them at the table that sat in the front of the room.

"Sing at your what?" Shimone asked as they sat.

Nevaeh tried to suppress her widening smile. "Nothing," she said quickly as Ebony and Timothy joined them.

"Uh huh," Shimone said as she eyed her friends with a knowing grin.

"Hey, sis, you sang that song," Timothy said as Ebony climbed in her father's lap.

"Thanks," Shimone smiled as she saw her parents approaching the doors.

"Ladies and gentlemen," the wedding planner said into the microphone, "would you please stand and join me in welcoming Mr. and Mrs. Tyler Calhoun." Everyone stood and clapped.

Tyler and Misty walked into the reception hall and took their seats at the head table along with their wedding party.

Shimone leaned over and kissed both her parents. "Congratulations, you guys," she said. It was evident by her smile that she was more than happy that her parents were finally together.

Soft music played as the caterers served a light dinner.

People chatted at their tables and others went to the head table to congratulate Tyler and Misty or compliment the wedding party on their attire. Once the dinner was over, the wedding planner took the microphone again.

"At this moment, we are going to have the first dance," she announced. "I've been told that the couple had no idea what song to pick, so their daughter has offered to present us, once again, with her gift of music, and she has also chosen the song."

Applause erupted as Shimone took the microphone and the music began to play.

As she sung the words to "Inseparable," Tyler led Misty to the center of the dance floor. Singing the words along with his daughter, he stared into Misty's eyes and thanked God once again for this second chance.

When the song ended, immediately, K.C. & Jo Jo's "All My Life" came through the loud speakers. Ronald led Nevaeh out onto the dance floor, followed by Marques and Shimone and Timothy and Ebony, who begged her uncle to take her out onto the floor. Soon, Imani and Eddie, Nicole and a male friend she'd invited, their parents, and other guests came out onto the floor to enjoy the moment in the arms of the ones they loved.

"Happy anniversary," Ronald whispered in Nevaeh's ear.

They'd been dating, almost nonstop, for seven years and Nevaeh savored every second she spent with her man. She smiled as Ronald tried to serenade her while they danced. She loved him to death, but he could leave the crooning to her. She allowed him to continue, though, because even though he was way off key, she loved the fact that he felt he had waited all his life to find someone as special as she.

Tyler smiled as Misty told him how much she loved him. He pulled her closer to him and whispered in her ear, "I love you more than I could ever say. I know it's been a long and tough journey, but we finally made it, and whatever tests our relationship may go through in the future, I want you to know that I will always stand by your side." He pulled back and looked into her eyes. "I promise." He leaned down and kissed her. Everyone around them delighted in the couple's love.

Group Discussion Questions

1. What relationship issue was most interesting to you? How would you have handled the situation differently from the characters in the book?

2. Marques had vowed to never be unfaithful to Shimone and had seemed sincere in his promise. What do you think caused him to break his promise to Shimone and Ebony, knowing what the consequences could have been?

3. Though his issues weren't discussed in detail throughout the book, Jeremy dealt with a lot of emotional baggage concerning his parents' marriage, and more specifically, the abuse he endured from his father. How realistic do you believe his reaction was toward his parents' separation?

4. Tyler's entrance into Misty and Shimone's lives stir up strong emotions in both women. While Shimone is hesitant to receive Tyler into her life as her father, Misty seemingly welcomes him with open arms, despite their past together. Do you believe Shimone was too harsh or was Misty too lenient in accepting him?

5. Do you think Imani was being selfish by spending so much time with Eddie, even when she knew Nicole needed her emotional support?

6. Since Alexia had no family and serious issues with her self-image, do you think she was simply using

Marques for his companionship and to build her own self-confidence?

7. Do you believe Nicole's reason for dating Shawn was legitimate?

8. Tyler and Misty's relationship seemed so sudden, in spite of their painful past. Why do you feel Misty was able to so easily forgive Tyler for all he'd done, and even go as far as accepting him as her soul mate?

9. Do you think it was easier for LaToya to simply accept Jayson rather than leaving Jamal after finding out that he'd been lying to her for the last two years? What would you have done if you were in her position?

10. Nicole's low self-worth was the result of her relationships with her family and friends, but how could she have prevented allowing the actions of others to dictate how she should feel about herself? How did you react when she first began harming herself?

11. After his and Shimone's breakup, Marques tried several times to coax Shimone into reuniting with him. Had Shimone taken Marques back sooner than later, would he have been motivated to make spiritual changes in his life?

12. Do you believe that there were signs LaToya could have been aware of that would have made her more alert of Jamal's infidelity throughout their relationship?

13. Eddie and Imani's willingness to push aside their spiritual morals and values in order to appease their flesh showed their spiritual immaturity. How spiritually grounded is a relationship if both parties are weak when it comes to battles between the spirit and the flesh?

14. Malcolm allowed his stresses at work to impose on his family life, causing him to lose everything he had. How could he have handled his emotions differently? Was there anything Jeremy or Nicole could have done in order to stop the physical and emotional abuse before it got out of hand?

15. Ebony seemed to play a prominent role as Marques's confidant when he was feeling down about his relationship with Shimone and the twins' death. Why do you think that is?

16. Many of the strained relationships throughout the book were held together by the individual's faith that God would pull them through whatever issues they were dealing with. How important do you believe this faith is when dealing with various issues, including relationships?